D1009832

DEMON'S FURY

The screams filled Kesira Minette's soul with searing acid. She resisted closing her eyes or putting her hands over her ears to block the farmer's hideous shrieks. To do so would give Ayondela too much pleasure. The jade demon sat on her throne of blue-white ice, sneering, her tusks gleaming with shining green. Ayondela tossed her head and sent a cascade of hair floating out gently; she had been lovely once, Kesira knew.

Only stark, ripping hatred showed now.

Other Avon Books by
Robert E. Vardeman

THE QUAKING LANDS: BOOK 1 in
The Jade Demons

Coming Soon

THE CRYSTAL CLOUDS: BOOK 3 in
The Jade Demons

Avon Books are available at special quantity discounts for
bulk purchases for sales promotions, premiums, fund
raising or educational use. Special books, or book excerpts,
can also be created to fit specific needs.

For details write or telephone the office of the Director of
Special Markets, Avon Books, Dept. FP, 1790 Broadway,
New York, New York 10019, 212-399-1357. *IN CANADA:*
Director of Special Sales, Avon Books of Canada, Suite
210, 2061 McCowan Rd., Scarborough, Ontario M1S 3Y6,
416-293-9404.

THE JADE DEMONS #2
THE FROZEN WAVES

ROBERT E. VARDEMAN

AVON
PUBLISHERS OF BARD, CAMELOT, DISCUS AND FLARE BOOKS

THE FROZEN WAVES is an original publication of
Avon Books. This work has never before appeared in
book form. This work is a novel. Any similarity to actual
persons or events is purely coincidental.

AVON BOOKS
A division of
The Hearst Corporation
1790 Broadway
New York, New York 10019

Copyright © 1985 by Robert E. Vardeman
Published by arrangement with the author
Library of Congress Catalog Card Number: 84-091828
ISBN: 0-380-89799-7

All rights reserved, which includes the right to
reproduce this book or portions thereof in any form
whatsoever except as provided by the U.S. Copyright Law.
For information address Howard Morhaim Literary
Agency, 501 Fifth Avenue, New York, New York 10017.

—

First Avon Printing, May 1985

AVON TRADEMARK REG. U.S. PAT. OFF. AND IN
OTHER COUNTRIES, MARCA REGISTRADA, HECHO EN
U.S.A.

Printed in the U.S.A.

WFH 10 9 8 7 6 5 4 3 2 1

```
10 PRINT "FOR GORDON GARB"
20 GOTO 10
```

THE FROZEN WAVES

Chapter One

THE FRIGID WIND gusting from the southlands cut into Kesira Minette's face like jagged-edged razors. The woman pulled the cowl of her battered gray robe futilely around her face to prevent the tendrils of cold from sneaking in to torment her further. The wind acted as if it had a mind of its own, intent on punishing her for sinful deeds. Strands of short brown hair caught on the wind and whipped about in front of her eyes, almost blinding her.

"Hard to believe this is early summer," she said to the lump under her thin robe and heavier cloak. The large mound stirred. Heavy talons cut into her shivering flesh.

"Too cold. Want to go where warmth is," came the cracked words. Kesira nodded, even though the *trilla* bird hiding under the cloth couldn't see the motion. She worried about the fragile creature. Zolkan belonged in warmer climes where he might preen his brilliant green plumage and flutter in cloud-dotted, syrupy warm skies. For a tropical bird, this weather must be pure horror not even her robe and cloak could fend off successfully.

Kesira found the wind unbearable. It stunned her even more when she realized that this *was* summer, that the air should be as a lover's caress and the full yellow sun smilingly benevolent in its warmth. Winter had been driven off by spring's fine weather, but there the usual wheeling of seasons ceased.

The demon Ayondela brought the freezing winds, the ice storms, the sharp pinpricks of flesh turning to stone. And she delivered the punishment to the land because of Kesira Minette.

Kesira jerked about when something large and powerful

jiggled her elbow. Her stone-wood staff dropped to protect her from a predator. She relaxed when she saw her traveling companion, Molimo.

"I am sorry," she said. "You startled me."

The young man's solemn expression didn't change. He held out his hands, palms skyward, and shook his head.

"No luck hunting?" Kesira waited for him to acknowledge what she had already surmised. The game, normally plentiful along the Pharna River, had been killed by the preternatural weather. Before the polar sentence passed, much of the world might lie in permafrost graves.

Molimo edged closer. Kesira shuddered but opened her cloak for him. The youth whirled in and immediately closed it so that it enveloped both of them. Kesira's heart beat a trifle stronger, Molimo's presence now warming her with a rush of—what?

Love? Kesira did not discount this, though it struck her as impertinent on her part. She was a nun of the Order of Geyla. About her waist hung the knotted blue cord of her Order and intertwined with that rode the gold ribbon showing her to be Sister of the Mission.

The last Sister of the Mission, Kesira thought bitterly. The world had turned inside out, normal becoming unusual and the horrible commonplace. Unthinkable deeds had been committed, and all of her Order perished or wantonly abandoned their vows. The demons had begun a war for dominance that entangled her repeatedly until she sought only vengeance for a single life-changing atrocity. When the demon Lenc had partaken of jade he began the power of transformation into something more than demonic. Lenc hungered for control over the world and all those on it.

For centuries the demons had remained aloof, encouraging humans to worship them. Kesira had fallen in with the Order of Gelya, and Gelya was a kind patron, free with his wisdom and caring of his charges. Life had been simple and good within the walls of the nunnery. If Kesira had not been sent to the distant city of Blinn for lamp oil, she, too, would lie charred with her Sisters. Of them all, she alone had survived. And alone of them, she had sought out other missions, only to find the teachings of her patron discarded in favor of carnal pursuits and, worse, the ways of doubt. They had turned from Gelya and left her alone in the world to carry on their patron's work.

Molimo stirred. Kesira felt his arm circling her waist, pulling her closer. Not for the first time she wished the handsome, darkly complected man could speak, but his dumbness was another atrocity brought by the jade demons. Somehow, Molimo had become embroiled in a battle between two of the demons and had been caught in a rain of jade. The forbidden green mineral had burned and scarred his strong young body, and he lost his tongue to one of the demons.

Kesira had found him at the side of a road, battered almost to the point of death, and had nursed him to health. But even the healing skills learned in her twenty-two summers failed to alleviate the problem of Molimo's sundered tongue.

Or a deeper, more troubling problem.

Even though they had been through much together, Kesira felt a thrill of danger when Molimo was near. The jade rain had seared his physical body and destroyed the natural balances. Molimo often lost control of his human shape and altered into a wolf, uncontrolled and at the mercy of bestial urges.

She turned slightly, brown eyes meeting his ebony ones. Molimo shook his head the slightest amount, assuring her that he was not in danger of undergoing that transformation. Still, Kesira worried. If Molimo became too hungry, would his human feelings stay in control over his more elemental, animal urges? She would make a fine meal for a predator as strong and sleek as Molimo the wolf.

"Too cold, too cold," Zolkan complained. Kesira winced as the *trilla* bird tightened his grip on her shoulder. She reached up and stroked gently over the cloth-covered mound of bird, soothing and trying to reassure him.

"We will stop soon. We must. The storm grows fiercer. Never before have I felt such wrath in a southern-born storm in summer."

"Ayondela's doing. She brings this as warning."

"I fear you are right. This ought to give us even more incentive to reach her and speak with her, to tell her that her son's death was accidental."

Kesira bit her lip when she uttered those words. Beside her Molimo tensed.

"I meant no criticism, Molimo. You could not prevent it. Your other self killed her son. Rouvin's death served a vital purpose, also. It was not in vain."

Rouvin had been half-demon, his mother Ayondela and his father a warrior captain in the employ of the Emperor Kwasian. Demons sometimes left their arcane concerns and walked the lands seeking out diversions. Ayondela had found hers in Rouvin's father, and Rouvin had grown to be a fine figure of a man. Too brash, Kesira knew, but still devoted to that which is honorable.

"I only wish I could have loved him as he wanted," she said softly, more to herself than to either Molimo or Zolkan. Rouvin had died under Molimo's wolf fangs to free another demon.

At the memory of Wemilat the Ugly, Kesira lifted her hand and placed it over her left breast. The bright imprint of the demon's kiss still burned in her flesh, Wemilat's mark.

They had met and defeated Howenthal, one of the original trio of jade demons. Howenthal had shattered, exploded, turned to jade dust and, in so passing, had taken Wemilat also. Kesira mourned the loss of the froglike demon. He had been kind and opposed to the changes demanded by Lenc, Howenthal and Eznofadil.

Kesira swallowed hard. There were still three jade demons, even though Howenthal had perished. Ayondela had joined their rank because of Rouvin's death.

"I can convince her," Kesira said firmly. "I need only reason with her. She was once a patron held in great esteem by her worshippers. Forsaking honor to seek the power of jade is not her way."

Kesira closed her eyes to the icy gusts and let small tears leak out, freezing her eyelashes together. Molimo guided them as Kesira remembered that moment on the hilltop. The weather had been pleasant then, the blush of springtime bringing forth particolored flowers in wild profusion along the slopes. But Ayondela in her wrath had appeared, the icy blue scepter in hand. Every spot on the ground touched by the water dripping from that wand had wilted and died. The demon's anger had mounted, and she had partaken of the jade, placing a tiny chip under her tongue.

Kesira shivered, more from memory than cold. Fangs had grown even as Ayondela's complexion altered from flesh tones to a pale green. The circle of hoarfrost at her feet had expanded as the forbidden power of the jade insinuated itself through her body. Her powers had been augmented, but Ayondela had lost something of her sanity, too. The jade demanded its payment. In exchange for the heightened power, it robbed Ayondela of a considerable portion of her prodigious life span. How much, the nun didn't know, but Wemilat had told her that Ayondela's years were numbered as a mortal's now.

Kesira had no wish to meddle in the affairs of demons, but Ayondela's angry alliance with Eznofadil and Lenc threatened the world—and Kesira could never forget the death of her beloved patron. Gelya had stood for charity and peace, and had been destroyed by the other demons. While Gelya's teachings did not include revenge, they did not preclude it, either.

Kesira gripped her stone-wood staff even more firmly and bent her head to the wind. Zolkan protested with wordless squawks, but she ignored the *trilla* bird. He complained far too much.

But the tugging at her arm made her turn again, to look nose to nose with Molimo. The hard dark eyes bored into her softer ones. He opened the front of their shared cloak and pointed. Kesira almost fainted from the renewed assault of cold air on her body, but she saw what the man-wolf meant.

Shelter!

"We will soon be warm and dry, Zolkan," she told the bird. The uncomfortable shifting warned her that she'd better be right or Zolkan might rip off her left arm. Eyes watering constantly from the wind, Kesira forged ahead until the rocky outjut broke the cold grasp of the storm and let her breathe normally for the first time all day.

"Better," Zolkan confirmed. "But still cold. Freeze me, feathers and all."

Molimo agilely spun from the warm confines of the cloak and vanished. Kesira grabbed for his arm and missed. The youth vanished from sight, as if he had never existed.

Warily, Kesira followed and found an icy pathway leading
into a cave. Molimo had already gathered a few pitiful
twigs for a fire.

"The cave should stand us in good stead this night," she
said. Molimo nodded, and Zolkan poked his head out from
beneath the coarsely woven gray fabric of Kesira's robe.
The green-plumed head craned around and one large black
eye fixed on a ledge above their heads. With a squawk, Zolkan took to wing and landed adroitly on the shelf. He
turned and surveyed Molimo's handiwork.

"Not enough. Need heat. Lot of heat."

Molimo paid the bird no heed and continued about the
serious business of building the fire.

Kesira settled down and let the youth work. She found it
difficult to keep her eyes off him. The sleek, bronzed flesh
of his upper arms lay bare to the cold, yet he seemed not to
notice. If anything, it only firmed the muscles rippling beneath his skin. When satisfied with the way he'd placed
the twigs and dried branches, he rocked back on his heels
and pointed. Kesira bent forward, her fire kit already in
hand. A tiny vial held a white powder, which she gingerly
sprinkled onto the wood. The sudden flare momentarily
blinded her. When the dancing yellow and blue dots had
vanished from her eyes, Kesira smiled.

The warmth of the fire came to her almost painfully.
Rubbing her frostbitten hands and moving closer to the
dancing flames helped. She relaxed even more, content.

"Never find Ayondela," the *trilla* bird declared. "All die
here. All. No use to continue. Cold, too frigging cold." The
bird launched off on a biting, salty description of how cold
it was and how much colder it was likely to be. Kesira had
never learned Zolkan's origins, but from the way the *trilla*
bird swore, she guessed he had been the property of some
sergeant in the Emperor's guard. Zolkan had flown into
the Order's sacristy one winter's day two years ago, more
dead than alive. Against Sister Fenelia's advice, Kesira
had nursed the bird back to health.

Now Zolkan was her only link with those happier days—
except for her unshakable faith in Gelya's teachings.

"If Rouvin hadn't died, Ayondela wouldn't have brought
this foul winter down upon us," said Kesira. "But we must
accept what has happened and work to change it. We must

find her and persuade her of the danger, of the error in choosing the path she now follows."

"Impossible," grumbled Zolkan. "She is jade. She is evil."

To Kesira's surprise, Molimo shook his head vigorously. It was the first time she had seen him become so agitated over Ayondela. The youth traced words in the dust on the stony floor. Kesira read and as quickly Molimo erased them to make room for new words.

"Not so," Molimo wrote, his finger bending into an arch as he pressed down hard in his vehemence. "Ayondela is good. Zolkan is wrong. We must find her."

Kesira sighed. "Yes, I agree, but where might she have gone? All I know is that she is to the south." Kesira shivered. "To the now frigid south."

Molimo wrote more. "Isle of Eternal Winter."

Kesira frowned. She pulled her cloak tighter around her body and leaned forward, balancing herself on her staff.

"What is this Isle of Eternal Winter?" she asked, puzzled. She had been well schooled in Gelya's teaching by the Sisters, but parts of her education had been ignored. Geography was one. When an acolyte spent more time within the nunnery walls than without, why bother with learning more than necessary about the terrain surrounding the Order?

"Isle of Eternal Winter?" called Zolkan from his perch. "No! We never arrive. Oh, my feather oil is freezing. I shall surely perish in this cold. Die, I tell you!"

"What is it?" she demanded of Molimo.

"To the south," was all he wrote. Her eyes locked once more with his. The fathomless depths of the man's soul beckoned to her. Kesira felt herself being drawn in, tumbling, falling, spinning through infinite space. She jerked away, eyes averted to the campfire. Was this strange magnetism an aftereffect of being caught in the jade rain, or did it come with the shape transformation? Whatever caused it, it frightened Kesira a great deal.

Molimo started to write something more of Ayondela, then stopped. His ears twitched and his nostrils dilated. Fur popped out on his cheeks and bony ridges above his eyes buried those burning black eyes in deep pits. He shook all over and dropped to hands and knees—to his paws.

"Molimo, no!" the woman cried. She threw her arms around his neck, as if this would stop the shape change. If anything, it accelerated it. She found herself clinging to Molimo's clothing, the sleek gray wolf snarling and snapping at the wind just a few feet distant.

"Do not stop him. Let Molimo go," cautioned Zolkan. "His ears are sharp. He hears them on our trail."

"Them? Who do you mean?" she asked. Kesira had lost Molimo, at least for the moment. She turned to Zolkan, eyes hot and demanding. "Is there something you haven't told me?"

The *trilla* bird stuck its head under one huge wing. Kesira reached up and grabbed the wing, pulling it away from the bird's thick body. One beady eye peered out at her. Guiltily.

"Tell me, damn you."

"Gelya not like your word choice."

"Gelya taught that the sun also shines on the wicked." Kesira fought to control her anger. "It shines even on you, Zolkan, even though you have deceived me."

"No lies. I tell no lies."

"You haven't told me the truth. Where is the difference?"

The *trilla* bird said nothing.

"Who follows?" Kesira shook the bird; tiny pinfeathers drifted gently downward until caught by the cold drafts of air gusting around her ankles.

"Molimo thinks they are Order of Steel Crescent."

"But how? They were all destroyed in the Quaking Lands."

"No," contradicted the bird. "They sought Howenthal as patron, but many fled when we destroyed him. Nehan-dir and others still follow us."

Kesira hunkered down by the fire, hands automatically thrust out to the feeble warmth. The Order of the Steel Crescent was not a religious order but rather one of mercenaries. Their patron had sold them to a cruel demon in exchange for payment of gambling debts; this had warped their views. They followed only strength, gave their allegiance only to the patron promising the most. Howenthal

had done so and had recruited Nehan-dir and his mercenaries. Now that Howenthal was no more, Nehan-dir undoubtedly sought a new patron for his small but intensely
combative group.

"Why cannot they see that war is not inevitable, that it
comes only from the failure of human wisdom?" Kesira
had run afoul of Nehan-dir and the others in his Order and
knew they were driven by ambition as large as the entire
world. They saw in the jade demons the opportunity to
gain status, power, riches. For so long those of the Steel
Crescent had been outcasts. The woman couldn't imagine
what she would have felt if Gelya had sold her and all her
Sisters for debts. The demons possessed greater than human strength, longevity, and traits. Alas, with the intense
burning of the good came the venal. What magnified to ele-
vate the demons above humanity also magnified their
flaws.

"Nehan-dir will not parley," she said. "But why must he
seek our deaths?"

"Killed Howenthal."

"We had no choice in that," she said, her tone almost
pleading. "Howenthal wanted to reign over all the others,
to disturb the balance of the ages existing between demon
and mortal. The jade made him too greedy. Can't Nehan-
dir see that?"

"Sees only his own misfortune and that you are cause of
most recent setbacks," said Zolkan. The *trilla* bird shifted
from one foot to the other, the cold rock beginning to affect
his circulation. He sank down and let his bright green
feathers cover his feet. This satisfied him for the moment.
One eye fixed on Kesira.

"We should attempt to parley. We can . . ."

Kesira reacted instinctively. The scrape of leather
against stone alerted her in time to rise and swing up her
staff. The butt end caught the man squarely between the
legs. He let out an anguished, "ooophhh!" and dropped to
his knees, clutching his groin. Kesira brought the other
end of the staff about smartly, landing it squarely on the
back of the man's head. The dull *snap!* and the way his
head lolled forward at an unnatural angle told her she had
broken his neck.

Kesira stepped over the man's fallen sword, gingerly

moving it with her stone-wood staff. Gelya taught the evil of steel weapons; this finely wrought sword had brought only death to its wielder.

The nun examined the man and opened the front of his jerkin. Burned with cruel force into his left shoulder was an ugly half-moon of scar tissue. He had been a follower of the Order of the Steel Crescent.

"Are there more about?" she asked Zolkan.

"Molimo checks now. Maybe."

Kesira Minette turned and stamped her foot, a tiny cloud of dust rising. "Tell me. I know by your tone that you're holding something back. What is it, Zolkan?"

"More than Nehan-dir walks outside. Much more. Demons battle demons."

Kesira had never found out how Zolkan knew of these matters. Yet the *trilla* bird had intimate—and accurate—knowledge of so many demonic affairs that she never doubted him when he made his pronouncements.

"Molimo! He's outside!"

"Stop! Wait!" Over Zolkan's protests, Kesira bolted into the jaws of the storm once again to warn Molimo. He might betray himself in his animal form. Some measure of his intelligence fled with the change, replaced by strength and animal cunning. Against the jade demons those were feeble commodities.

Kesira rushed forth, then staggered as Zolkan landed heavily on her shoulder. She glared at the *trilla* bird, then opened her cloak and let him burrow underneath. Kesira did not tell Zolkan this, but she needed his reassuring presence. Dealing with demons lay far beyond the training of a nun, even a Sister of the Mission. Any words of encouragement or warning Zolkan might give would be appreciated.

It might mean their lives.

She stumbled into the wind, eyes watering anew. Of Molimo she found not a trace, although she did discover the dead soldier's horse tethered to the lee side of a low hill. Kesira mentally marked the location; it would be good to ride again. She and Molimo had run their horses to ground. The cold winds had finished them with wracking coughs that shook the noble animals all the way down to their hooves. Molimo had killed the animals out of mercy;

they had eaten well enough for the next week, even if the going had been slower afoot.

"Are there others of the Order of the Steel Crescent?" she asked Zolkan.

"How do I know?" The bird buried itself deeper under the coarsely woven fabric of her robe.

The thunder rolling through the hills stopped Kesira in her tracks. She looked up in time to see two demons atop a mountain. One she recognized as Eznofadil; he blazed with the inner light of the jade power. The other was human in appearance but definitely more than human. He withstood blast after fiery blast from the jade demon, turning aside the potent thrusts with easy contempt.

The contempt turned to fear when another demon joined Eznofadil.

"Ayondela!" cried Kesira, but the name was lost in the wind. The air turned noticeably colder and frost formed quickly on the woman's face. She had to continually brush it off to see how the battle progressed.

The tide turned against the unknown demon.

"Toyaga's power leaves him. Jade overwhelms him," said Zolkan.

"Toyaga?"

Zolkan said nothing. Kesira looked at the ebb and flow of the battle. Ayondela lifted her icy scepter and sent a hailstorm pelting down on Toyaga. The demon cringed; Eznofadil threw another of his lightning bolts. It struck Toyaga squarely in the chest and sent the demon staggering. Against either Ayondela or Eznofadil he might prevail. Their combined might—augmented by the green evil of the jade—proved too much.

Toyaga fled.

Kesira slumped when she saw Ayondela and Eznofadil so triumphant. She had no idea who this Toyaga was, but he opposed them and the evil they sought to impose on the world. They would upset the balance of the ages, to force their wills on humanity rather than allowing mortal rule and appropriate worship.

Numbed by the sight and the cold, Kesira responded too slowly when she heard steel being drawn from a sheath. Her stone-wood staff barely deflected the lunge. The sword passed so close to her head that a lock of brown hair fell away, severed cleanly by the honed blade. Zolkan emitted a frightened squeak, more like a *prin* rat than a bird.

Kesira stared into the set face of her adversary. Another mercenary of the Steel Crescent. Kesira saw the same triumph mirrored in his grizzled face that she had witnessed on Ayondela and Eznofadil's.

The man rocked back for the thrust that would pierce her heart and leave her body to freeze in the polar winds.

Chapter Two

GELYA HAD NOT taught the principle of honorable surrender. Kesira Minette's patron demon had preached a faith that looked through death, but also a tenacity to cling to life. Honor and duty were all. Acquiescence to death was not a part of that.

Kesira's staff came up to parry the sword blow. The impact knocked her flat on the ground, stunning her. Through dazed eyes she watched as the shiny blade rose above the man's helmeted head, his knuckles white as he gripped the hilt tightly.

Then the world turned red and warm.

She blinked, not sure what had happened. A trembling hand wiped blood from her eyes, but it was not her blood. Struggling to sit up, Kesira managed to push the heavy weight off her chest. The soldier's body slid off with a dull thud.

The woman wiped the last of the blood from her eyes and saw that the Steel Crescent soldier lacked a throat. Bloody ribbons remained of his flesh. And standing nearby, crimson trickling off his gray muzzle, stood Molimo. The wolf's green eyes blazed with hatred.

"Thank you," Kesira said softly, not wanting to frighten Molimo more than necessary. When the change came on him, his human conditioning fled. But Kesira had never satisfactorily determined how much remained. She took no chances.

Molimo snarled and advanced, fangs yellowed and sharp, yearning for still more blood.

A shrill squawk stopped Molimo. The wolf-man turned his mobile lupine head about to stare at Zolkan. The *trilla*

21

bird crawled out of his hiding place and began yammering at Molimo in a singsong that Kesira did not understand. The wolf turned and bolted into the gloom, illuminated only by occasional—natural—lightning bolts.

"Thank you," the woman sighed. "What is it you say to him when he is like this? You've spoken those words before."

"It's nothing," the bird said.

"Why won't you tell me? Aren't we friends? Haven't we been through so much together?"

"Cold. Feathers freeze to my body. Return to piss-poor cave."

Kesira levered herself to her feet using the staunch stone-wood staff. "Very well, but one day you *will* tell me."

Zolkan said nothing.

The fire had died to embers and required several minutes of tending to build back to its former cheering warmth. Kesira sat, warming herself. Zolkan waddled around the perimeter of the fire, long wings outstretched, bobbing in and out until his feathers began to singe. Only then was the *trilla* bird warm enough to take wing and settle down on the ledge high in the cave.

"Molimo returns," the bird announced.

Kesira waited, expecting to see the lean gray wolf with the insanely blazing green eyes. A naked, shivering man returned.

"Oh, Molimo. Here." She hurried to him with his discarded clothing. Even as she helped him dress, Kesira felt urges within her toward him—urges that she tried to deny. Not that Gelya taught celibacy; he said to suppress natural functions was as evil as exalting them. Yet it was wrong for her to desire Molimo in the ways she did. She had nursed him to health when he was vulnerable. She would be taking advantage of him even now, even with his body restored. The jade rains had left him afflicted and open to any kindness.

Kesira swallowed hard. The only victory over her love for Molimo might lie in flight.

The youth quickly dressed and sat by the fire. Zolkan squawked and fluttered and carried on the singsong speech. Molimo paid no heed. As suddenly as he had appeared, Molimo stood and left.

Kesira started to call after him, then stopped. Wherever he went, he would return. In less than ten minutes he did come back, arms laden with bloody clothing stripped off the fallen soldiers. Molimo sorted through it and passed over the smallest of the articles for Kesira to don.

"They hardly turn me into the Empress Aglenella's lady-in-waiting," said Kesira, pirouetting about in the too-large clothing. "And you," she said, having to laugh, "are hardly decked out as a courtier." If Kesira's new clothing flapped in the wind, Molimo's cut off circulation. The tightness of the fit made Molimo appear even stronger than he was. Bulges showed in places where none ought to have been and movement was restricted to the point of ripping the fabric as he bent down by the fire. But the added insulation against the frigid wind aided them both.

"Are there any more soldiers of the Steel Crescent awaiting us?" she asked.

Molimo glanced at Zolkan, then etched in the dust, "None. Those two were the only humans about."

"Only humans?"

"Demons walk now, too," Molimo wrote. "Eznofadil and Ayondela."

"And Toyaga," she added, wanting to see his response. A slight flicker crossed his dark eyes, but he might have been playing a game of three-match for all the information revealed. Molimo solemnly nodded.

"Tell me of Toyaga," urged Kesira. "Is he an ally?"

Molimo nodded, then wrote, "He and Merrisen were staunch friends."

"What is Toyaga's relation to Ayondela?"

"They were once lovers."

Kesira shook her head at this. It seemed all of the demons had been Ayondela's lover at some time. Many humans also, if Rouvin was any guide. The demons showed all the human traits but magnified, she reminded herself. Altruism and charity were there, but so was promiscuity and cruelty. Ayondela had to have spent more time seducing her lovers than Gelya did in teaching that kindness gave birth to kindness.

Her attention came back to Molimo. "Toyaga," the young man wrote, "was badly injured. The surviving demons have not united against those of jade. Toyaga might lead, if he were in a position to do so."

"How can we aid him?" asked Kesira. "Any opposition to the evil brought by Lenc and the others is welcome." The fire did not warm her as much as her passion for revenge. Lenc had killed her Sisters and robbed her of the only sanctuary she had ever found in this world. A cold white flame burned on Gelya's altar, the symbol of Lenc's triumph.

"He is a demon. What can we do?"

"You and Zolkan seem to know more of them than I," said Kesira. "Do you have any ideas?"

Molimo stared at her, black eyes unreadable. He finally shook his head.

"Then we must press on in our attempt to reach Ayondela and convince her that Rouvin's death was accidental and that she should oppose Eznofadil and Lenc. And if she won't fight them openly, then she ought to remain neutral."

Even as she said the words, Kesira knew the futility of their quest. The jade insinuated itself into the demon's body and took on a life of its own. Even as it gave, it took power in full measure. The virtually immortal demons would live out only a normal mortal's life span, but to Eznofadil and Lenc this had been worth it—or they did not believe they were burning themselves out in exchange for the additional power.

For Ayondela, it had been the mad act of a moment's wrath. That did not stop it from being permanent—and evil.

Kesira wiped cold sweat from her forehead at the thought that Lenc might be able to augment his already awesome power with the jade and not perish. Did he hold a secret way free of this trap?

She prayed to long-dead Gelya that this was not so.

Of Molimo she asked, "What is the Isle of Eternal Winter? You and Zolkan mentioned it."

The man ran thick fingers through his lank hair before sketching out the answer. Kesira saw the emotions playing on his normally impassive face. She wondered if imparting such information took so much from him. It obviously did. But why?

"The Isle," he wrote, "is Ayondela's stronghold. Even though it lies to the warm south, the summit of the mountain on the Isle is always covered in snow and ice."

"And now? With her bringing this permanent winter on us?"

"Even the seas may be frozen," Molimo wrote. He licked his lips, then wiped his finger on the front of his too-small shirt, indicating he had nothing else to say.

"The day has been long, but tomorrow we ride," she said. Molimo nodded. Zolkan already slept, his head stuffed under one wing. Kesira looked from companion to companion, wondering what they shared. And why they excluded her from the knowledge.

She wrestled with troubled dreams that night, getting sleep but little rest.

Kesira Minette reined in the horse. It stood, snorting kinetic plumes of breath into the frosty morning air. She pointed far to the south and the tiny village huddled on the banks of the River Pharna. At the headwaters, in the Yearn Mountains, had been her nunnery. The river meandered across the Roggen Plains and hurried south to this spot some ten days ride from the Sea of Katad. "We can make the Order's lands in another day," Kesira said. Zolkan stirred restlessly on her shoulder, only his head peering out.

"Why bother?"

"Zolkan," she chided. "We seek those who worship Ayondela. If they can lend their prayers and pleas to their patron, this gives us even more chance to sway Ayondela."

The *trilla* bird sniffed loudly. His contempt for the idea carried all too well, but Kesira was not going to argue the issue with him.

Molimo kicked at the flanks of his horse and came abreast Kesira. The man-wolf pointed to tiny dust clouds dotting the plains between them and the Order.

"Horses?"

Molimo gestured that it might be soldiers of the Steel Crescent.

"Can we avoid them?" she asked. Even before Molimo silently nodded, she had mentally added, *We must.*

She tapped the reins against the horse's neck and

nudged the mare down toward the plains and the Order of
Ayondela. This approach appealed to her. Who better than
the demon's worshippers to intervene? They had to believe
in their patron and would recoil in horror when they discovered Ayondela had eaten the jade. If for no other reason, they would intercede to return Ayondela to her former
status, to keep change from coming too quickly.

Kesira held her head proudly as she rode, a prisoner to
hope.

Under the cover of nightfall, after a long, bitter day of
following ravines iced over and robbed of their summer's
bounty, they arrived at the side door to the Order's head-
quarters. Molimo had chosen their path well; not once had
they encountered a patrol of the Steel Crescent mercenaries.

"We should hurry in," Kesira said. "I am certain they
bar the gates when darkness becomes absolute."

Molimo did not stir. The expression on his face, the set of
his body, told Kesira he wanted to bolt and run. Fearing a
transformation into wolf, she reached out and gripped his
sleeve.

"Are you all right?" she asked anxiously. He nodded, his
eyes never leaving the walls of the Order. Ayondela had
done well by those in this abbey. The walls were well
tended and the grounds minutely cared for, a fact apparent
even though the frost clung so perniciously to the soil.
Shrubs and other low bushes lined the road leading to the
main gate and fruit trees scattered themselves about to
lend shade in a summer now aborted and a windbreak during stormy months.

"They will not harm you," Kesira said. "The Orders of
Gelya and Ayondela have much in common—had much in
common," she hastily corrected. "They preach goodness
and humility, not death and conquest."

This did not relax Molimo. Like a *renn*-stone statue Molimo sat in the saddle, staring sightlessly ahead.

Kesira tugged at the reins of Molimo's horse. It started
forward even as Molimo shook himself out of his stupor.
Kesira often wondered what scenes he saw through his
other-eyes, the half-human eyes and the half-wolf ones.

"Cold. Too cold," Zolkan complained. "Let's fly in."

"No," Kesira said, too sharply. The bird's powerful beak

clacked in response. "We must not give the impression of spying on them. All must be open when we approach."

"Do it soon. My feather oil is stiffening. Never fly again. Never!"

Kesira rode boldly to the gate and waved to a solitary figure atop the wall. The sentry stopped pacing and peered down, giving no challenge. Kesira called out, "We are travelers in need of a night's lodging. Can we avail ourselves of Ayondela's hospitality?"

"Where do you come from?"

Kesira rocked back in surprise. Her horse tried to shy but she held the mare firmly. When anyone approached the nunnery of Gelya asking for aid, they received it without question. She had assumed such was the case at the Abbey of Ayondela.

"It is cold and we are tired and hungry," she said. "I am a Sister of the Mission of the Order of Gelya."

"Gelya's dead," was the only response from the sentry.

"I know." Kesira didn't try to hold back the bitterness she felt, both at the fact of Gelya's murder and the attitude of the person within the walls.

"One moment."

Kesira, Molimo, and Zolkan waited impatiently as the figure vanished into the gloom. In the far west the sun dipped below the horizon and took what little heat had been in the air with it. The sunsets had been spectacular due to the ice crystals in the air, but for such beauty Kesira had little time. She would have preferred the gentler hues of summer to the vivid, precise visions cast across the ice clouds.

After what seemed an eternity in the gathering cold and dark, the gate creaked open to reveal a pair of hooded figures.

"I am Kesira Minette, of—" The figure on the right cut her off.

"We know. Our Brother has relayed your name. Why do you come here?"

"Can we discuss this inside, out of the wind?" A gust of wind caught at Kesira's tattered cloak and momentarily exposed Zolkan. The *trilla* bird was more used to jungle climes than arctic winds. He shivered without pause now.

The two shadow figures consulted, then stepped back,

pulling wide the gate. Kesira rode forward but Molimo hung back. She turned in the saddle and motioned for him to join her. With great reluctance, he did so. She failed to understand the problem.

The gate swung shut behind them. A heavy iron rod dropped into place, securely barring it.

"Do you have trouble with brigands?" she asked.

"There are many along the river with whom we have no desire to communicate." The robed figure threw back her cowl. Hair of spun copper reflected the pale light gleaming through kitchen windows. The face might have been lovely, but the scars on both cheeks marred any true beauty and left even the soul touched by the disfigurement.

"Forgive my lapse. We seldom admit visitors anymore. I am Abbess Camilia of Ayondela's Order." She executed a short bow.

"This is my friend, Molimo," Kesira said, indicating the man. His dark eyes took on a haunted appearance. Kesira hoped that this did not signal the change. Too many other-beasts roamed the plains now, the product of the battles between demons. Rouvin had hunted the other-beasts with the ferocity of a trapped leopard. As more and more of the half-creatures came into weary existence, this attitude might spread. Kesira prayed to Gelya that those of this Order did not similarly hunt those unable to control their form.

Kesira did not bother to introduce Zolkan. The *trilla* bird cowered within her robe. While it gave her a slightly hunchbacked appearance, neither the Abbess Camilia nor the Brother with her commented.

The Abbess made a small hand signal. The man returned silently to his solitary pacing along the top of the guard wall to keep watch for other unwanted travelers. Seldom had Kesira been made to feel more like a burden and less like a guest.

"All we need is space in your stables. We won't disturb your routine or rituals."

"The rituals are seldom performed in recent times," said the Abbess with a sigh.

"Then you know?"

Camilia spun so that Kesira could not see her face. Without a word, the Abbess walked to the kitchen door. She held it open, beckoning to Molimo and Kesira.

Not wishing to shiver in the cold longer than necessary, and fearing Zolkan might be at the end of his avian tolerances to cold, Kesira hurried forward. Molimo followed but more slowly. Once in the kitchen, Kesira relaxed. Everything reminded her of the kitchen where she had grown up, surrounded by her Sisters, given shelter and peace and all she might want to eat. The odors of roasting meat rose and made her mouth water, and while she wasn't certain, she thought she smelled a fruit pie baking. Where they had found fruit after such a treacherous turn in the weather, Kesira didn't know. It was enough for her to pretend they had an orchard nearby laden with fruits of all descriptions instead of the barren trees she had seen riding to the gates.

"Eat," said the Abbess, putting plates before Kesira and Molimo. She eyed Molimo strangely, her left hand resting on the red knotted rope about her middle. Camilia's fingers traced out the knots and worried at the very end of her Order's cord in a way that made Kesira uneasy.

"We thank you, but again, we do not want to put you to any trouble. Simple fare is all we ask, and a warm place to stay. With our horses in the stable will be fine."

"You are of Gelya's Order?" asked Camilia.

"Yes." Kesira took a deep breath. The Abbess served them generous portions of cooked meat and stewed greens. As was the custom, no drink accompanied the meal. Kesira flipped back her robe and allowed Zolkan to waddle forth. The *trilla* bird eyed the meat skeptically, then attacked the greens with vigor.

"We see few such birds," Camilia said, frowning. "When we do, they end up in our stewpots."

Without lifting his beak from the plate, Zolkan managed to squawk out, "Butchers. Cannibals."

"Do you know of Ayondela?" asked Kesira, her voice rising to drown out the bird's comment. "That she has partaken of the jade?"

"That's a lie!" raged Camilia. The Abbess slammed her hand down hard onto the table. Flatware leaped upward and Zolkan had to catch a particularly toothsome piece of vegetable in midair.

"I speak only the truth, only what I have personally witnessed," said Kesira.

"There are others who make this claim, but they lie, too!"

"No lie. Traveling across the land signs are everywhere. The jade rains are partially responsible for Molimo's lost tongue. He cannot speak. And," Kesira went on quickly, "we have witnessed demons battling. Eznofadil and Lenc, who murdered Gelya and devastated my Order, carry the telltale green hue."

"Ayondela would never turn away from her duties to her worshippers. We adore her as our patron. How can any demon forsake such love as that which we give so willingly?"

"Love sought," Kesira said gently, "is good, but given unsought is far better."

The Abbess said nothing more, her eyes hot coals betraying her continued anger at Kesira's insolence.

"We have seen the demons battling—and Ayondela taking the jade." Kesira got no response to this. She pushed on, fearing that she trod on treacherous soils now. "She became wroth over the death of her half-demon son, Rouvin."

"We have seen this. Ayondela has told us in our prayers of Rouvin's foul murder."

Kesira shot a hasty glance at Molimo. He sat as if paralyzed.

"But Ayondela has not told you of her alliance with Eznofadil and Lenc—and the jade?"

"No."

Kesira knew that Camilia thought she lied about this and resented it. "I can show you the truth of what I say."

Camilia made a vague motion with her hand indicating that Kesira could do whatever she wanted. Molimo tried to stir, but only managed to shift slightly in his seat. Zolkan waddled over to Molimo's plate and began gorging himself on the greens he found there, not caring what went on around him. Kesira sometimes admired the *trilla* bird's ability to focus in single-mindedly on nothing but food.

"The rune sticks. I will cast them and show you."

Kesira closed her eyes and settled into the timeless calm so like when passions are spent. Her mind floated and sank lightly, to touch the hidden passages within herself.

Kesira opened her brown eyes and stared at the table, only vaguely aware that others had filed into the room and now lined the walls. She reached beneath her robe and pulled forth the box containing the bone rune sticks. With a flourish she cast the sticks onto the table.

"This is the future," she intoned. "Those of you who can also read the runes, do so. You see what I see, that Eznofadil and Lenc defile our world. That their ambitions soar too high."

"Men would be demons, and demons would be gods," someone in the room said softly. "I see it in the rune sticks."

"There is more," said Kesira. Agile fingers traced over the fall of the sticks, interpreting the patterns, pointing out the message given her. "There were three demons who originally sought the illicit power granted by the jade. Howenthal is dead, in his fortress in the center of the Quaking Lands."

"Wemilat," said the one who had spoken before. "The demon known as The Ugly died in the battle with Howenthal."

"That is so," Kesira rushed on. "And Ayondela replaced Howenthal in the unholy trinity of jade."

"They would conquer all."

Kesira warmed to the interpretation. Whoever it was reading the runes over her shoulder aided her with the telling.

"They bring only misery to our world. We must petition Ayondela for succor. Have her return to the serene ways before Lenc and Eznofadil. She is not evil, but the jade turns her so."

"Ayondela," came the voice, louder this time. "She weaves in and out of this casting. The runes . . . the runes."

"What do you read?" demanded Abbess Camilia.

Before Kesira could answer, the other spoke, firmly and accusingly. "This one. Kesira Minette of the Order of Gelya, she and the other were responsible for Rouvin's death and forcing our patron to forsake us!"

"Wait," cried Kesira. "That's not what happened. We—"

"The runes speak it," insisted the unseen speaker.

"They killed Rouvin and forced Ayondela to vengeance. Because of them Ayondela has brought perpetual snows and freezing winter during our growing season. They are our enemy. Give them to Ayondela and our wondrous patron will embrace us once again and turn the leaves green with the loving kiss of spring!"

Kesira launched to her feet, only to find her arms seized by strong hands. She struggled but there were too many for her to escape. Kesira heard Zolkan's outraged squawking as the *trilla* bird also fell to groping hands. Of Molimo, Kesira saw nothing. But from the lack of sound, she guessed he succumbed without a fight. He had been in that odd trance ever since sighting the Order's walls.

"To the dungeons," ordered Abbess Camilia. "We will pray to Ayondela all night if necessary, and tell her of our gift."

"Murderer." The single word rose from one set of lips, only to be taken up by all. As they shoved Kesira toward the stairs leading downward into the bowels of the earth, they chanted "murderer" over and over until she wanted to clap hands over her ears and shut out the sound.

The clanging of the heavy steel door to the cell came almost as a relief. At least now there was silence. Deathly silence.

Chapter Three

KESIRA MINETTE sat in the corner of the cell, knees pulled up to her chest and arms encircling them. Even this did not prevent the cold from seeping into her bones.

"We're out of the wind," she said.

"Still cold," Zolkan complained. The *trilla* bird fluttered around the tiny cell, barely able to get aloft before having to swerve to miss the stone walls. Watching his corkscrewing path made Kesira dizzy. The confusion of green feathers, blue wingtips and the rosy red plumage of his breast spun in wild circles that blended and blurred and gave her a headache. She closed her eyes and leaned back against the rough stone, fingers working over the knotted blue cord at her waist.

She had tried, but had not properly thought through her dilemma. If she could read the rune sticks, it stood to reason others could, also. Kesira had to admit the reading given by the Sister of Ayondela's Order had been all too accurate. But, like their patron, they had not given her a chance to explain.

All were too eager to accuse, then repent their error at leisure. She had to convince them that any mistake would be fatal, that there'd be no opportunity to change their minds later.

Kesira found some solace in her rituals. Peace descended and enfolded her in its velvet arms—or was it numbness?

"Escape from here. Not like this place. Too dark. No one can see my lovely plumage." Zolkan landed heavily against the bars in the cell door and clung with strong talons. Kesira heard the scraping of hard claw against

steel. She didn't have to examine the bars to know that
Zolkan's claws gave out before the tiniest of scratches had
been made on the tempered bar.

"How do you recommend we do this?" she asked. "Zolkan? Molimo?"

The bird squawked in frustration and returned to circle
nervously in the tiny airspace provided. But from Molimo
there came not a sound, no movement, no indication that
he even lived. Frightened at his complete lack of response,
Kesira slid across the rough floor and sat beside him. He
did not give any sign of noticing her.

His eyes were open and fixated on infinity. Only the
slow up-and-down movement of his chest showed that he
lived. Kesira passed her hand in front of his face to break
the gaze, but failed to produce any hint of life.

"Molimo, what's wrong? We're not in a hopeless situation. Molimo!" She shook him as hard as she could. Only
then did he stir—he pulled away from her.

"Zolkan, what's happened to him?" she asked the *trilla*
bird. "I've never seen him like this before. It's as if he is
stunned. Has he hit his head? Or"—cold fingers gripped at
her heart—"is this part of the transformation?"

"Not losing humanity," said Zolkan, now grounded and
waddling to where they sat. The bird launched himself to
land heavily on Molimo's shoulder. The man paid Zolkan
no heed. Zolkan began the singsong speech that excluded
Kesira totally. She listened, trying to find some sense in
what must be words. She failed. But the effect on Molimo
was all she could have wished. Slowly the man's eyes
focused and his head turned until his nose and Zolkan's
beak rubbed.

"Bad breath," Zolkan said, sidestepping along Molimo's
shoulder.

"Molimo, what is it?" asked Kesira.

He turned to her, a slight smile on his lips. A pile of dust
provided his writing material.

"Evil all about us," he wrote. "We must not linger."

"This is hardly my idea of luxury to rival the Emperor's
palace in Limaden," she said tartly.

This produced what passed for a laugh from the tongue-
severed youth. He quickly sketched out, "Magicks abound.

Saps my strength. Can hardly move. We must escape *very* soon."

"How?"

Their eyes met, then Molimo began to write quickly. Kesira caught her breath and started to protest what he had written, then changed her mind. It was dangerous, and she did not approve, but Gelya had said that to believe only in possibilities was not faith but mere philosophy. She had to put her entire faith in Molimo and Zolkan. In no other way could they escape from this cell—and the imprisonment and death offered by the Abbess Camilia.

"Do it," she said quietly. "But hurry. I do not like to watch when you change."

Even as she spoke, Molimo's body flowed and rippled, breaking free of the shackles of human weakness. Replacing the sleek, tanned flesh were furred gray flanks, powerful jaws, and eyes as green as the jade they fought. Molimo gave voice to a low, heartful howl.

Zolkan took flight and hovered above, straining to maintain his position. "He is strong enough," the bird told her. Kesira had to believe. She had to.

Molimo arrowed forward in the narrow cell like a gray battering ram. The wolf's full weight—and more—struck the steel door. Kesira clutched at her belly and bent double as forces beyond her understanding hammered against the steel forbidden to followers of Gelya.

Kesira clapped her hands over her ears as the door blasted outward, jerked free of its hinges. The loud clanging filled the dungeons as the door smashed to the stone floor. Molimo stood on all fours, panting, head swiveling left and right, fangs bared. When he looked over his shoulder, Kesira had the eerie feeling that he might consider her for a meal. But the wolf trotted off, growling deep in his throat.

Zolkan fluttered to her shoulder. "He gives voice to the rage he cannot as human. To lack a tongue. He will pay for that. Of all indignities, that is worst. He will pay."

"Who?" asked Kesira. "Who cut out Molimo's tongue?"

But the *trilla* bird had taken wing and fluttered down the corridor after Molimo. Kesira rushed after them, feeling alone. However it was, those two shared a common bond that she did not understand. Worst of all, they did not

take her into their confidence. She might have nursed Molimo to health after he had been caught in the jade rains,
but he was chary with information about his past. She had
thought it an aftereffect, just as the shape-change was.
Now she wondered.

If Zolkan knew, Molimo did also. Where else might the
bird have gotten the information? He had been with Kesira for almost two years—and she had nursed him back to
health as she had Molimo.

She thought she was following them, but the corridor
stretched, barren, in front of her. Barred cell doors stood on
either side of the stone tunnel. Kesira ran to one and
peered through. Inside huddled a skeleton with a chain
fastened to what had once been a living neck. She shuddered. Had the Abbess Camilia ordered some poor creature
imprisoned and then forgotten him? Or had they remembered?

Kesira pushed such thoughts from her mind. She spun
about and stared into the other cell. A small child crouched
in the middle of the enclosure, playing with a chitinous insect.

"Wait," she called to the child. "I'll get you out." Kesira
looked about frantically for some way to open the barred
door. The lock had long ago turned brittle with rust, but
still presented a formidable barrier.

Her eyes came to rest on her stone-wood staff. Not even
thinking why it was there or why she hadn't seen it previously, she hefted the staff and ran the end through the lock
hasp. Using leverage, what strength remained to her and
the full weight of her body, she broke the lock. Fumbling
in her haste, she cast off the bar and threw open the door.

"You're free now," she said, her words trailing off when
she saw the thing in the cell. It had been a small, abused
child. Now it filled the small space with scales and bulging
muscles and a mouth filled with multiple rows of glistening fangs. A bloated purple tongue lolled to one side
and, Kesira saw, all the way to the beast's belly.

The roar deafened her. Without thinking, she raised her
staff and found it had turned into smoke. The vapor drifted
away and left her helpless in the face of this monster.

"Away," she said, beginning to back from it. Her mind
fought for composure and control over her panic-wracked

body. She might get the door locked again. Bar the steel plate. Find another lock.

The beast rushed.

Only instinct saved her. Kesira dived and twisted in midair, landing heavily and rolling. She came to her feet, the creature in the corridor behind her.

Kesira Minette ran for her life.

Panting, gasping for air in the musty dungeon, she found herself making no headway. Her legs pumped furiously, and she stayed in place. As she slackened her effort, she was drawn back toward the creature's huge mouth and those long, savage fangs. Kesira grabbed out and tried to find a hold along the wetly seeping stone walls. Her fingertips turned bloody with the effort—and she failed to slacken her inexorable backward pace.

"Go from strength to strength," she moaned out. "It is Gelya's will. Use what lies within. Honor demands it. For life!"

Kesira began running faster and faster and kept herself just beyond the beast's snapping jaws. Hot red eyes burned like embers in the thing's head and bloated white nostrils dilated with the effort it expended.

Legs pumping, Kesira found the chance to calm herself. Her mind regained control of her body. People failed not from physical weakness, but from lack of resolve; hers stiffened. She would not provide easy dinner for this creature locked away in Ayondela's cellars.

Even as she concentrated on escape, a cold wind gusted across her back. She broke stride and fell facedown. She rolled over, legs coming up to kick away the beast as it sprang. No attack came.

Molimo and Zolkan stood in the corridor, the monster gone as surely as her staff had turned to smoke and wafted away.

"All right?" asked Zolkan. The bird waddled forward and hopped onto her leg. She felt sharp, familiar talons as it walked up to sit in her lap, one beady eye glaring at her.

"Did you see it? The monster chasing me?"

"Magicks everywhere. This place nexus for Ayondela's wrath. Power turned inward and down into earth. Bad. Cold, too." The bird fluttered up to her shoulder for a better purchase. "Get dirty. Will my feathers ever come clean?" Zolkan stretched forth one long wing and shook it until tiny green and blue feathers from the tip fluttered free.

"But the monster," she said, giving way to uncontrolled shaking.

"Magicks," repeated Zolkan. "Brought on us by Ayondela." The bird craned his head around and looked at the wolf. The green eyes blinked. "Eznofadil's magicks," Zolkan corrected, as if he had been so informed by Molimo.

Molimo spun and trotted off, head low, nose sniffing here and there as he went. Kesira got to her feet and followed, amazed that she actually traversed the hallway now. She forced herself to glance into the cell with the skeleton.

The cell stood empty.

And the steel cell door through which the fanged thing had rushed was firmly closed, its cell empty, also.

"Magicks," she muttered. These were far from her lessons in the nunnery. Kesira considered it a major talent being able to cast the rune sticks and divine some small measure of the past—and future. Many had considered this valuable. Rouvin had commented several times on how few mortals possessed the talent.

Kesira would gladly trade it now for a sight of the sun, even if it were wreathed in icy clouds and freezing winds.

"Stay," Zolkan warned her. "Molimo must bear brunt of attack. His duty, his punishment."

"What?"

She skidded to a halt and saw the wolf at a crossing corridor, head jerking to and fro, jaws snapping at thin air. Kesira frowned when she saw faint disturbances in the air, ghostly patches of glowing light flitting over Molimo's head.

"What are they?" she asked, and even as she spoke, the ghosts took substance and attacked Molimo.

"No!" she shrieked. Zolkan gripped firmly on her shoulder, talons sinking to flesh. Powerful wings beat and held her back. Kesira tried to spin free, but found the *trilla* bird too firmly lodged for that.

"He more powerful. Wait. Wait."

Molimo fought the nightmare creatures. They shapeshifted constantly, flowing for advantage over the wolf. Molimo fought them the best he could. Strong jaws clamped firmly, only to find ghost flesh. The wolf howled and fought and succeeded in herding both the other-beasts into one corridor. This prevented them from attacking him simultaneously, but Kesira still doubted Molimo could win.

The beasts turned from snake to owl to leopard to *chillna* cat and back into gauzy white light as they strove for supremacy.

"Molimo draws them," said Zolkan. "They sense otherness in him and hate him for it."

"We must help."

"No. No way. Molimo strong. Molimo good."

Kesira ripped Zolkan free of her shoulder and ran to aid Molimo. The wolf never looked up, but one of the other-beasts did. In that instant, Molimo attacked and found firm throat to rip out in a bloody fountain. Kesira blinked as the hot life fluid spattered her. Molimo freed his victim and pounced on the remaining creature.

The other-beast turned to dancing specks of light and *popped* out of sight. Even as she stared at the bloody corpse on the floor, it evaporated like mist in the warming sun. Of the fight, only Molimo and the blood on Kesira's gray robe remained.

"We cannot battle this way," she told the wolf. "Molimo, come with me. We must leave this awful place."

The green orbs still carried kill-lust within them, but Molimo's tension went away and the powerful shoulder muscles relaxed from the spring he had planned to launch.

"How escape? Where go?" cawed Zolkan.

Kesira didn't know. She pointed at random down one of the corridors, then started off, the wolf and *trilla* bird tagging along. As she walked, her confidence mounted. One direction might be as good—or bad—as another. It depended on what use they made of all they discovered along the way.

But confusion returned when she came to another juncture and another and another. All looked identical. She was at the point of tears when she spotted stairs leading upward.

"There!" she cried. "We'll be aboveground in a moment."

"Magicks," muttered Zolkan. "Molimo says—"

Kesira had no chance to hear the warning. She took a single step forward and found herself lost in a fleshy, pulpy mass. Air cut off, she battled to make a tiny pocket in the juicy, fragrantly enveloping crush around her. Her lips brushed over the walls of her new prison; Kesira tasted fruit.

Lungs at the point of bursting, she pushed away her curiosity and battled, using arms and legs. As suddenly as the crush had come, it ended. She dropped to hands and knees in the small tunnel and gasped.

Kesira lifted her head and peered into the dimness when she heard the slithering sounds.

"Gelya, give me strength," she gasped out.

In the tight circular tunnel came the most odious sight she had ever seen. A worm as large as she wiggled along, pulling up its hindquarters and then thrusting itself forward. The nictitating membranes over its dim eyes fell in protection as it attacked. The toothless mouth opened and cilia groped to pull her deep into the gut of this creature.

Kesira struck out awkwardly, her fist hitting the worm's side. The eye membrane tightened in a protective measure, but the forward motion stopped. Kesira began backpedaling as fast as she could. In the tight confines of the tunnel—no doubt chewed by this worm—she couldn't turn around to make better speed.

The worm regained its courage or hunger and started forth again, mouth cavity opening and closing in an obscene parody of a human kiss.

"Go away!" she shrieked. "Leave me alone!"

A cross corridor saved her. The worm had tunneled back and forth through the odd substance imprisoning her. Again Kesira's lips brushed the walls of the tunnel and fruit flavor came to her. Most important was the chance to spin about and face away from the worm. The woman hurried down the cross corridor on hands and knees.

This presented a problem she had not considered. The worm quickly came up from behind her now, its cilia licking forth to touch her bare legs. Sticky fluids impeded her progress and soon held her back.

Kesira tried to kick and found her legs bound too tightly. She was being sucked into the worm's mouth, inch by slow, agonizing inch. When digestive fluids touched her feet, she screamed.

Her faith in Gelya's teachings never faltered; one maxim rose in Kesira's mind: *Faith without deed is worthless.*

Her fingers closed on the softness of the tunnel walls and pulled free gobbets of the pulpy meat. She thrust it at the worm with little effect. Then Kesira spied a dark, round pebble in the wall. As she slipped further into the worm's interior, the digestive fluids burning worse and worse at her legs, she grabbed for the seed. It popped free. Hard, heavy, it gave her a weapon.

Kesira cried, "Die, you foul beast, die!" as she pummeled the head and mouth with the seed. The worm recoiled, but did not loosen its hold on her. Kesira kept fighting. And then was explosively shot out of the worm.

For an instant she was too dazed to think. The seed still clutched in her hand, she struck feebly at the worm. But the beast had turned away and tried to reverse its direction in the tunnel.

Hideous gobbling sounds came from out of her sight, from behind the worm. Something ate it as it had tried to devour her.

Tears flowed down Kesira's cheeks, leaving behind salty, dust-streaked paths. She clutched the seed to her breast as if it were the most precious thing in the world. Watching the worm perish was not pleasant. Even more unpleasant was the sight when the last of the worm was gobbled up and she saw what had attacked.

"Molimo," she sobbed out. The wolf stood in the tunnel licking off the ichorous worm fluids from his muzzle. He had saved her life, but she wanted to be sick to her stomach. "I want out of here. What is this place?"

Molimo came to her. She recoiled from the rough tongue licking away the worm's digestive fluids still searing her feet and legs. Tiny holes had appeared in her gray robe and the gold sash about her waist had developed two tiny burns.

"It's as if we are trapped within a fruit, and that was a fruit worm. This is a seed and the walls are the meat." She frowned. Folk tales of maidens lost within the realm of a flower came back to her. Sister Fenelia had told her those stories when she was small. She had believed them possible, and the Sister had never disputed it.

"Magicks?" she asked. Molimo bobbed his head up and down.

"There is a way free," she said with growing determination. "If magicks placed us within the fruit, then we can win free because of faith. Nothing is stronger. Nothing. Not even steel."

Molimo did not appear impressed with her catechism. She crawled along the worm tunnel until she found a tight brown barrier that yielded like tough rubber.

"The skin of the fruit. We can get out here." She placed her feet against the soft walls and found some small purchase. Using her legs, she shoved against the skin. It stretched but did not break. Just as she neared the end of her strength, Molimo growled and savagely ripped at her feet. She jerked away and his fangs caught the tough skin. A ripping sound echoed along the pulpy tunnel, and a hole appeared in the skin.

Kesira blinked in surprise. They *were* in a fruit at the bottom of a bin, but if they crawled out would they remain this size?

The possibility they might meet another fruit worm decided Kesira. She boldly gripped the ragged skin and levered herself through. She shrieked as she emerged outside the fruit. Arms and head banged painfully against walls and door as she regained her normal size. When Molimo joined her they were jumbled together in an ungainly pile. And when Zolkan erupted from the tiny hole in the fruit the three of them more than filled the bin.

The door latch popped and they tumbled into the kitchen, landing on the floor.

Molimo scrambled to his feet first, nose sniffing the air, muscles bunched for attack. Zolkan fluttered up and alighted on the doorsill leading outside. Kesira finally got to her feet, legs wobbly. She saw her stone-wood staff leaning against the wall where she'd left it on entering the abbey's kitchen. Hesitantly, she took its cool length in hand, expecting it to turn to smoke.

The substantial weight of the staff comforted her.

"Go. Leave this magick-damned place," squawked Zolkan.

"I must speak with Camilia," the woman said. "There must be a way to convince her to implore Ayondela to change her ways."

"That fruit was demon trap," said Zolkan. "Molimo agrees. Eznofadil plays with these people. They worship Ayondela, but Eznofadil plays with them. Ayondela does not care."

Kesira nodded. "What you say is undoubtedly so. I must try to change Camilia's mind, however. An ally is better than an enemy."

"We go," said Zolkan. "Get ready to flee."

"Find Molimo some clothes first," commanded Kesira. "When he changes back into human form, we don't want him to freeze to death."

Molimo and Zolkan exchanged that damnable look that excluded her, then left without further discussion. Kesira settled herself and straightened her robe and cloak the best she could. Fruit juices and blood now added to its patchwork appearance.

She cautiously explored. When Kesira heard low chants of a ritual response, her footsteps quickened. All the Order would be gathered in the chapel. When Kesira found the sacristy and peered out onto the altar a coldness swept through her. She'd thought she had experienced the depths of despair when locked in the Order's dungeons but now the nun's spirit plummeted even further.

A cold white flame burned at the altar of Ayondela. The sigil of Lenc held the Order's full attention as they worshipped. They worshipped death and destruction, the end of the world and the establishment of a newer, crueler one.

The Abbess rose and addressed the assembly. "Sisters, Brothers, we find ourselves awakening to the dawn of a new day, a new era. Our patron Ayondela implores us to find new paths as we abandon the old. This flame is the symbol of our future, our hope!"

The chants were unfamiliar to Kesira, but she guessed they were part of the ritual established by Ayondela for her worshippers. They were being perverted now. The words called for harmony and faith.

The deeds would carry them to death and turmoil.

Kesira Minette gave up all hope of convincing Camilia that her patron had forsaken her Order and turned to the forbidden jade. The nun quietly slipped back to the kitchen and out into the wind's cold knife-thrusts. Somehow, even the inclement weather was more comforting than the scene she had just witnessed.

Kesira went to find Molimo and Zolkan and leave. If Ayondela's followers could not plead their case to their patron, Kesira saw no way other than meeting with Ayondela and personally trying to convince the jade demon of her error.

The wind felt even colder as the woman mounted her horse.

Chapter Four

THE TINY SHRINE provided some shelter from the raging blizzard. Gelid snowflakes hit with the fury of tiny, wet fists and made riding impossible. When Kesira had seen the isolated shrine, she had steered them for it, over Zolkan's protests. Now that they were within the confines of the shrine, she grew increasingly uneasy.

The *trilla* bird had been right about this place. Most Orders had a Brother or Sister responsible for alignment of buildings within the compound, and of the furniture within the buildings. Proper placement guaranteed good health, answered prayers, and imparted general prosperity to the occupants.

Everything within the shrine reeked of wrongness. As Kesira had knelt to begin her meditation, she had jerked about and glanced over her shoulder, certain that someone spied upon her. Only Molimo and Zolkan rested within the shrine, and they worked at spreading their blankets on the stone floor and tacking up a horse blanket in such a way that it cut off cold winds working through the doorless entryway.

"Wrong," complained Zolkan. "All wrong."

"I know," Kesira said. "But why? There is no danger lurking. I hear nothing but the wind and snow outside." She glanced up at the well-sealed roof. There was no danger of leaks allowing cold water to drip upon them this night. The sturdy stone walls fully thwarted the force of the south wind and the floor, while cold, was dry.

Kesira found herself unable to begin meditation. Restlessly, she rose, using her staff for support and paced the perimeter of the room searching for the cause of her nervousness. The altar stood unsullied by the white flame sent by Lenc to other altars she had seen—that of Gelya and also of Ayondela.

"Positions wrong," said Zolkan. "No planning. Makes me feel dirty."

"You always complain about being filthy," she told the bird, but conviction was not in her voice. She had the same sensation, and it did not please her. True, they had been on the trail for long days since leaving the Order of Ayondela and had found no time or place to bathe. The weather had grown progressively more bitter and made travel well nigh impossible.

The Sea of Katad lay, by Molimo's estimate, some six days travel to the east. They had crossed and recrossed the frozen Pharna River four times after fleeing from the abbey. Then the river had straightened and flowed like a hunting arrow, a sure sign that the sea was not far distant. All the while they had ridden they watched for soldiers of the Steel Crescent. They had seen none, though spoor abounded.

Sere bramble grass had been grazed, tracks in the iced-over snow indicated recent passage of dozens of cavalry, and Molimo had even sniffed out a lost dagger turning to rust in the inclement weather. The sigil on the handle showed clearly it had belonged to one of the mercenaries.

Kesira considered the possibility that not sighting the murderous riders had made her more upset during their ride to the sea. And the woman could not deny that she feared what they would find once Katad came into view.

The Isle of Eternal Winter.

Zolkan had tried to describe it, but Kesira had the impression the bird did so from secondhand information. From Molimo? How had the man-wolf given the bird such detailed descriptions? If he had written them out, why hadn't Molimo shared them with her? The few times they had been apart, Molimo had been in his wolf form and incapable of writing.

Kesira felt more cut off now than at any other time. Her Sisters dead, Molimo and Zolkan hiding information from her—she had nowhere to turn for solace.

Even worse, Kesira *feared* the Isle of Eternal Winter and Ayondela and Eznofadil and Lenc. True courage lay not in denying all fear, but in overcoming it. Kesira knew that there was nothing in the world she wanted to avoid more than meeting Ayondela to tell her the details of her son's death. Rouvin had been a doughty warrior, reckless and strong, handsome and endowed with more than human traits from his demon mother. Kesira thought mother and son shared much: defense of the weak; pride in accomplishment; ambition; ability.

She did not for an instant doubt they also shared fiery tempers. She had seen Rouvin's flare repeatedly, often in the midst of battle, when he turned into a juggernaut possessing berserk strength. Cooling had taken several minutes, usually long after the last foe lay slain.

Ayondela's immediate reaction to hearing of her son's death proved he had rightfully inherited the trait.

Kesira remembered how even Wemilat The Ugly had been forced to use extreme caution with the female demon.

"Must convince Ayondela," grumbled Zolkan. "Too cold for proper bath." The bird tried to preen his feathers and failed; the feather spines snapped from the cold and left bald patches. "Starving. No greens."

Molimo hurriedly wrote on a small tablet he had found somewhere in the Order of Ayondela's stable. He had erased their tally of hay and feed for their animals and now used it for his own communications. "The last you ate gave you diarrhea."

"Not my fault," said the *trilla* bird with a haughty upturn of his serrated beak.

"It wasn't Molimo's fault that my robe and cape have endured such indignity," said Kesira. She made brushing motions at the shoulder where Zolkan perched. "Whose could it be, then?"

"Greens poisoned. Only explanation."

"No poison," insisted Molimo, his stylus moving with assurance.

"What do you know?" demanded Zolkan.

All three fell silent when they heard wagons clanking. Molimo and Kesira went to the open entryway of the shrine and peered into the snowy distance. A fluke of wind opened a tiny patch and allowed them to catch sight of a large band of brown-garbed figures forcing their way into the teeth of the wind.

"They come here," said Kesira.

"Flee?" Molimo wrote.

"How?" she asked. "Our mounts are tired from battling the storm and we are in scarcely better condition. It is obvious they come here seeking shelter. Perhaps this shrine was erected by their Order, for they appear to be religious pilgrims."

"Hide?"

Kesira shook her head. "We must assume they mean us no harm."

"Bad place. Creepy," said Zolkan.

"I take that to mean you believe them to be somehow evil. We don't know that. Only our most recent experiences have us hiding from strangers and suspecting the worst of them. While true friendship is a tree that grows but slowly and needs constant nurturing, suspicion is far more apt to grow like a bitter weed." Kesira noted that the brown-robed men had moved closer so that their outlines were visible through even the heavily blowing snow. No trick of wind was required now to see them.

In spite of her confident words, Kesira gripped her staff a little tighter and widened her stance in case she had to defend herself. The tiny stone shrine would prevent more than a handful of armed men from engaging her and . . .

She shook off the panic engendered by the unknown men. It was truly as Gelya said: The less known, the more feared.

Molimo put away his tablet and stylus and pulled forth a sheathed sword. She had tried to dissuade him from carrying it, but her beliefs were not his. For Molimo the steel carried no religious burden. Gelya had taught that only the flexible survived, that the inflexible, like steel, snapped under stress. Or so Dominie Tredlo had told her. The Senior Brother of her Order had been unclear on this point and had allowed Kesira to invent her own rationale. When she had done so, he hadn't corrected her.

"Ho, who rests in this shrine?" came the loud hail from outside.

"Welcome, pilgrims," said Kesira. "We, too, are weary travelers. Where are you bound?"

The man pushed into the stone shrine and shook back his hood. The dark visage did not reassure Kesira as to the man's peaceful intentions. His hand rested on a dagger belted around his middle and she detected the telltale lumps of a sword beneath the robe. Heavy bony ridges raced above each eye, almost totally lost in the undergrowth of his black, snow-dotted eyebrows. Kesira wondered if the man had a neck; from all she could see his head seemed to be cruelly driven directly into his shoulders.

With a fluid grace that belied his heavyset build, he flitted around the room, returning with a broken smile on his lips. Kesira looked away from the yellowed, uneven teeth. She had liked it better when he tried not to be friendly.

"Just you two, eh?"

Kesira made a motion to silence Zolkan. The *trilla* bird settled down, obviously fuming at being overlooked.

"We are pilgrims on a holy journey to the Sea of Katad," she said. "And where are you and the others bound?"

"Mostly getting out of the weather," he said. "We hoped for warmer climes to the south. We travel along the banks of the Pharna to the sea, then farther along, praying that the storms lessen as we go."

Others crowded into the shrine now. Kesira noted that none of the men made any sign that they were in a holy place. Only when a smallish man in a robe of a different brown tint entered did Kesira believe they might be traveling monks. The man knelt quickly, head bowed, and went through a quick prayer too softly spoken for her to overhear.

"I am Senior Brother," the man said.

"Your Order?"

Frightened eyes darted to and fro, as if answering might bring down Eznofadil's full wrath.

The Senior Brother swallowed so hard Kesira saw his throat work as if fingers gripped it. His eyes continued to study his companions restlessly.

"Berura-ko," he said. For a moment, Kesira thought she had misheard. A particularly loud gust of wind had whistled through the shrine.

"A fine patron," she said. "Berura-ko and my patron were often partners in developing solutions to worldly problems."

"Who's that? Your patron?"

"Gelya." The Senior Brother slumped as if the weight of the world had been lifted from him.

"Gelya is dead," he said almost cheerfully. Kesira said nothing. The monk rushed on, "I did not mean it in the way you think. It . . . it is only that my patron is dead, also. Killed by the jade demons."

"Such rumors contain truth, then," Kesira said. "I had heard Berura-ko had perished, but I did not know."

"Lenc," the Senior Brother grated out. "Lenc did it."

Kesira started to tell the monk of their quest to find Ayondela, but Molimo's hand stayed her. She had to admit the wisdom in keeping her own counsel on this point. Silence never betrayed anyone.

"Your Brother said you journey to the Sea of Katad also," she said. "Perhaps we can join your band, until we sight the sea. Since we travel to the same point, I see no reason not to travel together."

"Nor I, nor I," said the monk, too quickly. He glared at the man without a neck, who smiled even more broadly. If Kesira had felt uncomfortable in the stone shrine before, she now felt openly fearful.

"Come, my dear, let us talk while the others fix a meal and prepare to bed down for the night. We have so much information about our respective Orders to exchange. Yes, I know it. I do."

The Senior Brother took her by the elbow and guided her away to a distant corner. For every snippet of worthwhile data the man imparted, he spent twenty minutes blithering about inconsequentials. Kesira was only too glad to beg off further conversation and slip into her blanket beside Molimo.

Molimo had written on his tablet, "Many of them are armed—not of Berura-ko."

Her hand rested on his arm. Molimo already slept. She silently mouthed, "I know." Sleep finally overtook the nun and she drifted along the pathways of her inner mind.

They had ridden most of the day, the Senior Brother staying close by Kesira's side. While the storm had blown over, the cold air cut to the bone and made Kesira even less willing to talk. But the monk chattered on, worse than Zolkan ever had.

"So glad to have you with us," he said for the hundredth time. "Livens up a dreary excursion. The others' faces get so tedious."

"As is yours," came Zolkan's muffled comment. Kesira thwacked the hidden bird with the palm of her hand.

"How's that?" asked the Senior Brother.

"Nothing. Just clearing my throat," Kesira said.

Molimo spurred up and rode on her other side. He pointed off to the left, the north, where rising columns of heat distorted the clear wintry air.

"We will have company soon," Kesira said.

"What? Where?" The monk swiveled about. When he caught sight of the approaching riders, he let out a wordless shriek that brought the man without a neck on the double.

"There," said the Senior Brother. "Brigands. I am sure of it."

The man nodded, put fingers in his mouth and emitted a shrill whistle. Their progress died as most of the monks broke ranks and pulled out wicked, well-used swords from beneath their robes.

"Th-these men are mercenaries traveling with us," stammered the Senior Brother. "W-without them we couldn't have got this far. So many brigands. So many."

"The cold's drove them out of their homes, more starvin' than whole," the mercenary said. His glacial eyes fixed on Kesira's trim form, visible when a quick gust of wind pressed her robe and cloak tightly against her body. "We give protection in exchange for occasional prayers."

Kesira said nothing. She wondered what else the mercenary took as pay. From the expression on the Senior Brother's face, she could guess.

A loud yell went along the front of their defensive line. The mercenaries charged in a ragged line, but even this ragtag advance threw the brigands into disarray. They were hardly experienced at thievery, Kesira guessed. It was as the one mercenary had said: These were not brigands, but farmers driven off their land by the unseasonably cold weather. By this time of year, they should have tilled and planted and been rewarded with the first green shoots poking above the well-tended soil.

That soil knew no cultivation; it lay frozen to a depth of

an inch or more. If Ayondela's frigid curse continued, the soil might perish totally.

"Th-they are very good at fighting. We of Berura-ko's Order do not fight at all. No," the Senior Brother said. In spite of the cold, sweat beaded his forehead. Kesira looked at him sadly. His patron had done a poor job of instilling in his followers the courage needed to face all the unpleasantness in the world.

One of the brigands fought past two mercenaries and rode toward her, screeching at the top of his lungs. Kesira eyed him, judged distances and speeds, then swung her staff. The butt end of the stone-wood shaft rammed hard into the attacking man's belly. Air gushed from his lungs, and he somersaulted out of his saddle. One foot caught in a stirrup, and he found himself being dragged along the frozen ground.

Kesira might have gone after him but another man, this one on foot, came at her. She brought the staff around in a vicious circle, smartly whacking him on the top of his head. He sank down without a sound.

"Molimo, no!" she called. Molimo settled back into his saddle, the wild expression passing. Kesira had cautioned him just in time. Another few seconds and he would have begun to change into wolf shape. As it was, only she knew the strain he endured to prevent the transformation.

"Run, you swine, run!" cried the mercenaries' leader. He strutted back and stared up at Kesira. "They've shown us their heel, the cowards." He thrust his bloody blade into the hard ground and drew it forth, cleansed.

"Let's stop for the day," the monk suggested. "We need to rest and recover from such a fierce battle."

"Fierce?" The mercenary laughed harshly. "This was not so fierce. Let me tell you about . . ." He went on with an increasingly ribald tale of his days fighting against Emperor Kwasian's army, then changing sides and fighting under the command of the Emperor's foremost commander, General Dayle.

Kesira grew tired of the man's boasting. She knew he did it only to impress her, but it only repulsed her. The mercenary took little notice. The tale took on its own rationale for existing, just by being told.

Camp was made and feeble fires started for fixing their

rations. From the depths of a huge saddlebag, the mercenary leader pulled forth a flask sloshing with liquid.

"Here," he said, thrusting it under Molimo's nose. "Take
a pull on this. It'll loosen your tongue. For such a man, you
don't have much to say for yourself."

"Don't talk to pederasts," came Zolkan's muffled words
from under Kesira's cloak.

"What did you say?" The soldier jumped to his feet,
hand on sword hilt.

"Calm yourself," said Kesira. "He said nothing. The
wind spoke, nothing more." As if to verify her claims, a
mournful howling drifted up from a distant ravine near
the Pharna. The sound came almost like a voice begging.

"Drink," the mercenary ordered. Molimo tipped back
the flask, making a face as the liquor burned down his gul-
let. The soldier laughed and grabbed the bottom of the bot-
tle, turning it up again for Molimo.

"Better," the mercenary said. He downed a goodly portion of the liquor, and by the time he thought to offer some
to Kesira, was roundly drunk.

"Filthy creature," murmured Zolkan. The *trilla* bird
emerged from under Kesira's stained cloak and took to
wing, the powerful downstrokes stirring snow all around.
In seconds, Zolkan had vanished into the black night.

"Your traveling companion," said the soldier, slurring
his words. "What did he say?"

Kesira looked at Molimo. The ebony eyes had glazed
over. The potent beverage had dulled his senses more than
she would have believed. It was as if the man had never
sampled liquor before, much less a vintage this strong. Kesira would have thought it drugged if the soldier hadn't
finished off the flask.

"He said the wine was strong," she said, smiling. Perhaps this would help Molimo lose some of his tension. Ever
since they had joined with the band of monks and mercenaries, he had been keyed up and jumpy. She had feared he
would turn into the wolf and, when he hadn't, she had begun to think the strain came from other repressed desires.

"He's walleyed drunk, that's what he is," laughed the
soldier. He slapped Molimo on the shoulder. Molimo
slumped to his blanket, snoring peacefully.

"It'll keep him warm through the night," said Kesira.

"Good, because he will need it."

"What do you mean?" Kesira frowned at the man's tone. It had turned vicious.

"You keep him warm a'nights, unless I miss my guess. But not this night. You sleep with a hero of the day's battle. You sleep with Civv Nimlaw and discover how good it can be!"

Kesira shoved him away. "Thank you, no," she said.

" 'Thank you,' the fine lady says," he mimicked. "You'll thank me the more when I've done with you."

"Stop it," Kesira cried. She drove a hard fist directly into the middle of Nimlaw's face. He twisted slightly at the last instant or she would have broken his nose. As it was, she felt the flesh under his eye tear and blood ran over her knuckles.

"You're the kind I like. Spirit. Not like the Chounabel whores. City of Sin, pigshit! There's no sin in that city. Too tame for the likes of me. I'm a hero."

Strong, thick fingers clamped on Kesira's upper arm. She winced in pain as she tried to fight free. But Nimlaw was a fighter trained in the most deadly school of all: life-or-death battle. She did little more damage to him as he pulled her closer.

"Molimo, help me," she begged. But the man snored gently on his blanket. The liquor had dulled his senses and left him unconscious. "Zolkan!"

"The demons won't hear you. Nothing but your cries of pleasure as I thrust my powerful sword into your sheath." He grabbed her between the legs. Kesira gasped in pain. "You like that, don't you, eh? You'll like it the more when—aieee!"

Kesira had been pressed close to the mercenary. Her groping hand fell on his dagger. She drew it and raked the sharp tip across his chest. A thin streak of blood dribbled into the cut fabric of his monk's robe. She tried to spin the dagger around and drive it into Nimlaw's chest, but he batted her hand away and her thrust missed.

"Hey, look at her!" came a voice from just beyond the circle of light cast by the campfire. "She's giving Civv a real fight. Fifty silver sovereigns on the vixen, that she holds him at bay for another five minutes."

The betting went around the circle, each mercenary feeding the next's need for a spectacle. Kesira was acutely aware of the eyes studying her, lewdly appraising her potential for use after their leader finished. Kesira would not be raped just once, but repeatedly.

"Zolkan!" she cried out.

"She brings down the wrath of her patron," said one.

"No, no," said another. "There is no demon named Zolkan. She is from the Shann Province. That's their women's way of saying, 'Oh, yes, Civv, you're such a man. Do it, do it!' "

Kesira struggled, but mercenaries came to hold her arms and legs spread-eagle.

"Senior Brother, please, in the name of Berura-ko, stop them! Please stop them!"

"Don't call for that toad," scoffed Nimlaw, hiking his robes. "He has no idea what to do with a woman. But I do."

"So show us, Civv. Show us," urged on the ring of soldiers.

"Let's see what I'm getting first," the mercenary leader said. He ripped open Kesira's robe to expose her breasts. They gleamed whitely in the flickering firelight. "See? She *does* want me."

"That's only the cold doing it, Civv. You're going to have to warm her up, from the inside!"

Again the taunting, hideous laughter. Kesira struggled, but with one burly soldier on each arm she had no chance to do more than wiggle.

"Our little virgin nun might not be a virgin," said Nimlaw. "Look at this." He ran his rough, blunt fingertip over Kesira's left breast, teasing it and tormenting her. She trembled when he touched the lip print left where Wemilat had kissed her. The demon's mark glowed with a pink inner light of its own. "She has marked herself so that I might know where to begin. How thoughtful."

Civv Nimlaw hunkered down and placed his lips directly over the demon's imprint. Kesira's bare flesh rippled at the light touch.

Then it vanished. She opened her eyes and saw the mercenary sitting upright, his eyes wide in horror. It was as if his worst nightmares had become real. He gasped and grabbed for his mouth, lips fluttering like a beached fish.

The shriek that rent the night was the last sound uttered by the soldier. He toppled over, dead.

Chapter Five

THE LAUGHING, JEERING mercenaries fell silent. Even the wind's continual moaning ceased. The soldiers stared at their fallen leader, alcohol-fogged eyes wide with fear.

"Civv?" one of them asked. He released Kesira's left arm. The woman jerked her right arm free. By this time the men holding her legs had released them, too. She sat up, pulling her robe across her. The spot over her breast where Civv Nimlaw had touched her burned like a forest fire, but the flames quickly cooled, just as the man's corpse did in the frigid night air.

"She killed him without touching him," said another.

"She's cursed. She killed Civv with a curse. She's a witch."

"A demon," murmured another, backing off. "She might be a demon sent to test us."

"She's no demon. She would have slain us all with lightning if she was. This one's mortal, just as we are. But she knows the magicks. The bitch killed Civv with 'em."

"Kill her," said another. The circle about Kesira began to contract once more. The mercenaries' fear had not gone, but their need for revenge—and to eliminate possible danger in their midst—overshadowed the ominous death of their leader.

Kesira grabbed her staff and swung. She connected with one's ankle and broke the bone. He howled in pain and hobbled away. She spun the staff around faster and faster, defending herself as best she could from a sitting position. When Kesira rolled and came to her knees, the fight became more vicious.

Swords had been drawn, and the men ringing her were

all blooded veterans. One lunge went by her head and barely missed laying open a gash that would have blinded her with her own blood.

"I'll put a curse on all of you. Your balls will fall off if you don't leave me alone," she cried.

"She killed Civv. Kill her," came the cold words from the tall mercenary assuming command. Kesira didn't know if he had been the second-in-command or merely promoted himself when he saw his leader lifeless on the ground.

Kesira fought to her feet, stumbling when she backed into Nimlaw's body. The firelight cast unearthly shadows on the dead man's face. The thick body had a curious flaccidity as if every bone had turned to dust. The eyes gaped wide and horrible, the last nightmare sights burned into the retinas. The mouth hung open, and the tongue lolled blackly. Kesira had not realized Wemilat had meant it when he placed the kiss upon her breast and told her the demon's mark would protect her.

The nun would gladly have traded a little of its killing power for strength in her right arm. She kept the soldiers at bay, but doing so tired her quickly. There were so many of them, and she was nearing nervous exhaustion.

Kesira made no excuses for her condition. Her spirit was at its lowest ebb. She was failing to live up to the high standards demanded by Gelya.

Kesira jumped a sword cut at her calves and tangled herself in her flapping robe. The woman hadn't had time to secure it properly, and it now trailed along the ground. She stepped out, planted her foot firmly on the cloth and tumbled forward. Even quick use of her staff did not keep her in a defensible position.

Facedown on the ground, she waited for the cold steel to skewer her body.

Instead a hot shower cascaded upon her.

Startled, Kesira reached up and touched the wetness. Blood. But she felt no pain. She rolled over and looked up in time to see one of the soldiers clutching his severed throat. Blood spurted darkly around his fingers, then turned redder as the cold winter's air touched it. The mercenary staggered a few feet, then fell, lifeless.

The deep-throated growling and the harsh snap of jaws

convinced Kesira that Molimo had come out of his drunken stupor and transformed into the savage wolf.

She found her feet again and took the time to properly fasten her robe. By then Molimo had come into the campfire light, muzzle caked with blood and green eyes flashing. The wolf head swayed to and fro almost like a snake's; the fangs, when Molimo struck, were as deadly, ripping and tearing instead of poisoning.

"She's enchanted him. She *is* a witch. Flee!"

The cry went up and the mercenaries faded off into the night. Kesira heard the thunder of hooves as they fled the scene of their defeat. They had faced armies and been victorious. Their leader had given them triumphs over dozens of brigands. He—and they—had fallen victim to a nun and a youth unable to control his shape.

"Molimo," she said softly, dropping to her knees and holding out her hands. "You do not have to stay in this form. You can change back into a man. You have done well, but do not stay like this."

It took all her willpower not to jerk away when the wolf snapped at her hand.

"Peace. Become tranquil. Force away the animal and return to humanity. You know the path. Think on Gelya's maxims, the ones I've taught you. Do it, Molimo. Do it for me!"

The green eyes filled with hatred and evil fire. The lips curled back to reveal the sharp fangs that had ended so many lives.

"Kill me if you will, but return to your human form." Kesira steadfastly faced Molimo.

The wolf cowered down, hindquarters tensing. The leap went past her, over her left shoulder. Kesira heard the wolf impact heavily on another. She turned and saw one of the mercenaries beneath the wolf. Molimo tried to savage the man's throat and failed. Teeth sank deeply into a protecting right arm.

Before Kesira could say a word, the man under Molimo's writhing, twisting gray body began to flow in a way all too familiar to the woman: The mercenary changed into a *chillna* cat. Powerful shoulders supported a drooping head; the creamy-furred belly vanished as the cat doubled up to use back claws on Molimo's exposed underside. Forepaws

raked on either side of the wolf's flanks while jaws even
stronger than Molimo's snapped and worked to find a
death-hold on a slender lupine throat.

Molimo was batted off by a powerful blow and came to
all fours, snarling and ready to continue the attack.

"Molimo, wait," Kesira ordered. The *chillna* was too
powerful, too heavy for the wolf. The cats had been hunted
almost to extinction because of their catholic tastes in
meat. They cared little whether they ate horse, swine, or
human—and, it was rumored, even dined on demon flesh
when they could. They hunted alone, and only because of
that had humans succeeded in eliminating them as a men-
ace to city and farm.

Kesira swung her stone-wood staff with all the power
left in her body. She had judged well. The butt end of her
staff crashed into the *chillna* cat's throat. The animal
choked and fell flat on its chest, wheezing noisily.

Before it regained its breath, Molimo flashed forward,
little more than a gray blur. Teeth ripped at ear and jowl.
The cat pawed weakly at the wolf. Kesira landed another,
far weaker blow to the rounded top of the cat's head. The
vibration along her staff shook her and forced her away,
pain lancing into her shoulders and body.

This time Molimo's strike went directly to the target.
The cat lay kicking feebly, its death throes pitiful in com-
parison to the heavily muscled body.

And, in death, a partial transformation occurred that
sickened Kesira. The hindquarters remained feline but
from the waist up, the mercenary reappeared. His naked
flesh shone with sweat in the dim light. Much of his face
had been ripped away, and his throat still drained a trickle
of blood. The half-human, half-bestial creature would never
again threaten anyone.

Kesira hoped that he—it—had found peace in death. But
she doubted it.

Molimo licked blood from his muzzle, then sank down by
the fire, the kill-lust gone from the green eyes. Whatever
drove the wolf had been sated. For now.

"Wh-what's happened?" came the timorous voice of the
Senior Brother of the Order of Berura-ko. "Oh, no. This is
awful."

"Do you have digging tools?" Kesira asked. "We should give him a proper burial."

"I wouldn't touch it!"

"Get the shovel," she snapped. The meek man trotted off to obey. Kesira forced him to dig a grave. It was far too shallow, but the ground had frozen and any digging proved difficult. Kesira worried that animals might unearth the body, then pushed the thought from her mind. If they found a meal in the shape changer, perhaps it would be for the best. She did her duty and could do no more.

Kesira pulled the carcass into the grave the monk had dug, then motioned for the man to cover the body. He did so hastily, not wanting to prolong the chore.

She stared at the tiny mound of dirt covering the body. "Can honor mend a broken arm?" she asked softly. "Can honor keep the people from starvation? No. Then what is honor but emptiness?" She swallowed and wiped her lips. "Honor shows our path through life. I did not know you, changeling, but I do hope that your path was straight and lined with decency and good deeds."

"We should leave," said the Senior Brother. "There might be others like it coming."

Kesira looked around and saw Molimo sitting beside the fire, returned to his human shape. He had dressed hastily, putting his shirt on backwards. She doubted if the monk would notice this, or even ask how Kesira had killed such a powerful other-beast.

"They are demon spawns. The demons test us with them. We . . . we ought not to allow it."

"Complain to your patron," Kesira said viciously, knowing Berura-ko had perished by the jade demons' hands.

As had her patron.

"What happened to the mercenaries?" the Senior Brother asked. "They rode off. They can't just leave us. We . . . I . . . where is Civv Nimlaw? I want to speak with him. We had an agreement."

"You would see him?" Kesira said in a deceptively mild tone. "I think he is yonder. Just on the other side of the campfire."

The monk hurried off, muttering to himself. The muttering stopped. Kesira heard a sharp gasp, then, "He's dead. Foully slain!"

Kesira walked to the Senior Brother's side and laid a hand on his thin, stooped shoulder. "Your wonderful body-guard tried to rape me."

"You did this to him? But how? There's no mark on his body, but he obviously died in agony."

"I hope so."

"But you must be wrong. He wouldn't . . ."

"Rape a woman?" Kesira's brown eyes bored into the monk's watery blue orbs.

He quickly glanced away. "We should be on our way."

"We stopped to rest. I haven't yet slept—or been allowed to sleep," Kesira said primly. "We will do so now."

"But Civv. We should bury him, shouldn't we? The other-beasts. The real animals."

Kesira picked up the small folding shovel and silently handed it to the Senior Brother. He looked from the shovel to the mercenary leader's body and back. With shaky hands, he took the shovel and began work on a second grave, next to the one containing the other-beast.

"All is fuzzy," Molimo wrote on his tablet. "What happened?"

"You don't remember?" Kesira asked. Molimo shook his head. "Don't worry, then," she told him. "It is only the strong drink. You shouldn't partake of it in the future."

Molimo nodded. Kesira wondered if this was good advice. Anything that brought forgetfulness to the young man might be a blessing rather than a curse. Still, she had some idea that his lack of control over his shape came from the liquor. Not that he always managed to hold back the change even when he was clearheaded.

It was a terrible curse Molimo endured, she thought. Perhaps Ayondela might lift it when they spoke and all was straightened out. Perhaps.

With this running through her mind, Kesira Minette dropped off to sleep.

"The brigands," complained the monk. "They are every-where. We cannot hold them off. We can't. Not without the mercenaries."

Kesira tired of hearing the man's whines. The monk's courage had died with his patron.

"No one's attacked in three days. And we are almost to the Sea of Katad. What do you do then?"

The monk looked about and bobbed his head up and down, as if it had come loose from his neck. The other monks in the party—all six of them still loyal in some fashion to their patron—rode apart and out of earshot.

"I think I shall go my separate way," the Senior Brother said, as if confiding a deep, dark secret. "There is nothing to hold me to my Order now that Berura-ko is dead."

"Does the death of a patron spell the death of the Order?" Kesira asked.

"Of course. The demon gave us purpose, continually fed us new ideas. The influx was required. Without Berura-ko, we are nothing."

"It takes no courage to die," Kesira said, "but it does take courage to live. You are forsaking all your patron taught. Because he is dead, does that make his teachings wrong?"

"Of course not, but . . ."

"Gelya's words were strong—and true. His death does not alter that. I am now the Sister of the Mission and carry on the teachings. If they were a proper course for patterning lives while Gelya lived, they are no less so now that he had been foully killed by the jade demons."

"You will draw their ire. Live small, and they will ignore you."

Kesira snorted, white clouds of crystalline air gusting under her nostrils. "Live small and you will be stepped on. Where is the honor in not trying to do your best in this world?"

"You think you can matter?" the monk shot back, his anger surfacing for the first time.

"Yes."

He shook his head. "I no longer wish to try. Let *them* go their own way." He indicated the other monks. "One of them will be selected as the new Senior Brother and who will remember me—or care?"

Kesira had pitied the man before. Now she felt only contempt; he had turned from all he had lived for. She wondered if the flaw lay in the monk or in Berura-ko's teachings. The nun knew little of other Orders and their beliefs, but she did know Gelya's preachings. They gave strength when she weakened, they provided strong guidance in what was proper and what was dishonorable. All the Senior Brother said smacked of faltering honor. While she might die trying to speak with Ayondela, the attempt would be bathed in honor.

Kesira Minette would do the proper thing. There was nothing more her patron could ask of her than this.

Zolkan circled above, giving voice to shrill cries of warning. She stood in her stirrups and peered out along the banks of the frozen river. At first she did not see what had alerted the sharp-sighted *trilla* bird.

Then she saw the four beasts scrabbling over the ice, coming from the far side of the Pharna.

"Molimo," she called back. "Is there a chance to outrun them?"

He shook his head, eyes fixed on the beasts. She knew from his expression that he recognized the creatures' otherness. His hands had curled into fists and he shook, not with cold, but with the strain of maintaining his human form. Kesira said nothing. She wished she could fight this battle for him, but it was not that easy. Molimo had to learn control.

If only he would pay more attention to Gelya's teachings. But the man didn't. It was as if he had a course of action of his own. Kesira wished he could speak of it so they could compare, discuss, argue.

"No, the demon spawn. No!" The monk sighted the creatures struggling toward their small band and panicked. He rode ahead, calling loudly to the other monks and leaving Kesira and Molimo behind.

It was all she had expected from the Senior Brother.

They had encountered only one group of other-beasts, the day after the mercenaries fled. Without much effort, they had outpaced the beasts. These approaching, however, were fleeter of foot—and more dangerously taloned and fanged.

"We find more and more, the closer we get to the sea," she observed. "Do you think these might be the product of Ayondela's activities?"

Molimo made a gurgling noise deep in his throat. She had heard it before.

"Lenc," she agreed. "Yes, it must be Lenc's doing. We

must kill them, yet it carries a burden of such sorrow." Kesira said no more. Molimo knew her conflict. She loathed the creatures while sympathizing with their plight. Even the man-wolf; Kesira fought against loving him, yet she had to. She had nursed him to health and cared for him then and now, but the sudden changes from man to wolf carried with them intense danger. Her love for him had to be muted by this consideration.

That did not stop her fear of the other creatures.

"Demon spawn, the monk called them. Do you think so?"

Molimo only shrugged. Whatever had produced this horrid configuration of man and animal was unnatural by its very nature.

"One day the world will return to its normal course. There will be demons content to stay apart from humans, giving only of their philosophy and charity, and there will be mortals, living out our span content with the knowledge there are others greater than we in the world. Gone will be the overweening ambition of demons striving to be gods and gone will be humans suffering for the vanity of demons."

Molimo stared at her strangely.

Kesira laughed without humor. "No, I don't truly believe that. We can never go back to the ways of our teachers. The Time of Chaos has seized our world and can never let go, not until there are gods to replace the demons."

Zolkan screeched from above, then plummeted earthward like a green arrow. Talons flashed and ripped the eyes out of the leading other-beast. The others rushed Kesira and Molimo.

Kesira's staff held two at bay. Molimo thrust with his sword and killed another. The creatures did not immediately renew their attack. Rather, they crouched just beyond weapon's reach and made odd, cooing sounds.

"Trap, trick. Don't approach," warned Zolkan. The *trilla* bird landed on the saddle just behind Kesira and gripped down. She heard his talons just cutting through tough leather as the bird cleansed them of blood and gobbets of eye.

"Are they demon spawn or other-beasts?" she asked the bird.

"No difference."

"Demon spawn cannot change shape. The other-beasts are like . . ." Her words trailed off. Kesira had started to say, "Like Molimo."

"Both deadly. Leave them. Escape now."

"I will see what they want."

"NO!"

Kesira ignored Zolkan's warning and dismounted, staff in hand. As she approached cautiously she saw no hint that these were shape changers. The grime had become a part of their scaly hides, and their frightened looks bespoke long hardship. The unnatural winter took its toll on them, just as it did on the humans.

"I won't harm you. Can I help?"

One made a tiny gesture imploring her to come nearer. The beast pointed to an injured foot, turning black with gangrene.

"This one's hurt," she said. "I'll see what I can do."

"No, trap. Don't." Zolkan's voice turned into the singsong speech that somehow communicated with Molimo.

Kesira turned her head and started to scold Zolkan. She saw Molimo flowing into his wolf form—and she sensed rather than saw the creatures rising up before her.

Molimo blasted past her, fangs reaching out for one of the beasts. It died in a messy flood of its own life fluids. The other struck out for Kesira, a talon raking her arm. She dropped her staff and gasped with pain. Green feathers exploded around her as Zolkan's wings beat at her attacker. This brief but furious defense allowed Molimo to dispatch another and finally the last of the demon spawn.

They lay on the ground, no hint of humanity coming to them in death.

"Not shape changers," said Zolkan, perching on Kesira's shoulder. "Always ugly. Always deadly."

"They might have been."

"Pity for shape changers gets you into trouble," the *trilla* bird said.

"It worked out well with Molimo," she pointed out.

"Special case. Molimo different."

"How?"

The bird took wing without answering, flapping powerfully and returning to his position aloft to scout.

Kesira sighed and started to coax Molimo back into human form. It wasn't necessary. The man had already donned his loose clothing and sat asaddle waiting for her.

"How is it that Zolkan can speak to you?" she asked.

Molimo only pointed. The monks had ridden hard and fast; to catch them would take some doing. Kesira worried over whether this was a reasonable course of action. Still, a group offered some safety. Together, they might frighten away the less bold of the beasts roaming the riverbanks in increasing numbers.

She put her curiosity aside and rode hard beside Molimo, glad for the feel of the cold air against her face. In less than an hour, they overtook the Senior Brother and the other monks.

Kesira started to speak to the monk, then changed her mind. What was there to say? Gelya taught that kindness gives birth to kindness. Kesira added that fear feeds on fear. The monks were proof of that.

"You outran them?" the monk finally asked.

"Yes," was all she said.

"They are treacherous. They . . . they gull you into traps. You should never show them mercy."

"I'll try to remember that," she said tartly.

They hadn't ridden another ten minutes when faint sounds echoed along the river from down a ravine.

"What was that?" asked Kesira. "It sounds like someone in pain."

"I heard nothing. Just the wind," the monk said too hastily.

"Which is it? Nothing or wind?"

"More beasts. They lay in wait to catch us."

"The cries are human," Kesira said, reining in her horse to hear better. "They come from that direction." She pointed off and to the right, down the ravine. "We should make sure that someone's not seriously injured."

"It's the beasts, I tell you." The monk almost screamed the words. "Leave them. You'll get us all killed."

"The cries sound very human," she said. Kesira glanced at Molimo, who shook his head. Even his sharp ears could not differentiate.

"We must make camp soon," said the Senior Brother. "If we make the cliffs near the Sea of Katad before dusk, we can get out of this awful wind."

"We must help whoever that is."

Zolkan fluttered down from his aerial station. Kesira winced as the bird dug talons into her shoulder. "Once today you find demon spawn. Just because monk is coward doesn't mean he is wrong now."

"It doesn't mean he is right, either, just because we were attacked by those poor creatures."

"Pity for other-beasts leads you astray," said Zolkan.

"Sympathy," she corrected. "Can we turn away if someone needs our aid? What is the difference if it is an other-beast? Perhaps we can help, as we did with Molimo. Or with a disgusting-looking mass of green feathers who flew into our sacristy, starving and more dead than alive."

Zolkan snorted. "Molimo good. Other-beasts not all good. And I not demon spawn." The bird sounded offended that she compared him with any of the creatures they had fought that day.

"The cries died down. That might be a human, not some poor soul trapped between animal and human."

"We ride on," said the monk."

"So ride and be damned by all the demons," she snapped. "We go to see if we can be of assistance." Kesira glared at Zolkan and Molimo. "At least *I* go. They can do as they please."

Zolkan launched himself and circled, but Kesira smiled when she saw the bird flying in the direction of the piteous and all too human sounds. And Molimo rode at her side.

Kesira might find disappointment or danger, but she knew where honor lay. She put the spurs to her horse and dropped down into the rocky ravine, bound for the source of the noise.

Chapter Six

THE MOANS AND CRIES turned into sobs. Kesira Minette spurred her horse faster, positive that this was not a trap set by one of the demon spawn or other-beasts. A human in pain needed her assistance.

The ravine walls towered above her and turned into a small canyon. The rocky floor made going slower than she would have liked, but it gave Zolkan a chance to scout ahead. Without his aerial reconnaissance, Kesira knew that her life would have been in much more jeopardy. She did not even slow the pace as the *trilla* bird came back, landing on her shoulder.

"Hut quarter-mile ahead," the bird announced. "No windows. Door off hinges. Looks dangerous."

"But did you *see* anything dangerous?"

Zolkan admitted that he had not.

"What did you hear?" she asked.

"More human cries, like you made when Gelya died."

Kesira said nothing to this. She faced straight ahead and rode with new determination. If the rising power of the jade demons brought forth unnatural creatures, so be it. She knew her duty. A human in danger required her aid.

She reined in less than a hundred yards from the hut Zolkan had sighted. Rude walls of split tree trunk required caulking. Wind whipped past and produced a mournful whistle in the holes between logs, but it was not this that she and Molimo had heard.

"Help me," came the faint words from inside. "Oh, Rael-lard, why don't you help me?"

Kesira dismounted and tethered the horse to a stubby

tree. Walking the distance to the hut might be dangerous, but she didn't want Molimo any closer than necessary.

"Stay with the horses," she said. "I'll be all right. Zolkan will serve as extra eyes for me."

"Why?" Molimo quickly wrote on his tablet. He erased the word by pressing the clay back into a flat surface, then quickly traced out a new question. "Why won't you let me help?"

Kesira couldn't give the man the real reason, though she knew he sensed it. If it were a human inside, she wanted to take no chances on Molimo shape-changing into a wolf. She had seen what happened when he spotted a helpless soul; that part of him dominated by the wolf spirit demanded the easy meal. Kesira wished the man-wolf was better able to contain the change urges.

"I'll be all right," she said.

"Trap?" he wrote.

"Zolkan will call for you if anything happens to me. No more argument. Stay with the horses. Be ready to ride, if the need arises. But I doubt that it will. Truly, Molimo." She took his right hand in both of hers and squeezed reassuringly.

Kesira saw the hurt in his dark eyes, but there was no easy remedy for it. She turned and walked toward the hut, eyes seeking out the slightest detail to indicate a trap and ears cocked for more of the sounds from within the hut. A steady sobbing came forth now.

Kesira hesitated a few yards from the hut and looked around. From the way the canyon formed, the sounds were caught by the walls and magnified many times over. The echoes bounced about and finally emerged down by the Pharna River where she had heard them. Atop the canyon walls stood lines of scraggly, stunted trees, failing in their bid to survive the inclement weather. By this time of year, the warmth ought to have coaxed them to full greenery, roots powerfully thrusting into rocky soil and seeking out ways of spreading seeds to the surrounding area.

With Ayondela's winter locking the land in a fatal grip, the trees stood like skeletal sentinels.

Around the hut evidence of the discouraging weather was even clearer. A barn, partially burned for firewood, held no trace of the animals that should have been inside.

Kesira guessed that they might have been eaten. What could have been a pleasant pasture stretching back along the canyon was now coated with dead grass, as brown as it had been in midwinter. The slopes of the hills farther back along the ravine hinted at good cropland in most years.

The ordinarily prosperous had become fatal.

Kesira used her staff to open the door even more. The sobbing noise inside stopped, but a new sound replaced it.

A cry, low and choked.

"Who's there?" Kesira called out. She stepped away from the door so that she wouldn't be silhouetted by the weak sunlight behind her. The woman heard muffled noises as if someone covered a baby's mouth to prevent further crying.

Zolkan circled above, sharp eyes watching her. She waved to the *trilla* bird. A squawk combining indignation at this and disgust with her drifted back down.

"I am Kesira Minette, Sister of the Mission of Gelya. Do you need help? Please, I want only to aid you, not harm you."

The cry sounded again. Kesira went through the door into the dank, almost freezing interior of the hut. As wan as the sunlight had been, it was still much brighter than the light within the hut. It took almost a minute for her eyes to adjust.

Kesira found herself staring at a scrawny woman holding a pathetic dagger.

"Get out. Leave us. My husband returns at any time. He'll kill you!"

"Why would he want to hurt me?"

Kesira's calm words did not soothe the woman. She broke down and cried, shudders wracking her frail body.

"How can I help?" Kesira asked again.

"He's been gone for almost a month. A whole month! He must be dead. Or . . . or he's left me." The woman became incoherent, trying to stop her tears and failing. She made tiny hiccuping noises as she moved about and sank down to a thin blanket spread on the floor.

"He's not abandoned you," Kesira said gently. "I am sure there is a reason for hope. Why did he leave?"

"To hunt. The farm's gone. We had to eat the animals

just to survive. Raellard said there'd be no crops this year. He was right. Cold. Always so cold."

"Raellard's your husband?" Kesira saw the woman make one quick jerky movement that she took to mean yes.

The interior of the hut had been stripped bare, everything flammable having been burned for warmth. Kesira heaved a sigh. It was a good thing the roof was constructed of sod or that would have gone also. The log walls were too thick for easy burning or the desperate woman might have tried to cannibalize them too.

"I heard your call for help. When did you last eat? I have some food in my trail kit. It won't be much but . . ."

"Food?" The woman broke down and cried. "I . . . I'm sorry. It's been so long."

"Why didn't you leave with Raellard?"

The woman's dish-sized eyes stared up at Kesira, then darted off to the far corner of the room. Curious, Kesira followed the haunted look.

"A baby!"

"No, leave it alone. Don't touch it," shouted the woman.

"But it's so thin. It's almost starved to death. Can he take some broth? No, I see that he can't. How old is he?" Kesira couldn't guess from the baby's condition. The infant might have been as old as a year—and starved—or newborn.

"He's not human," the woman declared. "Touch it at your own risk. He's evil, evil."

Kesira started to speak, then firmly clamped her mouth shut. The woman had gone out of her head with hunger. The baby appeared ordinary enough, except for the starvation.

"Awful things being birthed in the hills. They come down to our fields and prey on each other. Can't hunt nearby. Dangerous to leave the hut. They want me, oh yes, they want me. Nothing else to eat but me. And they won't get me. I'll show those hideous creatures."

Kesira held the baby close, giving it warmth and some comfort. "When was your son born? Not long ago?"

"A week. Took me that long to find out it wasn't human. It's an other-beast. Wants to devour me!"

Kesira went to the door and saw Zolkan waddling along

the ground just outside. She held the infant up for the *trilla* bird to see. She inclined her head in Molimo's direction to indicate that it was all right for him to approach. The bird squawked in protest at being used as a mere messenger, preened for a moment, then took two cumbersome steps and gracefully became airborne. Kesira went back into the hut.

"There is nothing wrong with your child. He is not a demon spawn. They are permanently locked in twisted animal form. Nor is he an other-beast."

"How do you know?" The woman fingered the knife she still held. "You might trick me."

Kesira saw that the woman was out of her mind with hunger and fear. While she wasn't certain anything would soothe the craziness, Kesira tried soft words and nonsense stories.

"I am a nun of the Order of Gelya. I am trained in such matters." She hoped that the slight quaver in her voice did not betray her. Until Lenc had destroyed her secure home, she had never once seen an other-beast. The rambling stories she'd been told by Dominie Tredlo and others amounted to little more than ghost tales meant to deliciously frighten the small child.

"You can see?"

"I cast the rune sticks and predict what will be," Kesira said, more truthfully. "I also have the talent of 'feel.' "

"What's that?" In spite of herself the woman had become intrigued and some of the madness left her.

"By touch alone I can tell if someone is demon cursed and might become a beast. Your son is not cursed."

"You might be one of them," accused the woman. "Yes, that's it. You are trying to gull me."

Molimo and Zolkan appeared in the door bearing food supplies. The woman cowered, forgetting the pitiful knife in her hand.

"This is Zolkan. As you can see, he is a *trilla* bird from Rest Province. The jungles there abound with them and it is said even Emperor Kwasian has a *trilla* bird as counselor on weighty matters."

"I have heard of such," the woman said.

"She thinks of me as stew meat. How disgusting,"

sniffed Zolkan. He hopped to Molimo's shoulder and used this perch to work his beak over dirtied feathers.

"The other is my friend Molimo. He lacks a tongue and cannot speak, but his heart is good."

Molimo dropped the food and pointed far up the ravine, past the snowy meadows and to the hills rolling away from the Sea of Katad. Zolkan supplied the words. "Molimo says danger comes down the slopes. We go to see."

"Must you leave?"

"Isle of Eternal Winter lies to east and south along coast. If we not back soon, go ahead. All danger to north now. Be wary."

"All right, Zolkan. May Gelya's blessing rest with you, Molimo."

"May Merrisen's," squawked the *trilla* bird.

They vanished from sight, leaving Kesira alone with the woman and her baby.

"Merrisen?" asked the woman.

"He was killed by the jade demons, as were Gelya, Wemilat, and Berura-ko and perhaps others of the demonic rank. A great war goes on for supremacy, a war not even the Emperor can fight."

The woman's hunger-enlarged eyes stared at Kesira. The nun didn't know if her words made any sense to her or if it even mattered.

"What is your name? If I am to help you, it would be nice to know."

"You told me yours, didn't you?" the woman asked. "And the others. You called them Zolkan and Merrisen."

"Zolkan and Molimo," corrected Kesira.

"I . . . I sit down." The woman slumped to her blanket, visibly wobbling about. The light-headedness passed and she said, "It's been three days since I had any food. I melt snow for water since our well's frozen over. Never been like this. Not in my recollection. Name's Parvey Yera."

Kesira almost missed the woman's name in the unconnected rambling. She had placed the baby back in its corner and had started preparing simple fare. She dared not give Parvey too much to eat or it would make the woman sick. Kesira remembered Zolkan's reaction when he had devoured all the greens at the Abbey of Ayondela.

"Gnaw on this," she said, giving Parvey a piece of stale

bread. The woman might have been Molimo wolfing down a portion of a recent kill. She gave the baby a few drops of water but it needed milk, and only from its mother might this be forthcoming.

The tiny fire would not burn for long. Parvey had exhausted all nearby wood but the few twigs were sufficient for Kesira to boil snow into hot water and to make a broth from meat in her provisions. This, too, Parvey slurped up greedily.

"Do you feel better?"

"More."

"Soon," said Kesira. "It'll take a while to fix. Have some more bread while it brews."

"Winter's so cold. Husband can't find food nearby. Baby came a month premature. He's supposed to be back by then."

Kesira had wondered why a man would leave a pregnant woman; this explained it. The cruel grip of winter had never relaxed, thanks to Ayondela. With food running low, the farmer had taken the chance of leaving his wife to bring back supplies, but the baby had arrived earlier than anticipated. It did not seem a pretty picture to Kesira.

"You expect your husband back soon?"

"Raellard's a good man," Parvey said, almost defensively. Kesira did not even hint that he might have gone seeking food and just continued on to Chounabel or Blinn or some other city, abandoning his wife and unborn child. Or that he might have fallen prey to the other-beasts roaming the territory in increasing numbers.

Kesira felt a weariness heavier than ever before settle over her. The suffering brought by the jade demons grew with every new day. Why had they not been content with the old order of things? But some always aspired to more power and the familiar had been disrupted for the ambitions of a few.

"More broth?" Kesira dished it out to Parvey Yera, who drank this with less of a famished air.

"Good."

"And your son? When might he dine, also?"

Parvey stared unseeing into the corner.

"He is human, not an other-beast. He deserves life."

"They came down from the meadows. Where they en-

tered our fields I do not know. They stalked me for days.
Killed one, I did. Rolled a rock down onto it from up there."
Parvey made a vague gesture indicating the top of the can-
yon wall above her hut.

"It is all past. You must look to the future."

"Why are there other-beasts? Where do they come
from?"

Kesira knew that Parvey didn't want a literal answer to
that. Kesira had seen how Molimo had been trapped in the
jade rain as a demon blew apart. That the other-beasts
were the product of demonic ambition wasn't the proper
answer to Parvey's question.

"I was told a tale when I was a very, very young acolyte
in my Order," said Kesira. "There is little truth in it, or is
there only truth? It is not for me to say."

"What story? I remember my mother telling me
stories."

"As you will tell your son," Kesira said, handing Parvey
another hunk of bread.

"Where do they come from?"

"In a time now past," Kesira began, "the Emperor desired a bridge built between two mountaintops so that he
could take his entire court from one to the other without
traversing the treacherous land between.

"The Emperor was a mighty ruler and commanded
many demons. Such power was envied, but because he was
the Emperor none opposed him. He ordered the demons to
build this fabulous bridge, but to only work at night because he found their visages horrible, and he did not wish
to frighten the Empress."

"These were other-beasts?" asked Parvey, her mind
being taken from her own plight.

"All were demons. There were no other-beasts—not yet.
The demons did not like being told they were hideously
formed, but the Emperor's command was not to be ignored.

"The demons toiled for many months, and the work was
still not finished. The task was monumental, even for ones
so skilled and using magicks no mortal might understand.
The Emperor became increasingly angry that they did not
complete their task and threatened them with severe punishment for disobeying his commands. He desired, above
all else, to be able to move from his winter palace to a sum-

mer palace cresting the far peak. Without the bridge to speed his journey, he might spend most of the pleasant months in travel."

Parvey, like a small child, sat and shook her head in wonder at this. The Emperor's command was law. No one disobeyed. To do so was totally unthinkable.

"What did they do? The demons?"

"Well," said Kesira, warming to the telling of her tale, "they knew that working only in the darkness of night would hinder them and keep them from finishing the bridge speedily. They begged the Emperor to be allowed to work during the daylight hours. He refused. His command had to be obeyed exactly.

"One of the demons, more fearful of the Emperor's wrath than the others, suggested recruiting human workers. The demons argued among themselves over this, but finally decided to do as the fearful one said when the Emperor began punishing the demons for their failure. And it was then that the other-beasts were born. The fearful demon placed a curse on the Emperor's human servants so that they changed into hideous creatures at night. The Emperor saw them hard at work and believed they were only demons, unable to recognize them as his loyal retainers. And thus the bridge was finished."

"But the other-beasts," said Parvey. "What happened?"

"The demons were not pleased when the Emperor rode across the bridge and never once thanked them for their efforts, but because he was the Emperor they were unable to take revenge on him. Instead, they left the curse upon his human servants. During the day they remained at the Emperor's side, loyal retainers, but at night they took on the likeness of the animals and roved the land, seeking their own revenge for being trapped in such hideous shapes."

"I had never heard this story."

Kesira smiled. She had embellished it a little from when she heard it as a child. Sister Fenelia had been able to tell the wildest stories and make them seem plausible to a juvenile mind. Then the smile faded as she considered the reality of the world. Molimo was no simple servant seeking revenge on the demons for being forced to build a bridge between mountains. Day, night, it mattered little when

the transformation occurred. It was a curse that scarred
Molimo's very soul—a jade curse.

"Rest now," Kesira urged. "And when you awaken
you'll feel much refreshed. Your son will want his meal
then."

Parvey looked apprehensive at this. She still believed in
her hunger-induced craziness that her son was an other-
beast. Kesira wanted to reason with her, to tell her it made
no difference. Even if the baby were an other-beast what
might it turn into? It was only a mewling infant, unable to
cause any true harm. But Kesira knew better than to even
hint that the child might be cursed.

"Rest. All will be better when you have taken the edge
off your fatigue."

Parvey lay down and slumped into heavy sleep almost
instantly. Kesira went and covered her with the thin blanket. She wondered if this were all Raellard Yera had left
the woman, or if Parvey had somehow burned heavier
blankets for the brief warmth that they gave.

Kesira picked up the baby and noted its eyes were open.
The child was so famished it did not even cry. Bones poked
through the skin and made the burden as light as feathers.
She doubted the tiny boy would have been able to survive
much longer. Her heart went out to him as she rocked the
baby to and fro and even slight twitches subsided. She only
guessed that the boy slept rather than died.

After returning the infant to its grubby corner Kesira
explored the tight confines of the hut but found nothing.
The place had been systematically stripped while Parvey
had fought for survival. Kesira looked closer at the knife
Parvey had dropped and saw that what she had first taken
for rust was blood.

Other-beast's blood?

"You are a noble woman," Kesira said softly, "to endure
such bitter hardship. As Gelya said, adversity introduces
you to yourself. But I only wish that the introduction had
not been so lengthy or torturous for you."

Kesira settled down and began her meditations. Reaching inside, she found serenity and renewed her flagging
spirit. But before she had gotten halfway through her rituals, a scraping noise from outside brought her fully alert.

Clutching her staff, Kesira rose and turned to the door

just as it was jerked open. She blinked at the sight confronting her. At first she thought it was a compost heap. Leaves and twigs moved as one in a huge mound. But the mound had legs and arms.

And the right arm waved about a spear with a gleaming, razor-sharp tip.

Before Kesira could speak, the mountain of debris lurched forward and sent the spear directly for her heart.

Chapter Seven

"THEY COME DOWN from mountains. We must stop them soon," urged Zolkan, in the shrill singsong speech Molimo understood. "Kesira will not be hurt by any within cabin."

Molimo stared back at the pathetic wood hut and wondered if the *trilla* bird only tried to comfort him. Kesira had found others to comfort and help, but she needed protection. And did not know it.

Where? Molimo directed to the bird. Zolkan spiralled upward and studied the terrain. The grain fields had fallen to hard-crusted snow, with only bare stalks poking through the ice. Heavy tracks crossing the field betrayed passage of the other-beast. Zolkan swooped down, sharp black eyes studying the ragged tracks for the most minute detail, then returned to Molimo.

"Only one. Must be a huge pile of shit. Big enough to eat my lovely tailfeathers." The bird twitched, fanning out his tail, then neatly refolded it behind him.

It stalks Kesira?

Zolkan bobbed his head up and down, then extended a wing in the direction taken by the stalking other-beast. "Changed from human to other in middle of field."

Molimo skirted the deserted grain field, choosing his path carefully. Even though his feet made slight crunching noises as they broke through the thin icy crust of the snow, the wind blowing against his face would muffle such sounds or carry them back down the ravine. His keen nose sniffed the wind, too, for any hint of the other-beast. When the fetid odor struck, Molimo made a face.

"Needs bath. Smells like shit," said Zolkan. "So do we. Long since I properly bathed. Too long. Look at me. A mess. Hungry, too." The large bird stretched its green-feathered wings more than a yard wide and batted them against the breeze. He seemed to hang just above Molimo's shoulder.

No change. Not yet. I now sense when it comes upon me.

"All right," said Zolkan, settling back down to his perch. The *trilla* bird didn't mind not flying; riding on a human's shoulder was far easier and allowed him to sleep. "You get horses and ride after beast?"

On foot. Better this way.

They stalked the other-beast and found it easier than anticipated. The creature had scented Kesira and the woman and child within the hut and had single-mindedly fixed on them as its dinner. It foolishly ignored all else. This proved its downfall.

The burly, lumbering creature emerged from behind a rock near the edge of the ravine. For an approach to the hut, it was well shielded. From Molimo's position, it was exposed and vulnerable.

Zolkan flapped his wings for balance, saying as quietly as he could, "Strong beast. Be careful."

Molimo studied the other-beast and the way it moved. Long, curved arms swung in front of it as it moved on its stubby hindlegs. Patches of its reddish brown fur had been torn away in other battles, and heroic fights they must have been. The vicious talons popping from the heavy paws promised nothing less than instant death to any careless enough to receive a blow. The short black muzzle was lined with broken yellow teeth and deep-set eyes peered steadfastly at its target.

The thick body rippled with fat and muscle—the hunting in this area had not been poor for all. The other-beast lurched forward, talons clicking against stone.

"Molimo?"

Zolkan, it comes on me. The force is too great to resist.

"A blessing, this time. Only your other self can destroy this shit pile monster."

Molimo shuddered and felt the cloak falling from his shoulders. Zolkan took to the air and hovered nearby, working furiously to maintain his position. The jerkin strained in all the wrong places. Shoulders narrowed and arms shortened; muscles became like steel wires. Molimo's nose twitched and hurt him as it elongated.

He snarled and shook free of the mortal clothing. Only his sleek gray coat stood between him and the biting wintry winds. And this was all the wolf needed. A second snarl died on his lips. When hunting he never made a sound to warn his prey. The rugged fight he'd have when he attacked this other-beast would require stealth and cunning—and all the strength locked in his lupine form.

Molimo vaulted easily to the top of a large boulder and hunkered down, waiting.

The other-beast came beneath him, passed his position. Molimo tensed his hind legs, then blasted forth into the air. His front paws raked feebly at the other's back, but his hurtling weight unbalanced his victim.

The other-beast slammed forward, doubling into a furry ball and trying to roll. Molimo's jaws clacked shut; succulent hot juices spurted as his teeth ripped at a heavily muscled arm and prevented those raking talons from ripping his belly open.

As quickly as he had attacked, the wolf danced back, crouched and waiting. The incautious beast opened from its defensive posture. Molimo exploded forward once again, teeth sinking into exposed throat—but the wolf paid the price. One arm might have hung useless but the other's strength was augmented with fear and fury.

One talon ripped at Molimo's flesh and caked his gray coat with his own blood.

Again the wolf danced away, but the fight was now on even terms. The other-beast, though wounded, had the advantage of bulk and power. It reared up and fell forward, almost crushing Molimo beneath its body. Snapping, snarling ferociously now, Molimo rolled free, shaken and unable to retaliate quickly. For the briefest of instants, Molimo had the chance to end the battle. The other-beast exposed the back of its neck to powerful jaws. But Molimo missed and the fight continued.

The wolf retreated steadily in the face of the other-beast's power and would have been backed into a small, rocky box had it not been for Zolkan. The *trilla* bird lanced down from the heavens, picking at ears and eyes, tweaking the bloodied nose, ripping at reddish fur and distracting the other-beast's attention whenever it began its attack on Molimo.

The wolf rested, regained strength, coordinated well with the *trilla* bird. This attack finished their adversary. The other-beast shrieked for as long as air passed through its throat. Then only frothy pink foam gushed forth. It kicked and clawed, but Zolkan and Molimo continued to chase it.

"Dead," said Zolkan. "And about time. My feathers are all dirty again."

The bird landed beside the carcass and waddled over. Zolkan burrowed into the fur and found a warm spot. He sighed, enjoying true heat for the first time in days. Riding on Kesira's shoulder, under the woman's cloak, provided some heat, but in recent days even this had not been enough for the feathered Zolkan.

Its body cools soon in this wind, Molimo told him.

"What does it matter? Nice now."

A wolfish growl came from Molimo. Zolkan poked his head up as the wolf began to rip at the softer portions of meat on the other-beast. In death parts of the creature had returned to human; these Molimo left and dined only on the fatty, animal parts. Zolkan sampled a bit of the flesh and spat it out.

"Your tastes are deteriorating, Molimo," the bird said. "This is awful. Piss-poor meat. Yaaaa!"

Halfway through the bloody feast, Molimo involuntarily shape-shifted back to human. Zolkan sighed and left his warm niche beneath the other-beast's arm. The bird took to wing and swooped down on Molimo's clothing. Scooping them up, the bird returned and dropped them near the shivering human.

"Dress," commanded Zolkan. "Not even demons can save you if you freeze to death."

Molimo wiped his body as clean as possible on the other-beast's fur, then quickly donned the clothing. His flesh had begun to turn bluish white with frostbite.

The wolf's hide has definite advantages to my bare skin, he told Zolkan.

"Too bad you cannot control change—or stop partway. Human with wolf fur. Ha!" The bird crowed at his joke.

It is needed in Ayondela's winter. How many die because of her curse?

Zolkan alighted on Molimo's shoulder and buried his body under the cloak. "Back to Kesira?"

When Molimo didn't answer, Zolkan craned his head around, sniffing, keen eyes studying the dark sky.

North, Molimo indicated. *There is trouble to the north. We must help.*

"Who?"

Toyaga struggles to regain his power. He does not fare well. We can help.

Zolkan nodded. "We can use allies. Even a brass-ass like Toyaga."

Molimo went to where the horses stood tethered. For a moment, he hesitated, thinking to see Kesira again before he rode off. He changed his mind and stepped into the stirrup cup, heaving himself onto the horse's back. The animal protested the weight, then settled down into an easy walk as Molimo turned the horse's head toward the north. To the east, past a line of high hills, lay the Sea of Katad. Behind, the River Pharna emptied into the sea. To the west rose the low mountains forming the other side of this once-lush valley.

But Molimo concentrated on the feelings he had about what lay to the north in a small box canyon. The demon Toyaga rested there, fending off the occasional attacks mounted against him. Toyaga's effort was futile, however. Molimo sensed the gathering strength soon to be applied against the solitary demon. None could withstand those forces, not even a demon.

Scout for us, Molimo commanded. *We need to ride fast, if we are to be of any use to Toyaga.*

"Any other-beasts in air?" asked Zolkan. "I have no wish to be gobbled up by aerial beasts."

Fly, said Molimo. *Let me worry on such matters.*

"Easy enough for you to say," grumbled Zolkan, but the *trilla* bird flew with deft wingbeats toward the north, guided by the diamond points of stars and the cold wind against his face. Soon even Molimo's sharp eyes lost sight of the bird.

Molimo flicked the horse's reins and started across the fields, into the low foothills and farther back into the twisting, turning maze of the low mountains hugging the coastline.

Molimo stood beside his horse, looking down into the canyon. Ragged upjuts of stone rose in their immaculate white raiment. The serenity tore at Molimo, pulling away tiny pieces of his very soul. How could such beauty hide the ugliness he knew was there? Crystalline flakes of snow gleamed through all the colors of the rainbow as sunlight caught the delicate branchings. He turned his view from the tiny to the large. The vastness of the mountains was as rocky arms cast outward to embrace him. At any other time he would have been content simply to stand and watch the eons pass by, marching in step with the geologic changes wrought in the very mantle of the planet.

"Toyaga fights well, but he weakens," reported Zolkan. The green bird landed on Molimo's saddle and looked the man-wolf in the eye. "Think he can help you?"

Can we help him is a more pertinent question, replied Molimo.

"There is only narrow trail down side of hill. Want me to go on and tell Toyaga you come?"

No. Molimo considered the matter from different aspects. *There is no need to warn those attacking him. Let our arrival come as a surprise to them.*

"Not possible. Toyaga battles another demon."

The demon is not of the jade. Her powers are vastly inferior, Molimo pointed out. *Eznofadil corrupts many, and lures Urray astray. She is not evil.*

"Yet," Zolkan amended, "Eznofadil corrupts her and lures her with promises."

He would slay her if she tried to use the jade. There is room for only one jade demon after all is finished. Such power as they seek cannot be divided.

"Ayondela fights only for revenge of her lost son. Rouvin meant all to her." The *trilla* bird took to wing and allowed Molimo to begin the tedious downward trek along the narrow path.

She cared little for Rouvin. This has been building for centuries with her. It disrupts the routine and makes her existence more thrilling. That is all. She lives only for the instant, like a mortal.

"Which she becomes because of the jade."

Molimo said nothing. Zolkan's assessment hit close to
the truth. For all Ayondela's increased powers, her life
span neared an end because of the toll taken by the jade.
Eznofadil and Lenc paced themselves, allowing her to ex-
pend her energies. The true conflict would come between
those demons—Eznofadil and Lenc—when the world lay
hollow and conquered.

He did not want to see that conflict come, nor did Molimo
want to see either of the pair emerge victorious and all-
conquering. The damage to the world was bad enough
without the gaping wounds that would be inflicted by civil
war in demonic ranks.

Sounds of conflict came to Molimo's sharp ears halfway
down the winding dirt path. At places he dismounted and
walked his steed past narrows, taking a maddeningly long
time. Molimo sensed the ebb and flow of power beneath
him. The fight between Toyaga and Urray raged, and Toyaga was gradually weakening.

"Soon, hurry," urged Zolkan as Molimo gained the bottom of the path. "Not far. Toyaga needs you. Now!"

I know.

The *trilla* bird stopped his singsong speech. To warn Urray might prove fatal. Molimo trotted his horse across the
frozen, rocky ground and halted a hundred yards distant.
While he couldn't see the actual conflict, the energies flowing between the two demons were more than obvious.
Streams of heat rose in thick, shimmering columns, melting snow to water that trickled away to join a small mountain stream. Wary animals came and lapped at the water,
then darted away when they saw Molimo.

His full attention focused on the column of heat. At the
base of that pillar stood two demons who had once been
friends—and more.

"Need me?" asked Zolkan.

Molimo nodded curtly. The bird perched on his shoulder.
Together, they approached the battleground. As they
neared the titanic struggle, they could see that not only
snow had melted. The very rocks turned viscid and tried to
flow away from the punishments being exchanged.

Urray might have been attractive at one time. No
longer. Her locks hung in thick orange strands that looked

more like copper wire than hair. The female demon's body had thickened and huge brown spots dappled her skin. Fingers elongated into talons pointed at Toyaga. Worst of all, the once pretty Urray's face contorted into a mask of pure evil as she strove to destroy her former lover.

"Urray, will it make your lot easier if I simply submit?" asked Toyaga. The handsome demon spoke in measured tones, but rivers of sweat poured from his face and body, mingling with the molten stone at his feet and sending tiny clouds of steam aloft.

"You cannot," Urray screeched. "Or you would have done so."

"I loved you, my dear one," Toyaga said. "I still do. Is my death such a vital matter to you? Have Eznofadil and Lenc seduced you?"

"I see how their power grows. I want it for myself. They are not fit to rule the world. But I am. I will destroy them and pluck the fruits of victory for myself!"

"Vain," grumbled Zolkan. Molimo silenced the bird with a single gesture.

Toyaga had seen Molimo enter the small clearing and dismount; Urray's back was to him. Molimo approached silently, hand on sword. He judged distances, estimated his chances. Whether or not a single sword thrust would kill a demon had never been satisfactorily decided. All Molimo hoped for was to distract Urray enough so that Toyaga might finish the task. It was a desperate act, but it was all Molimo could do. Toyaga was nearing death at the female demon's hand.

"There is nothing wrong with allowing mortals to run their own affairs," said Toyaga. "We were a contented lot, we demons. We had our little intrigues and our grand plans. Why should we add the burden of their petty, fleeting lives to our concerns?"

"Power. I want the power."

"You want the feeling of power, of being important. You could have it, Urray," the handsome demon said. "Look at Lalasa. She has the Emperor's attention. Hundreds of thousands attend her every word. Perhaps millions. I have no way of knowing."

"Think of that magnified, Toyaga," Urray cried. "It will be mine. Now!"

Toyaga fell to his knees. The magicks surrounding him crushed in like jaws of a vise. Urray chortled in glee at her impending victory. She shaped the cosmic forces and brought them together around her victim, squeezing, closing ever tighter around Toyaga.

Molimo stood within sword range of the female demon. The brown spots marring her skin pulsed with the power that used her body as a conduit. Molimo doubted she knew the source of that power or, if she did, even cared. He set his feet for the thrust.

No, not now! he shrieked. Zolkan took to wing, talons slashing at the female demon as Molimo shape-shifted into wolf.

Urray shrieked in rage at being thwarted in her attempt to destroy Toyaga. She spun and sent sizzling waves of heat at the airborne Zolkan. The *trilla* bird squawked in protest as his feathers smouldered and started to burn. Zolkan tucked his wings and dived directly into a pool of water.

Feathers and water rained down on Urray.

And a wolf tore at her throat.

The female demon staggered back, flailing with her taloned hands. Molimo knew better than to retreat. The animal urges were fully upon him, all human control gone.

Long red channels opened on his flanks as Urray raked his sides. And then he fought only thin air. A gauzy haze hung about him until a gust of cold wind pulled it away. The wolf stood, tongue lolling with breath coming in sharp, short pants.

"My friend," said Toyaga, limping toward Molimo. "You have saved my life. In a way, you have not done me a favor. I meant it when I told Urray she could have my very life. Now I must heal and continue the fight against Lenc and Eznofadil." Toyaga sighed. "And even Ayondela, poor, lovely, misguided Ayondela."

Molimo snarled.

"This is a rare affliction," the demon said, placing one hand on the side of the wolf's head. Toyaga jerked the hand away before Molimo snapped it off with a powerful *clack!* of his jaws. "Rather, I meant that it was rare, before . . . before we entered the Time of Chaos."

Toyaga sighed more heavily and sat facing the wolf.

Green eyes bored into him, as if sizing him up for a meal. Toyaga continued speaking, as if he had not a care in the world.

"It is an epoch of our development I have no wish to see. Urray and I have been through so much together, and now she turns on me. Her very flesh boiled with the evil Lenc channeled through her. And she never knew he only used her as a vehicle for his power. Urray was a tool, and an expendable one. But you know that, don't you?"

Toyaga took the wolf's head between his hands and stroked over the gray fur.

"Careful," squawked Zolkan, waddling out of the pool. The *trilla* bird shook and sent water droplets into the air. They hung in space and refracted sunlight, cascading down a myriad tiny rainbows. "He cannot control change."

"I guessed as much. I fear there is nothing I can do to aid him in gaining such control." Toyaga pried open Molimo's mouth and peered within. "The human form lacks a tongue, too. That lies beyond the scope of what I can heal."

"Help him?" suggested Zolkan.

"Yes, but how? What gift can I pass to him that will not attract Lenc and the others prone to abusing the powers given them by the jade?" Toyaga thought aloud, being mindful to stay away from Molimo's sharp teeth.

"Stop other-beast changes," said Zolkan. "Stop them!"

"Sorry, my feathered saviour. That is beyond my powers. I was always the poet among the demons, giving an instant's relief from eternal tedium with a witty phrase or a tart word. Only recently has it been necessary for me to learn to do things like this."

With a casual touch of his hand, Toyaga reduced a rock to dust. He shook his head in dismay.

"A paean to the seasons, a praising of the sun and moon, a glorification of the gentleness as warm winds touch our cheek, those are so much more important to me. Still."

Molimo rocked back on his haunches and stared balefully at the demon.

Can you do nothing?

"Alas, my fellow rescuer, I cannot," Toyaga answered

the plea. "No, that is not so. I might be able to give you one
gift. How does it go? Yes, a ward well against being sniffed
out by evil, magical noses. Something to make you go
unnoticed by them, as if you did not exist.

> The world about me,
> There are no eyes.
> Freedom of the air and sky,
> I fade into nothingness."

Toyaga nodded slowly as Molimo shifted back into human form. "I see that this is far beyond my feeble talents
to stop. But the words for the ward spell. Can you remember them?"

Molimo nodded.

"They protect from being seen?" asked Zolkan.

Toyaga shrugged. "Perhaps. Perhaps it will protect
only from magicks set to detect your presence. I cannot
say for certain. Words and phrases and emotions have
engrossed me for centuries, not such tedious magical
pursuits."

Thank you. Molimo held out his hand.

Toyaga grasped it, then laughed. "Clothe yourself. You
will freeze your pecker off and then what good would you
be to the ladies, eh?"

"Help us," said Zolkan. "We go to Isle of Eternal
Winter. Confront Ayondela."

"I know," said Toyaga. "I felt it within his mind." The
demon stared at Molimo. "Such changes. Perhaps the
Time of Chaos is a good thing. I cannot keep up with the
changes; it is best I step out of the way and let those who
can have their chance. Perhaps the era of demons is over."
A tear rolled down Toyaga's cheek. He quickly brushed it
away.

"I must go to heal, to rest, to lie in repose until the words
fit themselves together. I write an epic poem for the Emperor."

"Jade demons. Help us!" implored Zolkan.

"That would be worthwhile," Toyaga said. "Finding the

proper scansion for the poem is even more so. I wish you luck. It is little enough that I can do for you."

Zolkan sputtered incoherently and started to fly at the demon. Molimo's quick grab snared the *trilla* bird in mid-air.

We will meet again, Molimo told the demon.

Toyaga said nothing. The pity in his eyes spoke more eloquently than words. Then the demon vanished.

Chapter Eight

THE SPEAR DROVE directly at Kesira Minette's midsection. She inclined her staff just a fraction of an inch and deflected the deadly tip. Kesira felt the cold steel near her skin and slice away fabric, but she had escaped injury.

This time.

The woman danced back, getting both hands onto her staff. The pile of leaves and twigs filled the entire doorway, blocking any possible escape. She had to stand and fight.

"What manner of beast are you?" she asked, hoping to distract it. The ploy failed. Again the spear came seeking her heart.

This time the nun was better prepared. Her stone-wood staff parried the haft of the spear, and she spun the other end up and into the midriff of the animated vegetation. The "oof!" that came when she connected solidly told her of the human hidden under all the camouflage. As the man staggered a step back, Kesira brought her staff whirling about and lunged with it. Although she lacked a knife tip like a spear, the hard, rounded end of the staff sank deeply into the leaves.

Mud, twigs, and small bugs flew everywhere. Her adversary sat down heavily, but the spear remained in his hand.

Kesira got out of the confining hut and emerged into the cold, wintry night. Stars gave what pathetic illumination they could through the thin layer of high cirrus clouds, but the moon cast a ghostly, ghastly light that allowed Kesira to see.

Leaves and bits of caked mud fell away from her fallen

attacker. She thought she saw eyes, nose, and mouth through the clinging debris. Human hands and feet stuck out from the compost. And the hand tightened again on the haft of the spear to prepare for another attack.

Kesira stepped forward and brought the staff around in a low arc that connected where the side of the head ought to be. Twigs snapped, leaves crushed, and mud flew in all directions—and the man slumped to the side, unmoving.

"What *is* this thing?" Kesira muttered to herself. She used her staff to flick away the spear, then knelt and tentatively pulled away the cloak of leaves. A thin, not unhandsome face emerged from beneath the grime and caked leaves. Too thin, Kesira thought, but with winter gripping the world in such a deadly hold this was to be expected. Even she was not as plump as she had been when living in the nunnery.

More of the camouflage peeled away to reveal the black and purple bruise growing on the side of the man's head. She ran light, testing fingers over the wound. The man winced but did not regain consciousness. As Kesira continued her examination the leaves and other earth products fell free. Once gone, all that remained was a man dressed in the style of a farmer.

Hip-high leather boots sorely needed tending. The shirt had once been intricately embroidered with scenes of demons cavorting on their way to the Emperor's court, but now hung in tatters, bright threads dulled and broken. The short, heavy mid-thigh pants were totally inappropriate for cold weather but that never stopped the farmers from wearing them. With the high boots, only a few inches of bare, hairy thigh was exposed to the elements.

Kesira examined the spear. The shaft had been well worn by many years of use; the tip was shiny, sharp, and recently manufactured. She peered more closely at it and saw the name of the weapons maker and the faint imprint "Limaden" beneath.

"The Imperial Armorer?" she wondered aloud.

"Aye, it is, and give that back!"

Kesira instinctively swung her staff and connected hard with the man's wrist. The crack indicated a painful blow, but nothing permanently damaging; no bones broke.

"You'll get it back when I am sure you won't harm any of us with it."

"What?"

"Are your ears still ringing from my blow?" Kesira asked. She had seen cases where even a light head blow turned a man's brain to jam. It had not been her intent to addle her compost heap attacker, but if it had happened she wanted to know.

"No, nothing of the sort. I want my weapon back. And an explanation. What do you mean that I'd harm 'us'?"

"You are in no danger," said Kesira, "as long as you do not attempt violence. Till I am sure you are peaceful, I keep your spear." She used her staff to knock him back to a sitting position on the ground. "And I ask the questions. You intruded on us, not the other way around."

"Where's Parvey?" the man demanded. "Is she safe?"

"Parvey?" Kesira said, hoping she put enough query into her voice to get information from the man.

"My wife! Parvey Yera. I'm her husband, Raellard."

"You have a strange way of entering a home," said Kesira. "Do you always barge in, spear thrusting?"

"It's my house, and I do as I please."

She had offended his farmer's sense of possession. Kesira apologized.

"Who are you?" he demanded.

"Kesira Minette, Sister of the Mission of the Order of Gelya."

"Quite a mouthful. What have you done to Parvey? I want to see her." Raellard's eyes narrowed. "She's not been harmed, has she? The baby's not due for another week yet."

"Your son decided to make an appearance early. He arrived last week."

"Last week! *Parvey!*" he yelled. "It's me, Raellard! Get out here this instant!"

"She's been quite ill. Starving, because you left her alone."

"I left because we were both starving. Had to find food."

"You look well enough nourished," observed Kesira. Even through the dirt still marring Raellard Yera, he did not seem to be in as bad a way as his wife or newborn son.

"Hard to hunt and do more than eat it when you've

killed it," he said. "Tried smoking some of it. Got a few tubers and roots I brought back. Enough to keep us going for a few more weeks. Maybe by then the damnable winter'll have let up."

"I doubt it," Kesira said.

"It's enough, if we don't get gluttonish about it."

"The winter," corrected Kesira. "I don't think the winter will ease. I'm sure you brought more than an adequate amount of food back for your family."

"Want to see her." Raellard turned surly. Kesira silently motioned for him to go into the hut. She kept the tip of her staff firmly atop his spear so that he couldn't take it, though. Kesira did not trust the man. But she had to smile, and only through real effort did she keep from laughing, as he made his way to the hut. He left behind a trail of mulch normally seen only in the deepest of forests.

Kesira doubted he would harm Parvey or the boy. If anything, he'd keep Parvey from killing the infant in the mistaken belief he was an other-beast. While Raellard Yera was inside, she went exploring. Following the trail of leaves back down the ravine and around a bend, she saw where Raellard had dropped his burden of foodstuffs. She pawed through the rude canvas bag and saw green, decaying meat and the tubers and other poor viands described. She hefted them to her shoulder, staggered a little under the weight and started back toward the hut.

Raellard Yera blocked her way.

"Stealing my food, are you?" he raged.

"Helping get it to your wife," Kesira said angrily. "Why steal such pathetic fare? I could eat my horse and do better." The horse whinnied in protest from a score of yards away where it stood tethered. "Not that I would," Kesira hastily added. While she couldn't be sure the horse understood, it was best not to take chances.

And she and Molimo had regretfully lived off their steeds before arriving at the Abbey of Ayondela.

Raellard shifted uneasily from foot to foot.

Kesira dropped the bag and said, "Since you're here, carry your own load." She stormed past him, heading to the house. He made a choking noise, then grunted as he picked up the sack and followed. Kesira entered the hut and went to Parvey.

"Are you all right?" she asked the frail woman. "That is your husband?"

"Yes, Raellard came back. With food. Real food." Kesira didn't gainsay this. What Raellard carried in the bag was hardly what she'd consider "real food," but if you're starving anything looks delectable. Kesira stroked Parvey's stringy hair, thinking that a hungry person wouldn't listen to reason or be moved by prayer.

"Here it is," Raellard called, heaving the bag through the door. The bag landed with a *thunk!* in the middle of the floor. The infant began whimpering feebly at the sudden noise.

Raellard stood and stared for a moment, shifting weight uncertainly from foot to foot. He rubbed his lips and finally said, "Do something. The boy's bawling."

"He's hungry," said Kesira. "Only Parvey can do something about that."

Parvey cowered back. "It's an other-beast. It'll change on me and hurt me."

Raellard frowned, a look of concern on his face. Kesira saw that this was beyond his powers to understand.

"The baby is human," said Kesira in the softest, most comforting voice she could muster. "He will not harm you. He loves you. And you love him, don't you, Parvey?"

The woman shook her head and flinched away as the baby cried again.

"Eat some of the good food Raellard's brought and you'll feel better," said Kesira. "Eat and then let your son eat."

Kesira had no desire to intrude. She left the hut and went back into the cold, still night while Raellard fixed a meal of the provender he had scrounged. Kesira stood, arms crossed, trying not to shiver with the cold as she stared up into the now clear blackness of the heavens. Demon lights, someone had called them, but Kesira doubted that.

While the demons possessed powers, creating such artistic limitlessness lay beyond their ken. The demons might be superhuman in many ways, but they were not gods and only a god might form the vista Kesira gazed upon.

She had often wondered why the stars were not more

perfectly aligned, put into patterns, given outlines of distinct and recognizable figures. Sister Dana had told her that the confusion made it impossible to sort out such figures and that this was a mark of inspiration on a god's part—infinity had been created from a handful of stars.

Kesira played the game now that she had when Sister Dana told her this. The woman tried to find pictures where none were. Animals, birds—she found a dozen twinkling stars that might have been Zolkan's profile. The thought of the *trilla* bird filled her with uneasiness. Molimo and Zolkan had gone off on their quest without really telling her why they went. She had sensed the presence of other beasts nearby, but she also felt that this was only a part of why they'd left.

Food? Perhaps. But they could hunt together as easily as apart. She was no handicap and had proven it repeatedly.

Kesira's fingers traced over the bone box containing her rune sticks. If she cast, would it tell her the future? Her skill at this had improved dramatically. When she had lived in the nunnery, her ability had been minimal. Since Lenc had destroyed her patron and her world, the talent had burgeoned. Kesira had no way of telling if her readings were a product of her own skill or if some other force guided her hand, made the cast using her as a vehicle, sent her the interpretations.

"It was to keep warm," came the voice from behind her. Kesira spun, startled. "Sorry. Didn't mean to frighten you." Raellard stopped a few feet away from her.

"I was thinking of other things. It is my fault. What did you mean, it was to keep warm?"

"The leaves and mud. Couldn't get a decent fur off the animals I clubbed. All of 'em were poxy and hairless. The leaves and mud kept me warmer."

"They also served as a home for the insects." Kesira fancied she still saw the bugs crawling over the man's body in an undulating wave of browns and blacks.

"Good with the bad. Life's like that."

"You're not talking about the leaves and bugs now, are you?" Kesira asked.

"No. Parvey. My son. She still hasn't named him, and he's a week old. I told her I'd do it, but she got so upset I didn't say any more. Besides, that's the mother's responsibility. Not my place to even suggest it."

"Is she nursing him?"

"Finally. Not much milk, but then she's been starving herself. Enough food in there to keep her alive for a month."

"But not the three of you for a month," said Kesira.

"I eat more'n she does." The way Raellard said it was neither a boast nor a lament—it was simply stated fact. "Have to go out right away to do some more hunting about."

"And I must rejoin my party. We were traveling to the sea. They went north on a scouting trip."

"Nothing much to the north. Not the way to the sea, not for fifty miles unless you're up to crossing the coastal mountains. Only back down there, the way you came, maybe a day's ride on a horse." Raellard pointed toward the Pharna River.

"I'll be leaving in the morning. You won't have to worry about me interfering. Parvey will be just fine now that you're here."

"Leaving myself," said Raellard. "Can't afford to stay and nursemaid her. We'd both starve if I did."

"You can't just leave her."

"Can't take her and the boy with me, either, now can I? Weather's not so bad now, but another storm's moving in. Feel it in my joints. Stiff elbow always signals bad weather. Killing me now." Raellard held out his right arm and flexed his arm to emphasize the point.

"I may have hit it with my staff."

"Did," he agreed, "but this is a different kind of hurting." Raellard fell silent for a few minutes, then said, "You're good with that stick. Where'd you learn to use it?"

"I'm a nun. When my Order still thrived, I made many trips to Blinn for supplies." Kesira smiled wanly at her use of the word *many*. She had made only a few such trips, but to a young woman free of the confines of a nunnery, each one had been precious in its newfound freedom. Looking back, there seemed more than there actually had been.

"Brigands," said Raellard, nodding. "Had to fight 'em

off." He smiled almost shyly and added, "All the men, too, in this Blinn. Bet you had to fight them off, too."

"Thank you for the compliment," she said. "Truthfully, most of them would have nothing to do with me because I was a nun acolyte."

"Most?"

Kesira laughed. "I found enough who had no fear. Celibacy is not part of my vow to Gelya."

"Never had much time for such things," said Raellard. "The demons, I mean." Kesira wondered if the farmer blushed; she couldn't tell in the pale starlight. "No patron. Never found one that fit into what I believed, one who'd help me out."

"It usually works better patterning yourself to the patron's teachings," she admitted. "There is an order to life then. A system. A knowable pattern. The teachings make it easier to know where honor lies, what your duties are, your place in society."

"My place has been frozen away," Raellard said with a touch of bitterness.

"My friends and I are going to the Isle of Eternal Winter to speak with Ayondela. She is responsible for this prolonged winter. If we can convince her that she has made a mistake, summer might still reach us in time to keep many from starvation."

"Who are these friends of yours? Saw signs of them, but they're not around. Why'd they leave you all alone?"

"To tend Parvey," she said quickly. "And we will meet up again. The separation is a brief one."

Kesira stared down the valley, wishing for Molimo and Zolkan to ride into sight.

"Getting cold. Come back to the hut. Out of the wind."

"Thanks." Kesira started back when a sharp pain doubled her over. She gasped and fell to her knees, clutching her belly.

"What's wrong?" asked Raellard. The man hovered around her ineffectually, not touching her but wanting to help.

"Pain's going away. Been like this for a month or so," she said. "My cycle has turned irregular. Umm, it's easing more."

"Haven't been getting enough to eat," said Raellard. "You're as skinny as a rail."

"So much riding—and fighting," she said. "Those contribute to the problem. But I'm fine now." Sweat beading her forehead, Kesira rose on unsteady feet. The pain had been abrupt, a needle of fire ripping through her abdomen. She didn't push Raellard away when he put his arm around her and helped her to the hut.

"You can't go on alone," the man said. "I'll go with you in the morning. Together. For a while."

"There's no need."

"Owe you something for helping my wife. Parvey's not been right in the head for some time and you didn't have to even stop."

"I had to," Kesira said. "I couldn't let anyone suffer the way she was. Her cries carried all the way to the river."

"Then I can't let you go off feeling sickly like you do. It'll be just for a while, till I find good hunting."

"You must stay with Parvey. For a while until she's stronger. It'll be for your son's sake, too, Raellard. He needs a great deal of care now, being as sickly as he is."

"Shouldn't have come so early into the world," grumbled Raellard.

"But he did. You must stay with them."

"Duty's to see that they're fed. Can't do it here. Growing grain is 'bout all I know and I can't grow in frozen ground."

"We'll talk about it in the morning," said Kesira, having no intention of doing so. She would be off and away while Raellard Yera still slept. She would rejoin Molimo in a day or two and they could continue on to the Isle of Eternal Winter.

Kesira slumped down in the far corner of the rude hut and tried to sleep. She heard the muffled argument going on between Raellard and Parvey and wished she didn't, but there was no way for her to shut out the words.

Or the soft *click-click-click* of talons against the frozen ground outside. For a few minutes, Kesira wasn't sure she heard them. Then she sat up and strained. The pace was slow, sure, a four-footed animal's stride.

"Molimo!"

Kesira rose and went to the door, peering out through a

small crack. Her heart fluttered with joy when she saw a shadow-shrouded sleek gray body sniffing about outside. She pushed aside the door and slipped out.

"Molimo, where's Zolkan? It took you long enough to get back." The wolf wheeled and stared at her, as if he'd never seen her before. The mouth opened to reveal the sharp, flesh-ripping teeth.

"The Emperor take it! An other-beast!" cried Raellard Yera.

Kesira turned and saw the man, spear in hand, ready to cast.

"No, wait!" she exclaimed.

Raellard threw the spear with impressive accuracy. The sharp tip entered the wolf's shoulder; a last-instant twist prevented the point from entering too deeply. The animal vented a yowl of pain and turned angry eyes on Kesira.

"Get inside, damn you," Raellard ordered. "It's one of them other-beasts. Hungry lot will kill anything that moves."

"Don't bother me. Nothing is wrong," Kesira said.

The wolf pounced. She got her arm up and under the furred neck, forcing the snapping jaws away. Hot wolf breath gusted into face and drool dripped onto her arm.

"Molimo, stop it!" Kesira feared that the change had seized his mind and immersed him totally in the animal world.

She heard a grunt and felt the wolf tense. Hot fluids dribbled onto her arms and chest. The wolf rolled off her, kicking feebly. Raellard Yera had retrieved his spear and driven it with savage fury into the wolf's back.

"Broke his spine. Cut clean through it," the farmer said proudly. "But you shouldn't have stood there asking it to attack. Damnedest thing I ever saw."

Kesira paid no attention to the man. She got to her knees and cradled the wolf head in her lap. The sightless eyes studied the stars above. Already the body cooled in death.

"Molimo, no, no," Kesira sobbed.

"This'll feed Parvey good while I'm gone. Wolf meat's not the best-tasting, especially when it comes off an other-beast, but it'll have to do. We all have to make sacrifices."

Raellard pulled her away from the carcass. Kesira went back into the hut, oblivious to all Parvey said, oblivious to the baby, oblivious even to her own tears leaving cold, wet tracks down her cheeks.

Chapter Nine

"DID TOYAGA HELP?" asked Zolkan. The *trilla* bird fluttered around just above Molimo's head and caused a severe downdraft from his wings that made the man duck and dodge.

Who can say? I feel no different. The changes still come upon me, and I can do nothing to stop them.

"Pity. Toyaga can be such a fool. Always mumbling his shit-pretty words. Had hoped he might give you release."

His ways are different, admitted Molimo. *But he is not a fool.*

Zolkan did not answer. He rose higher, and Molimo escaped from the cold winds gusting down at him. The dark-haired man sat in his saddle and peered out over the land. Such beauty, he thought, and it had been blighted. For the depths of winter it was beautiful. Snow banked gently along the north sides of low hills and shone with a brilliance in the weak sun that made him squint. The crisp, cold air invigorated even as it sapped the heat from his bones, but Molimo withstood it more easily than either Zolkan or Kesira might.

Kesira.

His thoughts turned to her. By now she would have found her way back to the Pharna River and might even have reached the Katad. From there it was but a short journey along the coast to the prominence from which the Isle of Eternal Winter was visible. Crossing the sea to reach the Isle might prove dangerous, but Molimo failed to see one single moment of the journey south from the Quaking Lands that hadn't been. Even before, before they had left Howenthal's castle.

Every instant had been dangerous.

The battle with Nehan-dir and those following the banner of the Steel Crescent had been deadly. Wemilat had died. A kind and good demon, dead. For him Molimo mourned. And for Toyaga and the others.

Even for himself. He felt the urge to cry out, to shriek his name and listen to the echoes along the canyon walls. The hills would turn afire with his words and sear off this accursed winter brought by Ayondela.

Only tiny squeaks emerged from deep in his throat. The ripped-out tongue would never be healed, not in this lifetime. The jade rains had seen to that. He turned cold inside thinking of his fear as the molten jade had pelted his skin. Then he had been able to cry out in rage and pain. And he had.

A guttural growl now escaped him, the closest to an expression of stark anger he could voice.

"Feel stirrings?" came Zolkan's words from above. "Weak, ever so weak. But not far." The *trilla* bird let loose a string of curses that captured Molimo's full attention.

He sniffed the air for spoor, listened to the tiny slithers and crunches and snaps of moving wildlife about him, even experienced a slight drop in the temperature of the air moving across his face. But he sensed what Zolkan had seen with his eyes through an inner discipline that even the jade rains sent by Lenc could not extinguish.

Former power is not far, he told Zolkan. *I cannot get an understanding of what sort of power, though. It might be anything—and it is long gone.*

Zolkan's atonal complaints showered down on him from above. The *trilla* bird refused to ignore this.

We go to explore, Molimo said tiredly. *Then we leave immediately to rejoin Kesira.*

"You care for her, don't you?" the bird cawed.

My feelings are complex, as always.

"Don't give me that pigeonshit," said Zolkan. "She is a good woman."

She follows Gelya's teachings faithfully. She is honorable and shoulders her responsibilities, as is her duty.

"You love her, don't you?"

That path leads only to disaster for us all. You know the reasons why it cannot be.

"There is nothing to lose, not now," said Zolkan. "If we convince or defeat Ayondela, curse is lifted. If we don't, what's to lose?"

The battle is against Ayondela, Molimo said slowly, considering every aspect of the confrontation to come, *but Eznofadil is at the heart of the fight. He drives Ayondela, he goads her on, he is the source of the woe befalling us.*

"I gathered as much from Toyaga," said Zolkan. "Eznofadil uses Ayondela as peasant-minor in his game of conquest."

No peasant piece was ever so powerful. Ayondela is a major participant, at least a vassal-superior on this board.

"Is the Emperor piece in jeopardy?"

Molimo nodded. The jade demons' power grew daily, and he saw only small segments of their overall plan. Lenc was cunning in recruiting others to do his work for him. Whether that came from the jade turning his very flesh to stone, Molimo did not know. He did know that Eznofadil had always been cunning. None of the other demons played the strategy game as well.

The twitching within his skull alerted him. He kicked at his horse's flanks and urged the animal up a small incline and into a heavily forested area on the hillside. His every sense strained for a trap. The other-beasts saw nothing wrong in attacking those of their own kind.

Even one such as I, he said ruefully.

"What about you?" came Zolkan's muffled words. The tree limbs hid the sky and muffled the *trilla* bird's words.

Nothing. It lies ahead.

"I see shrine. An open-air rock altar. Old, very old. Predates even shit-eating demons and crotch-scratching humans."

You are so eloquent, Zolkan. Why do you not speak to me the way you do to Kesira?

"She is offended. Can I hide my origins from you? Old Garbgo sailed too long with me. Stole me from birthing nest when I was only chick. All life spent listening to him as he sailed coast along Rest Province."

The heat rises from the altar. I feel it almost as if it were physical.

Zolkan did not reply. Even the flap of wings disappeared. Molimo knew the bird flew on to scout the area for traps. As acute as his own senses were, the aerial reconnaissance provided by the bird proved invaluable. Many of the other-beasts lost large portions of their human intelligence and forgot to hide from all possible pryings. Zolkan spotted them easily.

The demon spawn were harder to trap or trick into revealing themselves. They were permanently locked into their deformed bodies, the product of intercourse between demons and animals. Molimo's gorge rose at the thought of such perversion, but he was in no position to pass judgment. Ayondela and a human had mated to produce Rouvin, a half-human, half-demon warrior of honorable deeds and a needful death.

Molimo licked chapped lips as he thought of Rouvin. The transformation had come upon him too quickly to warn Kesira—and Rouvin had not known he walked shoulder to shoulder with an other-beast. Molimo had shape-shifted and ripped the warrior's throat out before Rouvin's blade cleared its sheath. That the death had freed Wemilat and eventually led to Howenthal's downfall did not absolve Molimo's guilt in the matter.

He could not control the transformation in his body; he had slain Rouvin. Those were the facts. As it was a fact that Ayondela's rage froze the world.

The altar in the small clearing promised Molimo surcease from his uncontrollable affliction. While he doubted he could reverse the effect of the jade rain upon his body, Molimo did believe he might better control the change when it occurred. With the energies locked and dormant in this altar, he might be able to prevent unwanted transitions from one form to the other.

Molimo dismounted and tethered his horse at the edge of the wooded area. On foot he approached the altar. The stillness enveloped him like a warm, gauzy blanket. No wind. No sound. No odor, however faint. Each step he took made him think he moved that much closer to the end of the universe. Molimo wondered why no one had ever spoken of this place before.

He stood and stared at the rude stone block that served as an altar. Faint dark brown stains marred the sides; the top had been scoured clean by eons of wind and rain. The slow march of seasons, hot to cold, cool to warm, had cracked the stone and left fissures thick enough for a knife blade to penetrate. The living heart of the stone lay within.

Molimo stepped up and laid the palms of his hands on the surface. The stone warmed him in spite of Ayondela's winter. He closed his eyes and reached deep within himself.

Faint tendrils tried to touch him, to stroke the most afflicted parts of him. Then they vanished in the mist and left him as he had been.

There must be power given if power is to be received, he said. *Life must be exchanged for life.*

In the forest Zolkan squawked. He turned and saw the *trilla* bird perched on a thick tree limb just above where he'd tethered his mount. Molimo did not ask. He knew that the bird could come no closer. Faint though it was, the vestigial power of the altar kept Zolkan away.

With some reluctance, Molimo lifted his hands and backed away from the altar. He left the zone of silence surrounding it and again heard and felt and smelled the world.

"It still lives," said Zolkan. "Cannot get too close or burn me alive."

There are only embers, explained Molimo. *But it might help me to fan those embers into a fire.*

"Whose altar?"

Molimo shook his head. He had no knowledge of any before the demons with power to command such as this. But that did not mean they had not existed. Molimo considered what he was about to do and worried; it might be an error to bring back those who had left. Already the jade demons caused woes throughout the world. What might these spirits do if he resurrected them?

Zolkan read his face accurately. "Death now, death later, what difference? We all die eventually. Even demons."

The mortals call demons immortal, mused Molimo, *but this is not so. Demons merely live extended lives. As in all things, this human trait is only magnified and lengthened and augmented.*

"Their deaths are that much more spectacular," pointed out Zolkan. "To die nobly." The bird shivered. "I prefer to die quietly and not disturb my inherent beauty." Zolkan spread his wings and postured for Molimo.

Molimo shuddered and started to loosen his cloak, jerkin, and trousers. He barely got them off before his body flowed and twisted and grew and diminished, turning him into a sleek-furred wolf with snapping jaws and blazing green eyes.

"Change is slowed. Your control improves," said Zolkan, keeping high on the denuded tree limb to prevent the wolf from dining easily at his expense.

Molimo skirted the frightened horse with its kicking hooves and ran into the forest, more alive than before. His senses heightened. Every movement thrilled him; every odor burned in his nose. He longed to savor the coppery heat of a fresh kill's blood. Muscles responding smoothly, Molimo ran through the woods and rejoiced in the hunt.

A rabbit fell to his quickness. Four *prin* rats. A smaller gazelle. Molimo caught and maimed them all, careful not to kill. His almost human part fought the animal urges to rip flesh from the bones and dine on the tough, stringy flesh, even as that same part tormented itself over the creatures' sufferings.

While he was stalking another rabbit, Molimo shapeshifted back to human. He skidded along the dirt on his face, the ice and rocks cutting his chest and belly. Painfully, he lifted himself up and brushed off the freezing dirt. The rabbit had stopped and now peered at him curiously, unsure why it still lived. The rabbit's ears came up and swiveled around in wonder. The wolf had vanished. All it found was a clumsy human.

Slower, as grateful for miracles as a rabbit can be, it hopped off to return to its burrow. Foraging could wait till evening. It needed to recover from the fright it had received.

"Clothes," Zolkan said. A cascade of Molimo's clothes came from the sky. The bird swooped and landed deftly. It waddled around and pecked at the smell-weed and other hearty plants thrusting through the thin, icy crust coating the earth.

That will make you sick. Stop eating it, Zolkan.

"Dress. I only sample. It tastes terrible, anyway." The bird spat out tiny pieces of the smell-weed. Molimo donned his clothing and looked around. The world had changed on him. No longer did he view it from a height of two feet.

"Game still kicks back there where you mutilated it," said Zolkan with some disgust in his voice. "Clean kills are better."

I need living creatures.

Zolkan said nothing to this. He flew off and perched on the tree limb again, once more viewing all that happened within the small clearing. This time his expression, if the beaked face could show such, was only of disdain.

Molimo lugged the carcasses of the living animals and placed them on the altar. All about him he felt the stillness that had been present before, but now came a tension unlike anything he'd experienced previously. Molimo arrayed the creatures on the stone block and stared at them. No ritual came to his lips; none would have worked.

"Get it over with," urged Zolkan. "It will be night soon enough and I have no desire to be caught here in darkness."

Molimo ran his forearm across his dried lips. He stared at the animals and then did what was necessary. His sword flashed. One head, two, all. Life fluids returned to the stone, seeping into the cracks, seeking out the heart of the altar.

The curious bubble of nothingness he stood inside began to hum and vibrate with subdued energy. Molimo widened his stance, sword still clutched firmly in hand. Unseen beings brushed his elbows, touched his face, toyed with him.

What are you? he asked.

No answer.

Ghostly, almost-living veils fluttered before his eyes, nature spirits returning to a joyful existence after slumbering for untold years. The stone of the ages took on a vibrancy unlike any stone Molimo had seen. The blood had ceased flowing from the animals' bodies, but the stone took up a heartlike beat. Pulsations rippled from one side to the other. Molimo did not find this alarming, but it definitely unsettled him.

What have I returned to life?

—Nothing.

What are you?

—Spirits. Of trees. Of grass. Of life itself.

They spun around Molimo, ethereal fingers touching his body, yearning to be whole once more. The animal blood had revitalized long-forgotten nature spirits. They took on more substance, and he made out their silhouettes. A small bush shook feathery white leaves to the ground, then vanished. A larger tree poked its limbs to the very sky, only to falter and evaporate like burned-off fog. A small rabbit coalesced and stared accusingly at Molimo. He did not recognize the animal, but guessed it might have been one he recently killed. It started to hop away; its feet sank through the ground. The rest of the body dissipated, smoke in the wind.

Can you give me the power I seek?

—We have returned, for a moment, but it is a sweet moment.

Help me!

Mocking laughter rang inside Molimo's head.

—You who are so powerful, you who still hold possession of your corporeal body need our help?

Molimo sank to his knees. His hands reached for the altar. The warmth he had found there before now almost burned him, but he did not flinch away.

For this brief moment, aid me. Please.

—We can only try.

Molimo sucked in his breath when he felt lacy tendrils stroking over his face. The altar grew even hotter, a griddle for his flesh. Ghost fingers pressed his hands down to the stone. The pain lancing up his muscular arms and into his brain activated the transformation—and the change was aborted.

I did not change! he exulted. *Give me the power to hold back the shape changes. Please!*

Again he groaned as pain assailed him. The change to wolf began, then reversed. He retained his human form. Molimo dug down inside himself to find the mechanisms causing the change, the trigger that turned him beastlike, the trigger to be avoided.

—We weaken. This is strong. You are strong.

Try. Help me. I beseech you.

The spirits fluttered around him and began appearing and disappearing with increasing regularity. He saw small animals and large. Their spirits remained long after their bodies had been devoured by hunters, both human and nonhuman, to roam the woods seeking release or rebirth. They had found neither over the millenia.

Molimo allowed them to show him the corridors of his own mind and body, to examine spots hitherto blocked to him. But they could not give him the key to permanently lock his metamorphosis. Molimo railed at the idea of coming so close, only to fail. He fought and struggled, implored and cajoled them for help.

—You are mightier than the last who sought our aid.

Another has walked this path?

—A warrior named Piscaro.

Molimo had heard the legends of this mighty human warrior. He had died in service to the Emperor more than five hundred years ago. Songs told of his bravery and devotion to duty, soldiers raised their sons and daughters with his every deed ingrained so that they, too, might become great. And none dared speak evil of him, even to this day.

—He was a coward, before he came to this altar.

Molimo blinked in surprise. The spirits entering and leaving his body sensed his confusion.

—Before he summoned us, he was a weakling. In exchange for the life he imparted to us all too briefly, we gave him a part of us, a spirit indomitable and unbreakable.

His courage is legend.

—His courage comes from nature, a part of all that we are, a part of all that has been and has died.

Molimo continued his inner battle for domination over the jade-imposed shape alteration to wolf. He groaned and let the spirits aid him, but their help grew weaker and weaker. Molimo came no closer to conquering his problem.

Why do you hold back?

—You do well.

Molimo tried to lift his hands from the altar. This was not the same spirit that had come to him before. A different one, one of blackness and not light now seeped through him.

What are you? You are not the same.

—How astute.

The blackness welled inside him, forcing away the control he had so painstakingly learned. The spirits now boiling around him were of decay, of evil, the otherness of death that opposed life. The blood offering he had given to the altar no longer held the nature-life spirits.

Nature-death drew closer to him.

Away! Get away from me.

—When you summon a part, you summon the whole. Their time with you is past. Now comes our turn.

Molimo's battle became one of escape rather than self-understanding. The evil forces had almost tricked him into lowering all his defenses, as he had done for the other spirits. The altar turned cooler under his hands; the changing of polarities had occurred, but Molimo found himself unable to pull back and leave.

As surely as he had been held before, the power of death held him and sucked at his body and soul.

—You are a strong one. You will make an excellent addition to our rank.

No! I fight the jade power. I cannot give in to you.

—Piscaro did.

But the fainter voice of the life-spirit came. —Piscaro successfully fought and escaped. Do the same while you are able. Now. Fight, now, now. . . .

Molimo had watched as Kesira meditated, had gently touched her soul as she sank into the calm oceans of her deepest thoughts. He duplicated all the nun had done, found solace, found strength.

He slowly removed his hands from the frigid stone altar. Molimo was aware of the inky clouds enveloping him, but no worry tainted his thoughts. He was strong, he had his duty to do. Honor demanded that he face Ayondela and tell her of his responsibility in the death of her son.

The black spirits drew closer when they sensed his part in Rouvin's death.

Molimo rose to his feet.

He saw Zolkan wildly flapping in the tree, signalling to him to retreat. Unhurried, composed and able to hold darkness at bay, Molimo stepped away from the altar.

—You cannot leave. Please. Return. It will be long centuries before another comes to us. We want only to live again.

We all entertain hopeless fantasies, Molimo said. *This is yours. Rest in peace.*

He took another step. The tension around him mounted. Another step and another. The black tendrils slipped from his arms and legs and mind. With measured step, he returned to stand under the limb where Zolkan awaited impatiently.

"Evil. All around, evil. I feel it. My feathers fall out from it. I pile up shit under limb from fear for you."

Thank you, Zolkan. We can go.

"You got what is needed?"

Molimo only shook his head. The evil spirits had come as he felt control within his grasp. Now, he just did not know. But Molimo doubted he had full control over his shape alterings.

If nothing else, he had gained some insight. But would it do him any good if he found himself again locked within a wolf's body?

Molimo ducked the low branches of a tree and guided his horse to a more open trail. With luck, they might rejoin Kesira within a few days.

Chapter Ten

"KILLING THAT WOLF was a lucky thing," said Raellard Yera. "Keep Parvey in food for a while. Give her a warm blanket, too, even if'n there's not much time to cure the hide."

Kesira said nothing. She was too sick inside. The thought stuck in her mind and stung like a nettle: Molimo is dead.

"Don't think it was one of them other-beasts, either. This one looked to be well fleshed. Good body fat. Wolf meat's never been one of my favorites, neither for me nor the Emperor, but in this accursed weather, anything'll do, isn't that so?"

Kesira numbly nodded. She had grown to love Molimo. Not because she had nursed him back to health or because he carried the awful afflictions of the jade rain, but for his courage, his devotion, his sense of honor.

Molimo is dead. Feeding a woman already crazy with malnutrition. The winds felt colder to Kesira, the air a little more humid and stifling, the white snow too intensely brilliant, the world a grimmer place than it had just a few hours earlier.

"You all right? Not said a word."

"I have little to say, Raellard. Just meditating," she lied. "Performing the rituals was an important part of the Order of Gelya. But our patron's gone. All that remains of him are the teachings. And the ritual."

"Doesn't seem like much."

"No, it doesn't."

Kesira kicked at her horse's flanks and urged the mare to a faster walk. Being on foot, Raellard had to pump hard to keep up, but the man said nothing. His breath came more heavily now with the exertion. Kesira knew she punished him unfairly, but she didn't care.

Now and again her tear-fogged eyes turned to the perfect wintry clearness of the sky. She looked for some sign of Zolkan, the green of his feathers against the azure sky, the sound of his impassioned squawks as he protested some minor indignity to his feathers or his belly. Only the razor-slashing wind filled the day.

"Getting colder," observed Raellard. "Good to exercise hard. Keeps me warm."

Kesira reined in a little and slowed the pace to one that the man could more easily maintain. "Sorry," the nun said. She stared straight ahead, her cold-thickened fingers working over the blue knots in the cord around her waist. Occasionally Kesira touched the gold sash and resented the burden it placed upon her.

She might be the sole surviving—practicing—member of her Order. If Gelya's teachings were not to die, she had to recruit, to proselytize, to establish a new mission. Her Sisters in the nunnery were dead by Lenc's jade hand. Those in Chounabel had been seduced away from Gelya by the lure of the city and the mistaken belief that the Order had died with the patron. She was alone now in her faith.

Alone, without Molimo.

"I done something wrong. That's it. What was it? You don't want me along to chase off brigands? What is it?"

"Nothing, Raellard. I already told you that."

"More'n nothing. You were almost damn cheerful when we first met. You had fixed up Parvey and the boy. Now that you're away from them and with me, you don't make no more noise than a stalking leopard. Can't say that's nothing, now can I?"

"My journey seems destined to end in failure," she said. "I had a very fine ally, the son of Ayondela and a human warrior. He died. The demon freed by his death also perished. Now I . . . I fear for my friends who went to the north. I don't think they will return." A tear ran down her cheek, threatening to freeze against her skin.

"Why you want to talk to Ayondela? She's a crazy one. Always thought that, even when the weather was running warm."

"You know, then, that this is her curse for her son's death?" Kesira's wave encompassed the white countryside. In the distance, swirling above the Yearn Mountains, harsh black storm clouds were preparing another load of misery. Summer would be postponed still another week when that storm swept down the mountain slopes and across the Roggen Plains. Cities would be buried under the snow and the Pharna would freeze even more solidly, if that was possible.

A wink of vivid blue-white lightning confirmed Kesira's fear that this storm would be worse than the ones preceding it. Ayondela's power and wrath grew with every passing day.

"You able to deal with Ayondela all alone?" asked Raellard.

"I must. That seems to be the destiny cast for me. It is certainly my duty."

"Might be other people who'd follow along with you."

"You, Raellard? Thank you, but I can't ask that of you."

"You took care of Parvey, and you didn't have to."

"Gelya taught that kindness spawns kindness. But it is my burden that I cannot let people suffer, if I am able to help. I wanted nothing in return."

"Want to help, though. However I can."

"Escort me to the river, then go hunting for more food. In that you will have repaid me. Take care of Parvey and your son. Perhaps seek out a mission and ask after Gelya's teachings. There can be no better payment for me than that."

"Parvey's always been off in the head," Raellard said unexpectedly. "Even before. Before she got the notion the baby's an other-beast." The man scratched his stubbled chin. "You don't suppose she can be right about that, do you?"

"The son is yours."

"Don't know. Parvey's crazy. Might have taken up with a demon wandering by or even some weird creature out stalking around in the woods. Never could understand her."

"You're saying you don't think you're the baby's father?" Kesira frowned. This was a serious allegation. The sanctity of family ranked only under loyalty to the Emperor as a basis for their society. And even then . . .

"She's the mother, there's no doubting that. But I been gone lots trying to find food or something to hunt. The times I was back might not have been enough. Three others have died stillborn. It's a good piece of land I farm, but there's not been much other luck."

"Wait," Kesira said, coming fully alert. She had been away from her nunnery long enough to develop the feel Molimo referred to as "trail sense." Something stalked them.

"Can't say I mind you being skeptical on this," said Raellard.

"Quiet. Someone is behind us, hunting us."

Raellard fingered the worn shaft of his spear and looked around nervously. "Hate this. Don't mind it when I'm doing the hunting, but when they come after me, by all the demons, do I hate it."

Kesira used her superior height to slowly survey the terrain. They had left the hillier section where Raellard had his farm and reentered the ravine leading to the Pharna River. The bends in the ravine precluded spotting anyone behind. Kesira saw enough of the tall, stony banks to know they were relatively safe from attack in that direction. But ahead? The same problem lay ahead as behind: no visibility through the twists and turns.

"Let's step it up," suggested Raellard. "Might outpace them."

"Or wear ourselves out," Kesira said. "They might be herding us into a trap."

"Up the bank?"

"Why not?" said Kesira, not seeing any better solution. This would give them the advantage of high ground and increased ability to watch their surroundings.

The idea was fine, but Kesira had difficulty getting her horse up the steep bank. The ground had turned brittle with frost and broke under the horse's weight. Tiny avalanches showered them with stones and ice and left no easy way up.

"Go on," said Kesira. "You scout. I'll stay here with my horse and wait."

"We're not splitting forces. The only strength we have

lies in guarding one another's back. If you're right about going into a trap, they'll hit us from both directions."

"I might be wrong. There might be nothing—or just a solitary beast stalking us."

"Never go against a hunch. Besides, you said you have the ability to read runes. Might carry over into seeing the future without the sticks, don't you think?"

"Since the jade power came over the demons, it takes no seer to know that danger is everywhere." Kesira sighed, thinking of the lost innocent days past. She had traveled unescorted to Blinn. The occasional brigand proved little problem, and there had never been other concerns. Not like now. Not like it had been since the jade released half-creatures and demon spawn and held an entire world in icy bondage.

"Might backtrack and take it by surprise," said Raellard.

"Better to find a good place to make our stand and wait it out, whatever it might be."

"Here looks good to me." The man stared at the tall banks Kesira's horse had been unable to scale. Those provided a measure of lateral protection. From either direction they had an unobstructed view of almost fifty feet. This would prevent anything from creeping up on them unseen. "Just a matter of how long we wait."

"Not long," Kesira said.

They stood back to back, tension growing. No attack came. Kesira knew she might have been wrong. Her worry over Molimo's death might have confused the growing awareness of her surroundings. She found out how astute her feeling had been when the attack came—not from the floor of the ravine but from above, along the ravine's lip.

The first hint of danger came as snowflakes fluttered down wetly. Kesira brushed them away and stared at the cloudless sky, wondering where they had come from. The sight of the dirty snow heap rearing up brought an involuntary scream to her lips.

The heap lumbered to the edge of the ravine and launched into the air, falling directly for her. Kesira felt Raellard shove her to the ground. Only vaguely aware of all the man did, she cowered, sobbing. Wetness exploded around her. At first she thought it was blood, then saw it was melting snow.

Kesira rolled over, gripping her stone-wood staff, ready to rush to Raellard's aid. The man stood stupidly, the butt end of his spear firmly planted in the rocky soil of the ravine bottom. All around him lay fresh patches of fluffy snow.

"It vanished. It touched the tip of my spear and turned into a blizzard. Never seen anything like that, never, never."

"There's another!" Kesira cried. She struggled to her feet, staff protecting her head from anything thrown from above.

The mound of snow burst out into the air. Again, when it touched the tip of Raellard's spear, it blew apart in a frenzy of tiny eddies that whipped dirty snow around and deposited fluffy white banks. They stood knee-deep now.

"Let's get away from this spot. Whatever these snow creatures are, they aren't dangerous. But my feet are getting frostbitten." Kesira kicked free of the snow and found walking difficult.

Raellard destroyed another of the odd entities.

"Not like anything I ever saw."

Another hurtled downward and blasted apart around the pair. The snow banked up waist deep. Then it flowed, shifted by the wind, and came to mid-chest. Kesira fought against it. She saw the edge of the tiny snow field and wanted nothing more than to escape, but the hard gusts of wind kept blowing the snow against her, stopping her, holding her in the center of the heap.

"There's no demon cursed wind blowing!" shrieked Raellard. "I just saw there's none and yet more snow moved against me." The man thrashed furiously in a vain attempt to get free of the snow.

Kesira started to panic, then caught herself. Using the mind-settling techniques taught her over the years, she kept her composure enough to study this bizarre phenomenon. Another of the snow creatures fell heavily on top of them. She and Raellard were up to their necks now.

"They attempt to smother us," she said. "We must get to the edge."

"Trying. Can't move my arms all that good. Feet are

damn near frozen." He flailed about wildly and got nowhere.

More wet snow pelted down on them. Kesira barely kept
her head above the top of the snowbank. Another creature
and they would be totally buried. She moved her arms and
legs slowly, thinking to escape by slow inches. She had to
admit this was the best scheme because she made headway—but it wouldn't work. Another of the creatures
crashed down and plunged her into total darkness. Kesira
heard Raellard's muted groans and knew their time was
limited unless they somehow drove off the snow forming
their burial tomb.

Something nibbled at her mind. Drive off the snow. But
if the snow was somehow alive and endowed with rudimen-
tary intelligence, how could she do such a thing? These
were predatory animals. Of snow—and magic—but still
predatory.

Kesira drove her staff directly up into the snow above
her head. She began wiggling it and formed a tiny chim-
ney to admit the air. Through the snow tunnel she saw a
circle of blue sky. Not much, but enough to keep her going.
Failure came, not from physical weakness, but weakness
of the spirit.

Kesira Minette was strong.

She started digging for the blue sky and found another
blanket of white laid down. Again she poked her staff
through and got the air flowing, but she was that much
farther from her goal.

There had to be another way of escaping the deadly, cold
embrace of the snow.

Kesira reached down and found the pouch beneath her
robe. In it she carried the bone box with her rune sticks,
and the tiny vial of white powder for starting fires.

"Can't go much more," she heard Raellard cry. The muffled words told more than anything else. He was buried
and would soon suffocate. He might have only minutes—or
seconds—of air left.

Kesira did not hurry or fumble. Her movements were de-
liberate, precise. Her numbed fingers balked but she drove
them to their task. The glass vial of powder came into her
trembling hand. But what could she use for fuel?

The gold sash around her waist had been soaked, but it

was all she had easily available. She tied this to the end of her staff. Forcing it as far away from her face as possible, which amounted to little more than a foot, she poured the volatile powder onto the gold ribbon. Another mound of snow closed the air hole above.

Praying to her lost Gelya for patience, Kesira worried open a new hole.

The sash burst into flame. She winced, the sudden heat searing her eyebrows and hair. Swinging the staff away from her face the best she could, she felt the snow melting. Cold trickles ran down her body, inside her robe, over her face.

At first Kesira thought the tiny whimperings she could hear came from Raellard. Then she realized it was the snow beast, sobbing in agony because she melted its flesh.

Gaining a small chamber in the snowbank allowed her some small degree of movement. Kesira thrust the burning sash up and opened a tunnel to freedom. She scrambled up it, cutting toeholds in the snow as she went, using the burning sash to fend off more snow creatures throwing themselves to the top of the snowbank.

Gasping in the clear air, she settled to hands and knees, the staff stuck in the snow. The torch end blazed merrily as it fed on the air. She wiped away soot and water from her eyes and saw a spear tip poking through the snow a few feet away. Kesira wasted no time melting away the snow around it to reveal a cold and frightened Raellard Yera.

"Get out of there," she ordered. "The torch might go out at any instant."

Raellard scrambled to safety. A new blanket of snow fell around them, but the fire cut through its center and left them unharmed.

"Never seen beasts like that. Nothing but damned snow, but it was alive," muttered Raellard, backing away from the tiny mountain of snow in the center of the ravine. The snow left behind after Kesira's fiery attack began to flow together, a thing alive. It lumbered toward them, but Kesira held it away with her torch.

"Get my horse. Lead her down the ravine. We can outrun this thing now that it's lumped into a huge mound." She made tentative thrusts at the snow creature, but it had already lost interest. It began to split into smaller piles of snow, which moved off with a curious folding motion: They heaved up, fell down and flowed over the part on the ground. Repeating the motion provided slow but sure progress.

And that progress took the snow creatures away from Kesira and Raellard.

"They had enough, from the looks of it. So've I," admitted the man. "Never liked snow overmuch, and now I know why."

Kesira extinguished the burning sash by covering it with sand from the ravine floor. She hadn't wanted to ruin her symbol of her Order, but it had saved her life. Gelya had taught that only life brought hope; being dead availed no one of anything.

"It's not burned," said Raellard, more curious than frightened. He scratched his head and peered at her as if she had performed the miracle herself. "But I saw it burning."

"As did I. Gelya might be dead, but faith in his teachings works miracles," she said. "Minor miracles, but still evidence that all might again be well."

Kesira fastened the unharmed sash around her waist and motioned for Raellard to hurry. The man needed no second urging.

They traveled down the ravine, taking the left branch at every juncture for the rest of the day. By nightfall, they had reached the banks of the Pharna River—and the storm that had been brewing early in the day over the Yearn Mountains had ripped downward, smashing icy fists into anyone brave or foolish enough to stir.

"Shelter," Raellard called into the teeth of the high wind. "We need shelter and soon. I'm freezing my balls off."

Kesira set her mouth in a grim line but said nothing. All day she had ridden, wondering how to separate herself from Raellard's unwanted attention. He had been something of a solace by just being near, but the thought rose to the surface of her mind that this was the man who had killed Molimo. While Raellard's motives had been pure, the fact remained. He had killed Molimo.

"Toward the sea," she shouted. "There must be a traveler's shelter nearby. The Abbey of Ayondela maintained several along this stretch for their Order."

Whether those in the abbey still did was a question she could not answer. Ayondela had only recently been lured by the power of jade in her desire for vengeance. The shelters might stand as they had done for years.

"There," called out Raellard, pointing through the white veils pulled around them. A moment's unnatural calm allowed the snow to whirl in miniature tornadoes and leave a clear patch. The wooden structure had not fallen into disrepair.

Kesira dismounted and led her horse toward it. They pushed in and managed to bolt the door the best they could. The horse neighed and whinnied at being trapped within the small structure, but there was no proper barn, nor had Kesira expected to find one. Such huts as this were a boon to travelers, a blessing from Ayondela.

Now the female demon's blessing cancelled her curse: The hut protected them from the storm raging outside.

"No firewood," grumbled Raellard. "Wait. Will get some."

"You'll be lost before you go ten feet," said Kesira. "The blizzard's force mounts by the minute."

Raellard peered outside, his body blocking the door. When he heaved it shut and fumbled the bolt back across the door, he solemnly acknowledged what she had guessed. It was death to be outside in this weather. Raellard turned and patted the horse on the neck, soothing her nervous pawings and snorts.

"Good animal," he said.

"Would it bother you to know that I took it from a dead mercenary?"

"Not overly. Where do you think I got this spear? Found it buried in another man's back. The weather drives men to do awful deeds. Can't say I much like it, but I accept it."

Raellard Yera slumped down and pulled his thin cloak tighter around him. He hadn't bothered to coat himself with a fresh layer of mud and stick leaves onto it for insulation. Now Kesira wished that he had. Hers was the only blanket worthy of the name. Even her cloak provided scant protection against the penetrating cold of the storm.

"We should eat," she said.

"Tomorrow. Eat too much too soon and we might run out of food before the storm lets up. We're likely to be here for a few days. Seen other ear-freezers like it. Too many times before, I seen them."

Kesira saw that he was right. She had to remember that Raellard had survived in this area for long weeks while she rode, relatively flush with food and drink, from the Quaking Lands.

She fought back tears once more as she thought of Molimo lying dead on the ground outside Raellard's hut, the spear thrust through his spine.

"You said you did rune sticks. Will you?"

"What?" The words dragged her back to reality. Kesira did not want to go.

"The rune sticks. You can read them?"

"Yes, I suppose so." She found the bone box and opened it. The rune sticks lay inside, gleaming a dull white in the faint light of the hut. Even as she touched the rune sticks, the light dimmed even more. They were soon dropped into almost complete darkness.

"About sunset," observed Raellard. "Storm cuts off the sunlight, too. Nothing to worry 'bout, unless there's no light when the morning comes."

"It makes reading the runes difficult."

"What else we got to do?"

She smiled wanly. With a quick turn of her wrist, Kesira sent the rune sticks sailing. They landed in a tangled heap at her feet. She hunkered down and began sorting through them.

"They're glowing," said Raellard, a touch of fear in his voice. "All by themselves, they're glowing."

Kesira was surprised to see that he was right. Never before had this happened. She read the fiery runes easily, without need of additional light.

"What do they say?" he asked. He crowded a bit closer, his eyes locked on the rune sticks.

Kesira said nothing as she mulled over the meaning of the runes. The way they stacked, the ones visible, the ones half-hidden, the ones she could not read, all went into her interpretation. And more. From deep within came stirrings of just how much more the nun read.

"I see demons battling jade demons. Toyaga. Toyaga

and Eznofadil. Toyaga is . . . The runes fade on me when I look too closely."

"What of this one? The one that burns brighter than the others?"

"That is a strange configuration," she said. "One I have not seen before. Thwarted plans, perhaps. Or a mistake. It is close to a pair of rune sticks that mean friendship."

"Mistaken friendship?" asked Raellard. "Who gets this reading?"

"Either of us," she said. "Or neither."

"What of the storm? Will we survive it?"

Kesira studied the lay of the sticks a while longer, then let out a tiny sigh of relief. "The storm will pass by midday tomorrow," she said. "This is the rune of immediate departure. And this one," she said, pointing to another brightly glowing one, "tells of reunion."

Hope flared within her. Reunion? With Zolkan, perhaps?

"And that one?" asked Raellard. "The one that stays unlit?"

"That one is death," she said. "It lies across all the others. All of them. We will meet only death in the coming weeks."

The gusting wind drowned out her words. She pulled her cloak tighter and lay down near her mare. The heat from the animal helped and, when Raellard lay beside her, she did not even protest. Like sheep in a circle, they huddled and kept warm and survived the freezing temperatures.

Kesira survived—for death later on?

Chapter Eleven

THE STORM-DARKENED SKY split apart with thunder and fierce violet lightning. The jagged bolt of eye-searing energy struck a tree not a hundred feet away from Molimo, boiled the sap within and sent the superheated juices exploding outward in all directions. Droplets of the burning amber fluid touched his clothing and set it afire, but what bothered Molimo most was the deafness. The clap of thunder had robbed him of hearing.

Zolkan clawed at his arm, almost in a frenzy of worry. Molimo reached up and stroked over the *trilla* bird's crested feathers. Molimo saw his friend's beak opening and closing. Words no doubt issued forth, but he heard none of them.

He pointed to his ears, then his mouth. The message was clear. Zolkan subsided, but still craned his head from side to side. When he began pecking at the back of Molimo's cloak, the man realized he was on fire. He spun the cloak around and saw minute pinpoints flare from the sudden gust of air past them. Rolling the cloak into a tight ball, he thrust it into a snowbank. Tiny hisses issued forth as the burning sap was extinguished.

". . . they fight again," he heard Zolkan saying.

My hearing returns, he indicated. *Yes, you are right. The jade demons make still another bid for power. I cannot understand the protagonists in this, however.*

"Toyaga?"

Possibly. I wish we could find Kesira.

"She rides on to Isle of Eternal Winter." The *trilla* bird squawked loudly and shook a wing. A bit of sap had stuck to the blue feathers at the tip. Molimo plucked the offending feather and cast it away. Zolkan thanked him with ill grace, unhappy at having his fine plumage destroyed in such an ignominious fashion.

This trail follows a different ravine to the Pharna. We will emerge less than a mile from the sea.

"She will be waiting," Zolkan assured Molimo. "I have scouted. She is no longer at hut with woman."

How do the woman and her baby fare?

"Well enough, from all signs. They eat. Woman spends much time hiding from shadows."

You mean in shadows.

"From. Very frightened. As we ought to be. Demons!" Zolkan lifted a wing and spread it, feathers momentarily illuminated by a lightning flash of frightening intensity. He pointed at a peak to the east. From it Molimo guessed the demons had a splendid view of the Katad Sea. But they did not sightsee. They fought. With magicks that bemused him. Never had he seen their like, but then never had he thought about one demon attacking another in this way.

Molimo felt increasingly as if he belonged to an epoch now dying before his very eyes.

Pillars of green sprang up, gutting the nighttime sky. Those shining columns protected two of the jade demons. But which two? Ayondela? Eznofadil? Lenc? What combination fought the solitary demon on that far peak?

When lightnings lashed out and struck at the fighting demon, Molimo knew the identity of one jade antagonist: Ayondela. She used the elements to freeze and attack. The lightning was only a byproduct of her blizzards and ice storms wracking the feet of the offending demon.

"It is Toyaga," said Zolkan. "Can you help?"

I see no way. If only there were. Molimo railed at his own inability to fight the demons. Even when they lacked their jade-enhanced powers, he was only as a mortal against their demonic strength.

"Battle goes against Toyaga."

Molimo saw the handsome demon as if they were only an arm's length apart. Toyaga fell heavily, face upturned to Ayondela. A smile crossed his lips. Whatever powers he called upon, they protected him from Ayondela's wrath— but barely. The probing ice scepter Ayondela carried in her hand battered at Toyaga's defenses. Frost formed on the

ground and then turned into a small glacier. Toyaga
slipped and slid, futilely striving for traction. He fell heavily over the brink of the mountain and tumbled into nothingness.

"He is lost."

But Toyaga had not exhausted all tricks. He spun and
somersaulted in midair, held aloft by the high winds of the
very storm Ayondela had summoned.

The other pillar of green light moved, pushing aside
Ayondela. The female demon jerked about, her eyes glowing like intense green beacons. The fangs that had
sprouted since partaking of the jade matched her eyes in
hue and blazing brilliance.

A hand waved her aside, and, after fuming for a few seconds over it, Ayondela yielded to the other demon.

"Eznofadil."

*Truly, it is. He goads Ayondela on, but wants to be re-
sponsible for the final kill. Toyaga will not survive.*

Molimo found himself silently cheering as Toyaga
righted himself and floated like a bird on a summer's
thermal air current. The handsome demon wafted away as
gently as a leaf when updrafts tossed him higher and
higher, away from his jade foes. But Eznofadil had singled
him out. A pass of a green hand brought Toyaga back to
the edge of the mountain.

Toyaga took a desperate gamble—and won. He doubled
up into a ball and lost the airfoil that held him aloft. He
fell like a rock toward the base of the mountain. And at the
last possible instant, he winked out of existence and
popped back a few paces from Molimo and Zolkan.

"We meet again. I had not intended it to be so soon. I am
sorry to lead them to you in this manner, but unless I oc-
cupy them otherwise, they will slay me." True sorrow
crossed Toyaga's face. "I can only wish it had ended in
some other fashion for you." Again the demon shifted
away, leaving only footprints in the snow.

"We run. They come, we run!" urged Zolkan.

*We can try, but it is useless if they pursue him. Take to
wing, my friend, and find Kesira. She will tend your needs.*

"You need help. Now!"

The shock wave announcing Ayondela and Eznofadil's
arrival knocked Molimo off his horse. Zolkan grabbed

fiercely on the man's shoulder and brought blood, then released his grip and fluttered off drunkenly. The *trilla* bird fell to the ground and struggled to rise to his feet. By this time two shimmery green pillars rose from the snowbank.

"What have we discovered, darling Ayondela?" asked Eznofadil with mock seriousness. "Why, I do think we have made a discovery far surpassing that of the annoying Toyaga."

"It is the wolf who was with the bitch," Ayondela cried.

"Yes, I do believe it is. Has the wolf killed any more of our offspring, do you think?"

Ayondela spun around and faced Eznofadil. The taller demon smiled and crossed thick arms over his chest.

"What do you say? This wolf killed Rouvin? How do you know that?"

"Ayondela, Ayondela, the jade imparts immense powers. I see the past, as well as the future. You will, too, when you have experienced more of its ineffable qualities." Eznofadil lightly bounced a jade chip from one finger to the next as a juggler at the Harvest Fairs might do.

In other circumstances, this might have amused Molimo. Not now. A wolf's snarl rose from deep within his throat. He padded forward, jaws clacking shut powerfully. The animal urge struck him full force. He leaped, fangs intended for Ayondela's throat.

Her jade fangs unexpectedly parried his. Fat sparks crawled into the night like drunken red roaches from the impact.

"How lovely. Jade against natural tooth. I must study this phenomenon more carefully," said Eznofadil. "You do well, Ayondela. Remember. The jade will not permit failure."

Molimo cowered back, snarling. His green eyes met Ayondela's equally green ones. Neither flinched. He leaped again, teeth sinking into her wrist. With her icy blue scepter, she batted him away.

"Foul creature!" Ayondela pointed the scepter at Molimo. Caught in a circle of intense polar cold, the wolf sank to the ground, stunned. His drool froze his jowls shut. Eyelids refused to open as fur and eyelashes froze together. His breathing became labored; the air flowed like syrup into his lungs.

The wolf tried to stand only to fall belly-down on the ground, legs splayed out on either side. His matted tail flopped feebly, and the cold inside slashed fiercely at his lungs.

"You do that so well, my darling," said Eznofadil. "But for a moment, release the wolf. I would gloat at his death."

"He killed Rouvin? You are sure?"

"Ayondela, you have such a fixation on your son. He was hardly worthy of a mother so caring and thoughtful." Eznofadil smirked as he studied Molimo. The wolf's green eyes glared their hatred, life slowly ebbing from his body.

"A moment. No more."

Molimo howled with the cessation of the cold around him, but he was unable to move. His frostbitten paws hurt as much as if a million needles had been thrust into them. His nose burned with a fury that made him think he had nudged into a fire rather than cold. Worst of all, he had been drained of all energy. Molimo would not be able to attack again, now that Ayondela's spell had been lifted.

"You do not bleed?" Eznofadil asked solicitously of the female demon. "His teeth did not break skin?"

"How could they?" she said, anger fading. She thrust her bare wrist skyward. Lightnings arched down from the heavens and smote her fist. The green of her skin took on hues and highlights unnatural and unnerving. No trace of the wolf bite showed. "The jade protects me."

"It turns the flesh hard," said Eznofadil, as if lecturing. "Soon enough, you will be harder than any *renn*-stone statue. The jade protects its own."

Zolkan waddled over to where Molimo lay gasping for breath. The *trilla* bird cawed in the wolf's ear. Weakly struggling, Molimo got to his feet, wobbled and fell muzzle-down in the snow.

"Can you flee?" asked Zolkan.

Molimo shook his head.

"I distract them. Flee. You must. You must! To Kesira!"

Molimo fought to regain his feet again and once more failed. He wanted to tell the bird to save himself, that further effort was not possible on his part. But the green-feathered bird took to wing and circled above. Neither of the jade demons paid the bird any attention. Molimo tried to decide if they hadn't noticed or if they just didn't care. What could one lone fowl do to an invincible demon?

Eznofadil turned back to Molimo. "You understand too well what is happening, don't you, *wolf?*"

The demon taunted him with knowledge hidden from Ayondela. Eznofadil knew he was an other-beast. Molimo gathered what anger rested within the wolf-brain and directed it toward Eznofadil. He surged to his feet. While his legs were wobbly and weak, strength flowed once again. He recovered. And he would rip the greenish throat from Eznofadil, no matter that the jade veneer protected his soft tissues.

"There will be no attack," Eznofadil said softly, so that only Molimo heard. "She does not know you. Should I tell her? How great would Ayondela's wrath be then? The world plunged under a mile-deep glacier extending all over the planet?"

Molimo growled, low and deep in his throat.

"Ah, you see the problems with that, do you?" Eznofadil glanced at Ayondela. "She is but a moment's diversion. A useful tool and nothing more. She destroyed you for us, did she not? I really must speak to Lenc about this. He assured me that—"

Ayondela screamed as Zolkan arrowed down from above. Hard talons raked across her face, sought green-glowing eyes, caught on one of her deformed tusks. The *trilla* bird grabbed hold of the jade fang and twisted heavily in midair, using momentum and surprising strength to catapult Ayondela to the ground. She landed heavily, ice scepter falling from her grasp.

Zolkan flashed to it and hefted the wand in his talons. It weighed no more than a large rabbit. The bird took to wing, carrying Ayondela's symbol of power.

"Die, you miserable creature!" she screeched. The sky split asunder with the power of the storm she summoned to stop Zolkan. Molimo watched in helpless fascination as the green tint of the demon's skin darkened. The power of the jade possessed her spirit more and more. She hardly noticed when Eznofadil handed her the chip of jade he had been playing with. She slid it under her tongue; the hue deepened and her power grew.

And grew and grew.

Molimo wanted to call out to her, to tell her that she destroyed herself. Eznofadil and Lenc waited for her to die, a burned-out husk that had served their intermediate purposes. Ultimate rule would rest with either Eznofadil or Lenc, of that Molimo was certain. Ayondela would be discarded along the way.

"Return my scepter, filthy bird!" she called.

Rain and snow turned to ice in the air. Zolkan was buffeted violently, his escape with the scepter impossible. He dropped the wand into a snowbank and careened off, still caught in the windy fingers of the punishing storm.

"Ayondela," said Eznofadil, "why not retrieve your toy and return to the Isle of Eternal Winter? I shall be along shortly. After I have kicked this miserable cur a bit more."

"He killed Rouvin. You said so. He is *mine!* I will kill him. No one else. No one."

Eznofadil began to radiate an intense green light. He tapped into the power given him by the jade, and did so more effectively than Ayondela. Molimo caught the subtle power words of the spell Eznofadil employed on her.

"He is not the one who destroyed Rouvin. I made a mistake. Return to the Isle. I will join you soon. Go, darling Ayondela, and await me. Await me."

Ayondela fetched her scepter and vanished into the storm, not saying a word.

"She can be controlled, yet," said Eznofadil. "It becomes more difficult, however. The jade is a two-edged sword she has not mastered. Using it against her is so easy." Eznofadil looked down at Molimo. The wolf snarled.

"You would see what I will do to you? Yes?"

Eznofadil looked around and saw Molimo's horse nervously pawing the snow-packed ground some distance away. "That is a good model for my demonstration."

Eznofadil smiled, the lip curling into a sneer. He held out his hand, palm to the storm-wracked sky. The horse neighed and bucked, as if caught in a fence. Eznofadil slowly closed his hand. The horse let out a whine that sounded human as it intermixed with the thunder. Then the poor animal fell over, kicking feebly, its neck broken.

"So easy. Before the jade I moved small items. I cheated at three-match and dice. I even enjoyed moving about the rune sticks my followers cast. But you know all about moving the rune sticks, don't you, my dear friend?"

Molimo almost choked when the shape change again seized him and he shifted from wolf to human form.

"This is appropriate. Face death in your real form, not some surly wolf shape. Good-bye."

Eznofadil reached out, as he had done to Molimo's horse. Molimo felt invisible fingers around his neck, squeezing, cutting off wind, breaking fragile bones.

He refused to die easily, but struggle was impossible. The jade demon was invincible. But escape? Molimo grunted and croaked and made pathetic noises.

And he remembered what Toyaga had said to him. The spell. Toyaga had no idea what it might do, if anything.

> *The world about me,*
> *There are no eyes.*
> *Freedom of the air and sky,*
> *I fade into nothingness.*

At first, Molimo did not think anything had changed, that Eznofadil still choked him. Then he realized that the pressure at his throat had vanished as surely as a thirsty plant drinks rain water.

"Where are you?" raged the jade demon. "What did you do? Where are you!"

Eznofadil rushed forward to where Molimo stood. Molimo moved a few feet to the side and let the demon batter at thin air.

"You are full of tricks. Too full of them. I don't know where you went, but we shall find you. We shall!"

Eznofadil winked away, probably following Ayondela to the Isle of Eternal Winter.

Molimo wondered at the spell's effect until he heard Zolkan squawking above.

"Where go? Where are you?"

Even as Zolkan spoke, Molimo felt sharp pains in his gut. He grunted and doubled forward, panting like a wolf that has chased a rabbit overlong.

Zolkan landed on his shoulder, one beady black eye peering into his midnight black one. "A trick? You used trick on Eznofadil and vanished? Good!"

Good, Molimo agreed. *But he killed the horse. We have to walk now.*

"To Kesira?"

To Kesira, he agreed. Molimo staggered a bit and stumbled, but as he walked down the ravine, toward the Pharna River, his strength slowly reasserted itself. By the time he sighted the frozen expanse of the river, he felt confident that they might defeat the jade demons.

Almost.

Chapter Twelve

"THE ENTIRE WORLD comes to an end? Just like that?" asked Raellard Yera, frowning at such an idea. "Why do anything against the damned demons, then?"

"That's not what I said." Kesira leaned forward, her face flushed. She ignored the howling winds and the penetrating cold and even the way her horse stepped over her awkwardly inside the tiny rock shelter. She spoke passionately of her theology now, of belief, of that which drove her life forward.

"Thought you did," said Raellard. He looked skeptical at all she had told him.

"Let me go back and retell it. Perhaps this will be clearer. You know how the world came to be?"

Raellard shrugged. "It formed from the five elements."

"Yes, yes," she said, impatient to bypass such basics and get on with the telling. "Void, filling it came the world, the dirt beneath our feet, then covering it the ocean, above it air and burning in the air was fire. Each element is higher than the last, but not better."

"I don't understand."

"This is going astray from what I wish to say," said Kesira. "But quickly, the heirarchy of elements was established as I mentioned: void, substance, water, air, fire. Each added to the others before it, each gave new dimensions to the universe."

"The five comprise everything."

"Exactly, Raellard. Then came animals, then humans." Kesira swallowed and said, "Then came the demons. They are stronger than mortals and possess powers we do not share. It is said they can run all day and live forever."

"They are the product of human and animal," said Raellard. "I remember that much."

"True. They are a hybrid, with human traits accentu-
ated and strengthened, while still retaining baser animal
instincts and energies. If a mortal loves, a demon loves a
thousand times more. If a human hates, a demon hates
with the intensity of all in the world. And not all demons
possess all traits. Some are very, very good, like Gelya,
while others seek only to destroy."

"Ayondela."

"She is deluded. As a human may be led astray, so has
she been by Eznofadil and Lenc."

"They are the evil ones."

"Yes," said the nun, thinking of how Lenc had so viciously destroyed her Order. And her life.

"If they can be killed—and you said they were being
killed—why call us mortals?"

"This is at the core of what I said to you. They are not
truly immortal, meaning that they live forever, but their
life spans are immense by human standards. Their time
will soon pass. They can be killed by their peers, and their
rule nears its end."

"The Time of Chaos," said Raellard, shivering. Kesira
did not think it was from the cold. "All that is normal will
be gone."

"Chaos will not last. Nothing lasts save change. The
gods will rise to supplant the demons."

"What gods?"

Kesira shook her head. "Those of my Order argued this
point. The best that could be decided is a progression similar to that occurring when the demons came into being
through offspring of animals and humans."

"Human and demon breeding will produce the gods? I
don't want no part of this. I saw Ayondela—or what she's
done to the land. Froze it. She must be a coldhearted bitch.
What man could take her to his bed and enjoy it?"

"You did not know her son Rouvin. There was a majesty
about him, something more than human and even more
than demon, yet less than both. He was no god, but rather
a failed god. He combined the lesser points of each rather
than the greater."

"These demons couple with anything. I heard the stories."

"Rouvin told me that the Time of Chaos is when demons and humans die and the gods are born. I think he was wrong. Humanity survives and the demons perish—and then there will be gods."

"So? How is this any different from being under the thumb of a demon?"

"The gods will be different," she said with conviction. "They will be more humane, have higher principles, be dedicated to good works. The flaws of humanity will be erased and the best traits will remain, intensified, distilled, perfected."

"They'll bring us all we want to live off?" asked Raellard. "That would be paradise."

"Humans need to work to give themselves a sense of worth. Can you imagine how dull it would be not having the well-being of accomplishment from your toils?"

Raellard sighed. "I would give it a try. Not to break my back in the fields, not to starve because the crops failed through no fault of my own, not to have to scratch and scrabble out a meager living—I'd like to live as the Emperor for just a day."

Kesira shook her head, saying, "The Emperor's burdens are even greater. He has the welfare of all to consider. Only loyalty to him gives us the greatest good. The decisions he makes daily are far more difficult than working in a grain field. He must strive to hold the Empire together, so that we work united, to keep faith in him."

"My faith dims," said Raellard. "A hollow belly demands filling before any duty to the Emperor."

"This attitude is another sign that we enter the Time of Chaos."

She settled back, the rush of having a new pupil past now. Raellard was hardly as good as some of the acolytes who had recently joined the Order, but it did Kesira good to think she instructed, enlightened, brought new ideas to the man. Lenc tore at the very foundations of the empire when he destroyed the Orders and their patrons. Education became muddled and factions rose up to oppose authority.

She shuddered. Her hardest task since the advent of the jade demons had been working almost alone. Without her Sisters to bolster and succor her, Kesira felt lost. Zolkan and Molimo were more than friends for her; they had become her sole sources of support. Now even they were gone and she had to rely on a dirt farmer. Still, Kesira tried to tell herself, each citizen of the empire needed every other; Raellard needed her and she needed him.

Somehow, that did not seem right to Kesira, even though it should.

She dozed fitfully, dreaming of Molimo and Zolkan and even Wemilat and Rouvin. Kesira awoke to Raellard shaking her gently.

"What is it?"

"The storm," he said. "It's died down. We can be on our way to the Sea of Katad."

"There's no need for you to come with me," she said. "You wanted to hunt to supply your wife with food enough for the rest of the . . . summer." Kesira had a difficult time believing this weather might be called summer.

"Parvey's crazy as a wobble bug. Can't go back to her. Not soon. I promised to help you for all you did, and I will. Honor requires me keeping my word."

"You never gave your promise on this," Kesira said, but she saw where the conversation led and resigned herself to his company.

"Do now. Promise to help you get to Ayondela and stop this winter. Isn't this helping Parvey, too? I mean, get rid of the cold and grain grows again. Won't have to forage off the land and worry about wolves and the like."

The mention of wolves sent Kesira into a new depression. Molimo dead. His body slowly being eaten by the woman back in the hills. Kesira grew sick to her stomach but held down her rising gorge.

"We'll ride to the sea," she said. "By my reckoning we might not be more than a day or two distant."

"A day, no more."

Kesira led her horse outside. Again the weather had cleared to leave a brilliant azure sky with only traces of fleecy clouds whitely dotting it. She found it so difficult to believe that this ought to be warm and summery and lushly green with every imaginable plant in abundance. The snow fields extended across the Pharna, obscuring the banks of the river and the frozen surface. Kesira remembered tales of the river freezing as myths told to frighten; if the river ever had frozen solid this far to the south, it had been in days long past. Still, with every hardship comes an unsuspected benefit. Riding on the river itself provided easier going than through the snowbanks and drifted blockages formed by the high winds.

"Might fall through," Raellard observed when she told him of her intention.

"How thick is the ice?"

He shrugged.

"Find out. I'll wait. I promise not to take the horse out onto the river until you tell me."

Raellard returned a few minutes later. "Ice's thicker than I thought. I dug for ten minutes and got almost a foot down and still didn't break through to water. Must make the fish uneasy having a white roof over their heads."

"They might not even notice," she said. "Unless they like coming to the surface for sunning."

Kesira rode along, eyes flashing this way and that, alert for any movement along the banks of the river. She remembered all too clearly the beasts roaming the Roggen Plains—and the brigands. Times were hard for both man and beast. She and Raellard looked to be easy prey. The woman wanted to dodge or outrun any danger rather than prove that they were not going to give themselves up easily.

As hard as Kesira watched, Raellard was the one who spotted the spoor along the crest of a snowbank. He tugged at her arm and pointed, motioning her to silence.

Kesira immediately dismounted. While she might be able to see farther, she could also be seen more easily. She and Raellard went to examine the tracks. The nun didn't need the man to tell her that many mounted troops had passed by recently. The edges of the imprints were still crisp and sharp, not melted by sun or eroded by wind.

"A dozen. More," Raellard said. "Soldiers."

While it was a logical conclusion from the pattern left by the tracks, Kesira asked how he knew.

"The shoes on their mounts. All identical. Look." Raellard pointed to one imprint that had sunk through snow and found the dirt beneath. "A mercenary sigil."

Nervous sweat popped out on Kesira's forehead. She wiped it away before it cooled her too much. She recognized the pattern instantly.

The Order of the Steel Crescent.

"We're heading the same way as they," she said. "Down to the Sea of Katad."

"Might skirt around their flank," said Raellard, indicating a possible path to the north. "Or forge south and away from the river. They are doing as we do, using the iced river as a highway."

"Time works against us," Kesira said. She felt increasingly uneasy about how the winter gripped the world around her. "Ayondela must be convinced of her errors soon, or no one will survive."

"From all you say, will the other jade demons permit it to continue much longer?"

"There wouldn't be any humans left to rule, would there?" mused Kesira. "I had not considered that. They obviously encourage this for their own reasons." She considered the unnatural winter from this perspective, then shook her head. "We must reach Ayondela as soon as possible. How long can Parvey survive, even with the . . . additional food supply?"

"The wolf won't last more'n a week or two at the outside. The other stuff should last her that long and then some."

Raellard did not see her cringe when he mentioned the wolf.

Molimo.

"We go on, along the river. We can only hope that the Steel Crescent rides fast and for another destination."

"Not so fast. Horses are walking," Raellard pointed out.

She gestured for the man to continue. Kesira walked her horse now, to keep it quiet and to lessen the sound of its hooves on the hollow, ringing ice. By midday they had not caught sight of any other riders. They stopped for a brief meal.

As they ate, Raellard said, "Cast the rune sticks again. Let them tell us of danger."

Kesira already knew the danger. But she did as the man asked. The nun pulled out the bone box and opened it. The sticks lay inside, inert and unlike the night before. She cast them forth, letting them land on the ice.

"They're not glowing," Raellard accused. "What's wrong?"

"They are," she said, cupping her hands over the pile. "The sun robs them of much of their inner light."

"Read them."

"The rune sticks do not tell all. They can be cryptic." Even as she spoke, she studied the casual pattern formed. "They say I am wrong, mistaken. Again the friendship runes appear prominent." She looked up at Raellard, who munched at his ration with little evidence of intelligence showing. Wrong in friendship? Was she wrong in trusting Raellard? Did the runes tell her what she already knew, that Raellard had slain Molimo? Or did the runes mean something else? "There is little more to see. Clouded future. Blocked to me."

"Humph," was the only comment the man made.

They repacked their meager belongings into a sack slung over the saddle and stood. But Kesira froze when she heard the clank of metal on metal. She turned and saw the man standing atop the low rise by the river, hands on hips. Sun glinted off the steel of his armor and turned him into a shining, indistinct form.

"Can I believe my eyes?" came the mocking words. "Is this the woman who killed our patron in the Quaking Lands?"

Kesira gripped her staff and stepped away from her horse, ready to fight.

"You know this one?" asked Raellard.

"Nehan-dir, leader of the Order of the Steel Crescent. Yes, we've met before. Not pleasantly, either."

Others joined Nehan-dir on the hilltop. They stared down at the two, then laughed uproariously.

"What are you laughing at?" demanded Raellard. "What's so funny?"

"You, little man. A dirt farmer and a nun. We find that immensely funny."

"Come down here and I'll show you how funny it is!" Raellard waved his spear about ineffectually.

"Raellard, be calm. They are mercenaries."

"Never heard of this Order of the Steel Crescent," he grumbled. "Well, I have," he amended sullenly. "So what?"

Kesira prepared herself for battle, settling her mind, tensing and relaxing muscles to make sure she was loose and able to move quickly when the need arose. She did not bother explaining to Raellard Yera her horror at finding Nehan-dir here. The man had turned mercenary after his patron had sold him and all his followers to another demon in exchange for cancelling a gambling debt. Nehan-dir had rebelled; something within the man had snapped after being treated as little more than chattel. He and the others sought out only strong patrons, selling their services. Howenthal had hired them; they had worshipped Howenthal until Kesira destroyed the jade demon. She had no doubt that Nehan-dir now rode to the Isle of Eternal Winter to pledge allegiance to Ayondela. The Order of the Steel Crescent gravitated toward strength and the female demon's power gleamed whitely across the land. It made sense that Nehan-dir sought a patron not likely to be destroyed soon, who would grant him and his fellow mercenaries the security they had never gotten before.

"I would kill her," said one soldier. Nehan-dir turned and nodded, indicating that his permission had been given with pleasure.

The armored mercenary awkwardly came to meet Kesira in battle. The nun saw that her opponent was a woman, half a head taller, with a thick pink scar running diagonally across her forehead. As the mercenary drew her blade, Kesira attacked.

Her stone-wood staff whirled about in a blinding arc that ended squarely on the other's wrist. Bones snapped. The mercenary yelled in pain and twisted away. The staff rebounded and continued its journey in a circular orbit, landing behind the mercenary's knee. The woman crumpled to the ground, moaning.

"I have no desire to harm you," said Kesira, knowing this

would not work with Nehan-dir. Gelya had said that it was possible to purchase peace at too high a price, but she had to try.

"But I want to see your blood foaming in the snow," said Nehan-dir. "You robbed me of my patron. Howenthal was the perfect replacement, and you killed him."

"My patron is dead, also," Kesira said, widening her stance, waiting for Nehan-dir's attack.

"He died because he refused to walk the way of power. Alone, he died. Alone, you will die!"

Nehan-dir came down the slope and motioned to the woman, still clutching her broken wrist.

"She's mine! You promised!"

"You failed," Nehan-dir said coldly. "She is very quick, this little nun. You underestimated her." Nehan-dir bowed forward from the waist, hands above his head. The chain mail vest he wore slid over his head and landed in a heap at his feet. "Take my mail and wait with the rest. I'll show you how to deal with her."

Kesira attacked even as Nehan-dir spoke, but the man was wary. Her staff flashed through the air—to the spot where his head had been. He ducked, drew his dagger, and moved in to kill. She barely succeeded in getting her staff spun around her waist and back in front to parry the thrust for her belly. Kesira danced away.

"This will be interesting," said Nehan-dir. "I enjoy your death already."

She studied the small, scrawny man for some sign of weakness. Kesira saw it everywhere, yet she knew it was all illusion. His thin arms were strung with steel sinews. The spider web of scars across his face testified to the battles lost—and won. Sandy hair blew in wild disarray, making Nehan-dir look the part of a wild man. But his attacks came purposefully, deliberately, with measured power and always on target.

Kesira Minette fought for her life.

"Haieee!" Raellard Yera took the opportunity to attack. His spear darted for Nehan-dir's throat, caught the gorget and skittered away. The leader of the mercenaries stepped back, a surprised look on his face.

"The farmer can fight. Then fight!"

Nehan-dir attacked and snapped the point off Raellard's spear before Kesira could move. The farmer tumbled back onto his rear, sitting and staring stupidly at the skinny soldier towering above him. With only a dagger, Nehan-dir had defeated a man armed with a spear. All that had saved Raellard from a nasty cut on the thigh was the tough-leathered high top of his boot.

"Stay," Nehan-dir said to Raellard, as if speaking to a dog.

Kesira fought then, hard, pushing offensively, being forced into defensive postures. Nehan-dir smiled as he fought, enjoying the conflict. Freed of his chain mail he was as agile as Kesira and more highly trained in the ways of combat. Luck—not skill—kept her from perishing at the point of the man's dagger.

"Go on, slip and slide over the ice," he taunted. "It makes my kill all the easier."

"Nehan-dir!" cried one of the soldiers on the hill.

"Fool, can't you see I am busy?" Nehan-dir never took his eyes off Kesira. He had learned that her staff could deliver savage punishment and even death to the unwary.

The sounds of death echoed down from the hill. Nehan-dir took the chance to spin and look, then whirled back to face Kesira.

"Witch! How did you summon the demon spawn?"

Kesira was in a better position to see what happened to the mercenaries. Hideous creatures boiled upon them, snapping and clawing. The soldiers fought well, but there were too many of the demon spawn for them to evade.

Nehan-dir had to choose between killing Kesira and losing his followers or retreating.

"There will be another time, I hope," he said. "If not, I leave you to the demon spawn. May their bellies churn and bloat when they devour you!"

He hurried up the hill, dagger resheathed and sword hacking at the monsters. Kesira heard the shrill cries of pain as men and women were injured. Then came the thunder of hooves as the horses raced off.

Kesira and Raellard faced the thwarted demon spawn alone.

"This is a better death, in my eyes," said Kesira. "These creatures are at least true to their savage nature. Nehandir sells himself to the highest bidder."

She helped Raellard to his feet. With little more than their bare hands, they faced the half-dozen hungry beasts slithering down the hill toward them.

Chapter Thirteen

THE DEMON SPAWN stopped at the top of the hill and peered down at Kesira Minette. She took the brief respite in attack to settle herself. A moment's panic came when she realized how alone she was. Raellard Yera would prove little use in this battle. He was not up to fighting and might only get in her way. How she wished for Molimo or her Sisters in the Order. It was unnatural having to fight without someone's support near at hand.

The centermost demon spawn vented a roar that shook her. She quickly recovered, knowing that this cry was intended to frighten her into a mistake. The bulbous creature waddled down the hill, inch-long fangs snapping and clacking against the lower, solid dental plate. The beast appeared to be a combination of snake and bear with a goodly portion of vegetable added. It had the color and general shape of a turnip, the arms and shoulders of a bear and the fangs of a reptile; Kesira was not optimistic about the outcome of the fight.

She faced speed, strength, and ugliness.

"I will stop it!" yelled Raellard, rushing forward. He poked at the creature with his broken spear. One careless paw reached out and batted him away, as if he were nothing more than a minor annoyance. The demon spawn seemed to recognize Kesira as its primary opponent.

"Stay back from it," she cautioned. "It shows some small intelligence." Under her breath Kesira added, "More than you possess."

The others in the pack started down the hill, a frightening combination mixing both the animal and vegetable into a stew too odious to contemplate. Claws scratched and

146

teeth banged shut and the odors that assaulted their nostrils were almost worse than any physical attack. Raellard stumbled back to take up a spot at Kesira's side.

"We can run."

"Nehan-dir is no fool. He would have realized we were trapped by them. They will attack constantly until we are dead. How can we run from so many?"

"They look slow."

Even as he spoke, the bear-snake-turnip beast lashed out with a speed so blinding it took even Kesira by surprise. She lost the bottom four inches of her staff to sharp dental plates.

Almost by instinct, she brought the top of her staff down firmly on the top of the furred head. It bounced off impossibly thick bone. Kesira wasn't even sure the beast noticed.

Backpedaling, she swung and got the tip of her staff near the creature's eye. She lunged and missed.

"This isn't working," Kesira said, panting from exertion. "Nothing slows it. And the others . . ." The rest of the demon spawn slowly spread out in a fan shape and worked their way in toward the center where Kesira and Raellard fought. Kesira muttered constantly under her breath, half the time praying to long-dead Gelya and the other half cursing the demon spawn so intent on making her their supper.

She used staff and feet against the creature and only confused it. She had yet to produce a visible wound.

It lunged forward, snapping and clawing. Kesira had to retreat across the icy Pharna River. The woman slipped, caught herself, and maintained a semblance of balance. To fall now meant only death.

"What do we do? Never saw so many of the damn things." Raellard poked and prodded. He might as well have been scratching a pet's proffered ears. The demon spawn kept coming back for more.

Before Kesira could reply, a shrill squawk filled the air. The demon spawn hesitated. A new squawk, this one followed by singsong words Kesira recognized.

"Zolkan!"

The *trilla* bird alighted between her and the demon spawn. The incongruous face-off should have ended in the bird's death. One quick swipe of those powerful claws, a

gobble and a swallow, even a misplaced step would have
ended Zolkan's life. The brightly feathered bird snapped
another command. The demon spawn looked up at Kesira.
She thought she read sorrow in its bloodshot eyes before it
turned and lumbered off. Zolkan kept squawking and
flapping his wings. The other demon spawn reluctantly
turned and followed their leader.

By the time the beasts had vanished over the hill, Kesira had regained her composure.

"Zolkan, thank you. How'd you find us?"

"How'd the bird do it?" broke in Raellard. "How'd you
chase off those monsters?"

"They envy my innate good looks," Zolkan said haugh-
tily. He turned away from Raellard and jumped up to Kesira's shoulder. He craned his neck around and one beady
eye peered into the woman's soft brown eyes. "We must go
to sea. Now. No time to waste."

"The Order of the Steel Crescent," Raellard broke in
again. "What of them? They'll know we didn't get eaten
and stop us."

"Lose this bumpkin," advised Zolkan.

"Please, he has helped me," she said, but her own
thoughts had run along similar lines. As much as she
detested—and even feared—being alone, Raellard was not
fit company.

"Let him help from farther away."

"I stay with you," Raellard stoutly maintained. "Parvey
can do all right for herself. She has plenty to eat. You said
this weather can only be changed by talking to Ayondela."

A lump formed in Kesira's throat. Parvey Yera had
plenty to eat. Molimo's body lay outside in the cold, waiting for new pieces of flesh to be hacked off and eaten. Tears
poured down her cheeks.

"Travel. Now!" squawked Zolkan. The bird batted at
her with his hard wings. "Necessary. No time for cries."

"You are right," the nun said. She quickly traced over
the knots in the blue cord around her waist, said a traveler's prayer that helped settle her rampaging emotions,
and then she mounted up. The horse slipped and slid on
the ice, but the going was easier than amid the snowbanks
lining the river.

"Nehan-dir rides to the north. Stay on south side of river," urged Zolkan. "Ride like wind!"

Kesira angled across the river, but she did not heed the bird's advice. Raellard panted and puffed hard to keep up with the pace she set. As long as he walked and she rode there would be a difference in speeds. Kesira was not going to abandon the man.

"More, faster. Pigeonshit! Hurry!"

"Zolkan!" she exclaimed, shocked. "Your speech!" She had heard the *trilla* bird speak like this before, when he had been recovering at the nunnery. The wild tales he had told had aroused her imagination, opened up the ideas that whole vistas existed in the world to which she was not privy. Zolkan had obviously belonged to a soldier or perhaps a sailor for many years and had been sold to a wealthy merchant, but the details had never been clear to Kesira.

"Ride!"

She smiled now. Having Zolkan back did more to bolster her flagging spirits than she might have thought. Several times she started to ask about Molimo, how the two had become separated, why Zolkan hadn't been nearby when Raellard killed the wolf, but she held back. Simply feeling the talons cutting into her beleaguered left shoulder was enough for the moment. When she was better able to assimilate the story, she would inquire.

The untimely frost of Molimo's death would eventually melt within her heart, and then she could ask for details. But not now. Not now.

"Up banks. Snow not too thick," the bird told her when they finally reached the far side of the Pharna. Here and there Kesira had seen thinner patches of ice, the river beneath making its desperate, frightened path to the sea. She had skirted those spots and made the journey longer than either she or Zolkan desired.

Raellard complained, "Snow's damn thick. Damn near knee-deep. Hard going."

"Climb up behind me," Kesira told him. "We can ride together to the top of the rise. Then we'll rest."

"No rest," grumbled Zolkan. "Must reach Katad Sea soon. Must."

"Why?"

The bird didn't answer. It only grumbled and complained to himself.

"What I want to know's how you drove off those demon spawn," said Raellard. "You faced 'em down but good. They took off, not scared but really dejected."

"That is a good question, Zolkan. You seemed to be able to speak to them."

"Can. Told them you taste bad. Told them truth."

Kesira laughed. It wasn't as much the humor of the situation as it was a release of tension for her. "You must have a silver tongue to get rid of them so easily."

"They're not too bright." Zolkan grumbled some more, and Kesira heard him add, "Like humans."

The *trilla* bird spent their rest period preening himself, then urged them on. Kesira insisted that she and Raellard take time to eat again, even though it had only been an hour since their last meal. Zolkan waddled about, muttering, pointing, screeching.

"Chew faster. Eat, eat," he grumbled. "You tell me I think only of food. Look at you. Getting fat!"

Kesira involuntarily reached to her waist and felt. No ring of fat there or on her hips or behind. Since leaving the nunnery she had been on abbreviated rations. With Ayondela's curse upon the land, there was scant chance anyone grew fat.

"Zolkan, what is so important about reaching the sea? We'll be there. Does it matter if it is now or an hour from now?"

The bird let out an aggrieved cry and took to wing. He fluttered and flopped about as a downdraft caught him, then he found the proper rising thermal and soared. Kesira watched as the green dot dwindled and finally vanished in the blue sky.

"We'd best ride as he says."

"What is that bird?" asked Raellard. "Never seen his likes before. Looks to be good stew meat. Flesh on the bones."

"Don't let Zolkan hear you say that. He gets upset when he hears of peddlers selling *trilla* meat."

"A *trilla* bird? Guess I have heard of them. From way to the south. Wonder if it's warm there. Like it ought to be."

"That, Raellard, is something I don't know. I'd guess that Ayondela has been thorough in her curse."

The rest of the day passed by in an endless band of white and cold. As they topped a hill, Kesira reined in and simply stared.

"What by all the demons is that?" asked Raellard, stumbling up to stand beside her horse. "It looks like it cuts open the soft underbelly of the sky."

"It does."

Kesira had never seen the Isle of Eternal Winter before. But she knew that it had never before sported that towering, flickering, cold white flame in its center. Lenc had left his mark on Ayondela's private island. What other points of her life did the jade demon also claim as his own?

"Look at that," said Raellard, awe in his voice.

"I am," she said in some irritation.

"Not the island or that funny flame. The sea. Look at it. It's froze in the damnedest way."

Kesira's eyes widened. Raellard's description did not do justice to the truth. The sea had frozen, but not in the manner of a lake or river freezing over. The very waves had been caught as they pounded against the shore and had quick-frozen. All the way to the Isle of Eternal Winter, the jagged waves thrust sharply upward, etched in ice. It was as if she looked at a picture from a book drawn with ice as a medium and snow the brush.

"How do we cross *that?*" she wondered.

Kesira spun about in the saddle when she heard rocks being dislodged on the side of the hill. Her first thought was that Nehan-dir and his mercenaries had found them. Then she saw the handsome young man with the dark, flowing hair and penetrating midnight eyes. Kesira felt faint and rocked slightly in the saddle, suddenly weak hands gripping the saddle horn for support.

"Molimo!"

The youth smiled and pointed toward the island.

"You're alive. How? He— you— it can't be!"

Molimo frowned, obviously not understanding her. Kesira vaulted from the saddle and let Raellard take the reins of the bucking horse. She threw her arms around Molimo's neck and almost toppled him over. Kissing him, then burying her face in his shoulder, she cried unashamedly.

His hands stroked at her short brown hair, then lifted her face. They just stared at one another. Kesira swallowed hard. It was as if Molimo spoke to her, not with words but deep inside. Almost.

She struggled to understand the words, the feelings. Zolkan's loud squawk broke the spell.

"No time for that. To Isle of Eternal Winter. Need to hurry. Ayondela's curse killing off world."

"I know, Zolkan, I know," she said, tiredness overtaking her now. "But I've got to know. Molimo, why aren't you dead?"

His eyes widened, then he smiled. Molimo reached into his pouch and pulled out the writing tablet and quickly wrote.

"I am quick—hard to kill a man-wolf."

Kesira glanced back at Raellard, who stood shuffling his feet in confusion. "That man killed a wolf and left it for his wife—the woman in the hut. I thought it was you."

"Not me. Must have been real wolf. Zolkan and I explored." Kesira saw him hesitate, as if he wanted to write more. He rubbed out what he had started, then penned, "The Emperor is being forced to retreat on all fronts and return to Limaden. Crops are failing everywhere. Animals dying. Demon spawn are appearing with greater frequency. Other-beasts, too. The natural order is dying—being killed."

Kesira noted that Molimo's hand trembled the slightest bit when he wrote that.

"Magicks abound, unleashed by jade," he continued after he had erased the other message. "Cold feeds the demon's magic, killing off opposition. Emperor being unable to fight means the empire is totally under their control."

"Is the winter worldwide?" she asked. Molimo nodded.

"Ayondela must be stopped." Kesira frowned. "Can the other jade demons duplicate her spell and return us to winter if we do succeed in getting her to lift the curse?"

Molimo hastily wrote, "No. Takes too much energy, even with jade supplementing them. They use her as tool to be discarded when no longer worthwhile. Go to Isle of Eternal Winter. Stop her."

"You're beginning to sound like Zolkan," Kesira said. She heaved a sigh. She hadn't considered getting to an island to be any problem. Find a boat, one used by fishermen, perhaps, and sail to the Isle of Eternal Winter. Kesira had forgotten that appealing and easy approach when she saw how the Sea of Katad had been frozen. It was as if Ayondela had looked out and snapped her fingers, casting everything in ice in a split second. Crossing those jagged, knife-edged waves would be deadly—and there were rank after rank of them all the way out to the island.

"How?" she asked.

Molimo indicated that it would be difficult, but that he had no real plan. Zolkan squawked, "Why not fly? But no. You humans lack proper appendages."

"Chop our way through the waves," said Raellard. "The only road's going to be one we make for ourselves."

"I'm afraid you're right," she said, mind beginning to turn over the possibilities open to them. "But how? We don't have that kind of equipment with us. Your spear tip is hardly useful and Molimo's sword is not going to do the trick for us for long. The edge will blunt."

Raellard fingered the spear he had retrieved. The shaft had broken about a foot under the steel tip and provided only a cumbersome knife. Kesira's staff was hardly the tool for this task.

She sank to the ground, her mind falling in upon itself. She calmed her turbulent thoughts and concentrated, just as she would to do a rune stick reading. Inspiration and genius often walked hand in hand. Barely had she begun to consider the various avenues to be taken getting to the Isle of Eternal Winter when Zolkan let out an anguished squawk.

"Order of Steel Crescent. They go to island. Now we can never reach Ayondela's stronghold."

Kesira rose lithely to her feet and peered out over the blinding white expanse of the frozen wave crests. Even at this distance Kesira made out Nehan-dir's thin figure and that of the woman whose wrist she had broken in combat. The others worked with shiny devices, turning them this way and that, striving for whatever the proper position was.

"What they doing?" asked Raellard. "Never seen a thing like them before."

Molimo wrote quickly. "The devices capture the sun and turn it against the ice."

"They're melting a path to the island using the sun?" Kesira frowned. "Where would Nehan-dir get such a contraption? He did not strike me as mechanician enough to build it."

"One of the jade demons," wrote Molimo. "But which one? Which is now Nehan-dir's patron?"

"Lenc," spoke up Zolkan. "His flame burns on island."

"But Eznofadil has been very active lately," wrote Molimo. The bird nodded solemnly. Kesira wondered what had happened after they left her and Parvey Yera at the hut.

"Could Ayondela have furnished them the machine?" she asked. "What she does and doesn't do is something of a mystery. She is too destroyed by her grief to think clearly."

"Eznofadil," said Zolkan with some conviction. "This is his doing. Feel it."

"So what's the difference who gave 'em the burning plate?" asked Raellard. "Knowing doesn't help us any."

"But Nehan-dir having it does," said Kesira, an idea beginning to germinate. "They melt a road to the island. What's to keep us from traveling along that same path, after they've gone?"

"They'll see us." Raellard said it flatly.

"They work to reach the Isle of Eternal Winter by nightfall. We go out then. Can they see in the dark?"

"Demons can," muttered Raellard, not liking the idea of being on the ice after the sun set. "Be cold out there. Damn cold. Freeze our balls off, we will."

Zolkan screeched and landed on Kesira's shoulder. "Might work," the bird said. "I scout, you walk. No horse."

"Why not?" asked Raellard.

"Because the rider would rear up far above the waves." Kesira squinted into the glare again and said, "Those waves are about head-high. They provide ample cover for us as we go on foot, but not for a horse and rider."

"What does it mean to you?" asked Zolkan. "You don't ride. She does."

"Make getting away harder," was all Raellard would say.

Kesira shook her head. Already the farmer thought in terms of escape. While it might be prudent, she did not for an instant consider it. They had to reach Ayondela and convince her to lift her curse. Somewhere deep inside, Kesira had come to the conclusion that the only payment Ayondela would accept for this was a life.

Kesira would gladly give hers in exchange for the stolen summer's return.

"They cut through the waves as knife through water," said Zolkan. "Hate being in way of that. Singe your feathers, quick."

"We rest and wait for sunset," she said. "At the rate Nehan-dir is progressing, they will be at the Isle of Eternal Winter by then. And we can follow." She glanced from one to the other. Both men and the *trilla* bird agreed, each to a varying degree.

To Raellard she said, "You can return to Parvey. She needs you, and this isn't really your fight. Go, hunt, feed your family."

"Gave my promise," Raellard said, almost sullenly. "Can't back down." His face brightened. "Besides, I've always wondered how a demon lives. I'm curious about that house sitting atop the island."

Kesira laid a hand on his shoulder. "Thank you," she said. "We may need all the help we can get before we are finished this day."

She sat, meditated, watched the pale flickering of the cold white flame burning at the center of the island. It was twin to the one gnawing away at Gelya's altar back in her nunnery.

Soon enough, dusk cloaked the land and they gathered their belongings to begin the trek across the ice. Kesira almost turned and ran when she saw the razored waves rising head-tall along their mathematically precise rows. The melted area in front of her had lost its dazzling whiteness now that the sun had set.

She felt as if she marched between the teeth of some voracious beast and descended into its throat.

Silently, Kesira motioned for the others to start. Molimo stayed at her right and Raellard on her left, with Zolkan flying above. Even in the midst of such staunch friends, she did not feel more confident.

Chapter Fourteen

"THE BIRD KEEPING a sharp eye out for any stragglers?" Raellard Yera asked uneasily. "Wouldn't want to run into any of those soldiers. Not now, not in here."

Kesira shared the farmer's concern. She found herself glancing back over her shoulder, certain someone followed. No one did. A haunted feel about the ranks of waves made her wonder what had died so that this frozen tribute to Ayondela's power could exist. The endless motion of the surf against the beach had been stilled, yet the thwarted waves trembled under her feet and threatened to burst free at any moment. Or was this only imagination? Kesira knew only that she was getting colder and colder. Being in this ice forest robbed her of heat, sent tiny needles of pain up from the soles of her feet, made the slightest mistake painful as she brushed against the waves held in perpetual suspense.

"The Steel Crescent's contraption worked good," observed Raellard, running his hand over the edge of one wave and noting how it had been melted into a smooth curve. "We'd never be able to move so fast without this road already cut for us."

"Quiet," complained Zolkan from above. "I listen for movement. How can I hear with your grumblings disguising all?"

Kesira put her hand on Raellard's shoulder to comfort him. She understood that he spoke only from nervousness. The eerie expanse of water turned to ice gnawed at her courage, too.

They walked on briskly, making good time. Kesira had estimated almost two miles to the Isle of Eternal Winter and decided they had gone more than halfway in only an hour. They slipped and slid on the recently melted slick surface and studiously avoided the more dangerous areas on the edges of the waves.

But it was Molimo and not Zolkan who first alerted her to dangers other than those presented by the immobile sea.

The man spun and drew his sword, facing along the front of a series of waist-high waves. Kesira quickly moved to stand beside him, peering into the gloom. She heard before she saw.

Delicate chewing sounds. Then stronger vibrations in the ice. Finally an inky black mass erupted not ten feet away, bulling its way through the thick ice. Tentacles lashed toward her face; Kesira shoved out her staff and allowed the suckers to fasten on the stone-wood rod. But she made the mistake of hanging on, not allowing the creature its pleasure with her staff. It pulled her along the ice on her knees, shouting as she went.

"Stop it, Molimo, stop it!"

The man leaped forward, blade rising and falling in a short, vicious arc. Black fluids spurted from the severed tentacle. It did not release the staff.

"What is it?" she gasped out. Kesira fought to get to her feet, succeeding only in slipping and falling again. All the while she struggled to pry loose the tentacle from her staff. It was made from the wood sacred to Gelya and had been through much with her. More from sentiment than good sense, Kesira tried to retain it.

"Never saw anything like that before," came Raellard's quavering reply. Molimo continued to hack and thrust at the beast, forcing it to partially retreat back through the hole in the ice. He fought well, but the beast knew no fear. It squirted back through, new tentacles grasping out blindly.

One caught Molimo on the chest and batted him away as if he were an annoying insect buzzing around a giant's nose. Molimo skidded back into Raellard, sending them both down in a pile.

Kesira stood, ichor-dripping staff in hand. She faced the formidable black sea beast without Molimo's quick sword to aid her. One snaky tentacle passed near her head. She stood without moving. It took a few seconds, then seemed to home in on her. When the two tentacles whipped about, the woman acted without thinking. She dived over the waist-high barrier of the frozen waves and into the next rank running perpendicular to their path.

The tentacles swung up, then crashed down to grip her. The sharp leading edges of the waves neatly severed the groping appendages. Hot black fluid hissed and popped on the ice. Kesira rose up on her toes and swung her staff double-handed. It impacted so hard on the creature that Kesira lost her balance and went skidding along the icy surface in the pipeline of waves.

A muted shriek aimed at the clouds hiding the moon, then the beast sank back down into its hole. Kesira heard the water sloshing about the break in the ice. Silence descended. She watched in awe as the ragged hole mended itself, freezing quickly until no trace remained of the beast, except for the severed tentacles and the spots where black blood had steamed their way into the surface.

"Hurry, hurry," urged Zolkan. "Sounds have alerted Steel Crescent soldiers. Nehan-dir sends back one to check. Hurry."

Molimo motioned for her to follow. The man trotted off a few yards and hunkered down in the darkness between ranks of waves. Kesira saw his plan immediately; he hid, ready to ambush the scout.

"What're we supposed to do?" asked Raellard, confused. "If we go on, that thing might follow. Can't go back. So far to land. If it catches us . . ."

"Don't worry now. Get down. We have to make sure the scout does not report back."

"But if he doesn't, the soldiers'll know something is wrong."

"A good point. We have lost any hope for secrecy now. At best we'll gain a few minutes."

The sharp scraping of boots equipped with steel cleats rang out in the deadly night's silence. Kesira felt her heart hammering wildly. She stilled it by rituals but still her hand shook. She didn't know if anticipated discovery did this to her or if it was a reaction to the monster breaking through the ice.

"Behind bad luck comes good," she told herself. This was hardly anything Gelya would have taught—her patron did not believe in luck's existence. Good luck is born from hard work, Gelya taught. But Kesira needed comforting not available from the innumerable maxims she so glibly recited.

Strutting along came the woman whose wrist she had broken the day before. The warrior wore her right arm in a sling and her sword pulled around so that she might draw it left-handed.

Molimo gave her no chance to do more than gasp before he ran her through with his sword.

"Twice now that she was careless," said Raellard with no remorse. "More chance'n any I ever knew got." Molimo knelt and plucked the sword from the woman's belt and handed it to the farmer. Raellard stared at the fine steel blade as if it were a poisonous snake.

"Take it," said Kesira, heaving a deep sigh. "Gelya taught against the use of steel. I am bound by that; you are not."

"But I've never used a sword before. Hardly ever used more than a spear or knife."

"Take her knife, too," said Kesira. "Just think of the sword as a longer knife." Molimo glared at her, but the woman was beyond caring. Tiredness assailed her and forced her eyelids shut in spite of all that happened.

"Hurry, hurry, hurry," urged Zolkan. "No new scout has been sent, but will be soon if you don't hurry."

They raced along the notch carved in the waves, making better time now with the threat of discovery balanced over their heads. Kesira and Molimo had each taken one of the sets of cleats from the dead woman's boots. With the cleats on one foot, they skated along on the uncleated foot. Raellard scrambled along behind the best he could.

"Halt. Wait. Look up," came Zolkan's words. Kesira did not find the *trilla* bird aloft, but she knew he was there, watching out for them. Her eyes started low, among the waves—then paused for a moment. The direction of the wave crests had reversed.

"We're near the shoreline of Ayondela's island," she said, showing Molimo what she meant.

Kesira's attention turned up. She gasped. They had stumbled almost onto the beach of the island and had not known it. Rocky, dark cliffs towered above them, rising more than two hundred feet. Faint ghost light rimmed the cliff's top like ethereal lace, the product of the white flame burning in the center of the island. Dancing shadows flitted across the ice, ducking and dodging, belonging to nothing human.

"The path ends against the cliff," said Raellard, missing the beauty of the Isle of Eternal Winter. "May be a stairway up the face. Or even some ladder inside the rock. Saw that in a mine once. Went right up through a mountain to the top."

Crunching and gnawing sounds came from beneath Kesira's feet. She looked down. Through translucent ice she saw ominous dark figures moving. Cracks shattered the ice. She hurried forward, leaning heavily on Molimo as she did.

"More of the beasts eating upward," she said. He put an arm around her waist, and they worked their way closer to the base of the cliff. Only when they were sure that dirt stretched under the ice rather than water did they stop.

"Can't get up there, no way," said Raellard, scratching the stubble on his chin. "I'm no climber. Can't get up there, just can't."

As Raellard talked, Molimo studied the rock face. His grim expression told Kesira that Raellard had been right. When Molimo swung about, sword in hand, she was startled. The man peered past her, toward the acres of frozen crests.

A voice as deadly as the ice field said, "Kill them where they stand. All three of them."

Kesira spun and saw Nehan-dir a dozen yards away. A boulder had been rolled away from a cave mouth. The mercenaries with him drew swords and came forward—more than two dozen of them.

Kesira knew there was no way to fight them and live. Nor could they hope to run back into the notch cut through the waves. Already several of the soldiers cut off escape by that route.

"That one has Alir's sword. The misbegotten demon spawn killed her. I claim him for my own!"

Raellard stared in dumb fascination at the sword in his hand. He had never thought simply holding it would brand him as a murderer.

"But I killed no one," he blurted. "That one. He did it!"

Nehan-dir laughed. "See? They turn on one another. This is the loyalty preached by the weaker patrons. Not the strength of arms *our* patron espouses."

"Who is your patron now, Nehan-dir? Ayondela?"

An amused smirk crossed the scrawny soldier's scarred face. "Hardly. We serve Eznofadil."

Kesira drove back the first mercenary to reach her; Molimo gutted another. Raellard found himself flat on his back, a swordpoint at his throat.

Before the thrust came that would end his life, the very earth shook with the booming command, *"Wait!"*

The soldier staggered back, stunned by the vibrancy and power locked in that single word. All eyes turned to the top of the cliff. Standing there, bathed in luminous green, Ayondela stared at them.

"They are ours, mighty Ayondela," protested Nehan-dir. "Lord Eznofadil promised them to us."

"Bring them to my throne room. *Now,* sniveling worms!"

Her cold blue scepter pointed downward. A circle of wan light enveloped Nehan-dir. Ice formed on his sword, his flesh turned gray with frostbite and his eyelids matted shut as the fluids around his eyeball started to freeze.

"Do as she says, damn you all," Nehan-dir grated out from between chattering teeth.

Ayondela's wand moved back into the cradle of her left arm. Her fangs caught the light from the dancing white flame inland and her long, waist-length hair billowed out over the sheer drop as she turned and vanished from sight.

With ill-concealed disgust, Nehan-dir indicated that the three should be taken into the small cave from which the mercenaries had emerged. Kesira blinked at the glare inside. The very walls burned and molten rock dribbled down in sluggish rivers. Yellows and whites stabbed into her eyes and forced her to lift a hand to shade them.

"What causes this?" she heard Raellard ask somewhere behind her. The farmer grunted when one of the soldiers cuffed him on the side of the head.

She called out to the man, "Magicks, Eznofadil's magicks. He makes the interior burn even as Ayondela holds the outer world in frigid bondage."

Nehan-dir shoved her toward a crushed stone ramp leading upward. Kesira began to climb, taking the switch-backs one after another. After what seemed an eternity of heat and light, they emerged in front of a palace forged from blue-white ice glinting like a giant diamond.

"Ayondela's," Nehan-dir said, confirming what she suspected. "For whatever reason, she has always enjoyed being surrounded by ice. Frigid bitch. Who else would come to what should be a tropical island and turn it into her own Isle of Eternal Winter?"

"You don't like her," said Kesira.

"She has her uses. Eznofadil uses her."

"You worship the power he has?"

"Ayondela is a fool." Nehan-dir said nothing more as they walked along the path leading to the immense gates chiseled from a glacier. On either side of the walkway grew tiny white flowers, their blue centers glistening with ice crystals. Kesira stooped to pluck one of the flowers and jerked her hand back when she touched one.

"Cold, isn't it?" said Nehan-dir, smirking. "Everything is cold here. You will learn."

Kesira's brown eyes rose to the pillar of cold, heartless fire rising behind the palace. This provided the faint light suffusing the entire area.

"Lenc's doing. His bond with Eznofadil requires a symbol," said Nehan-dir, kicking at Kesira so she stumbled and fell headlong into the palace's entryway. Molimo tried to come to her aid, but a half-dozen swordpoints pricked his skin. He subsided.

"You show more intelligence than I'd've thought, mute one," said Nehan-dir. "Don't try to escape or help her. Ayondela's wrath will take its toll, I assure you."

Kesira looked around, awed in spite of herself. The entire structure had been carved from a single block of ice, yet the interior was warm. Paintings by both mortal and demon artists hung on the ice walls, furniture lined the corridor, all was sumptuous and elegant and expected—except for the ice construction.

Nehan-dir motioned. Twenty-foot-tall doors of clear ice swung back to reveal a huge audience chamber. Ayondela sat on a blue-white throne, scepter in hand. Kesira's heart pounded now. She had wanted an audience with the female demon, a chance to explain what had happened to

Rouvin. She knew she would get only a few words before
the demon's wrath erupted and doomed them all. Kesira
had to make every instant count.

"Faith and courage are partners," she muttered to herself. Molimo heard, turned partially toward her and smiled.
Kesira hoped that he retained his human form long
enough for her to explain. Otherwise . . .

"Mighty Ayondela, Mistress of the Isle of Eternal Winter, your humble servants bring these prisoners," said Nehan-dir, obviously loathing every formal word he spoke.

"Ayondela!" cried Kesira, dropping to give obeisance.
The floor burned at her knees and turned her robe damp
with melted ice. "I am guilty of your son's death. I killed
Rouvin. Take me and lift the winter curse you've placed on
the world."

Ayondela ignored her. The female demon's eyes blazed
with jade light. Her scepter rose and she pointed it directly
at Molimo.

"This one. He killed Rouvin."

"I am responsible," protested Kesira. A flick of the wand
sent waves of chilling cold against Kesira's face. The nun
fell forward, supporting herself on quaking hands, gasping
for breath in the magical beam that turned even the air
into a frosty liquid.

"He killed Rouvin," Ayondela repeated.

"I'm innocent," blurted out Raellard Yera. "Don't know
anything about these two. Nothing. They . . . they kidnapped me!"

"Silence!"

Raellard cowered back, then straightened. "I am a loyal
servant of the Emperor. Only he can speak to me in such a
tone."

"Careful," Kesira cautioned. "She is not in her right
mind."

Ayondela's fangs began to glow with the pale green inner light. She rose and her eyes flashed hotly.

"To the special room with them. And *him,*" the female
demon said, indicating Raellard with her wand, "I want
him to understand fear. It will be a good exercise to see
how well the device works."

Nehan-dir's soldiers grabbed the farmer by the upper
arms and lifted him onto his toes so he couldn't struggle ef-

fectively. They dragged him off. Raellard said nothing. The expression of contempt on his face told it all. He had shown a moment's weakness and loss of faith, then regained that part making him a man.

"Wait," Ayondela said, as the mercenaries started to escort Molimo and Kesira from the room. The demon's eyes narrowed as she looked hard at Molimo. "This one is familiar to me. Very familiar."

Kesira stumbled slightly when Ayondela said that. Currents flowed in the room that she did not understand. She saw Molimo's throat muscles moving, as if he spoke, and she thought she heard quick words. But that wasn't possible. Molimo's tongue had been cut out.

But what confused the female demon? She had been certain of Molimo's guilt in her son's murder.

"Never mind. Take them away."

Kesira saw the look of relief on Molimo's face and relaxed a little herself. Whatever had happened, the woman knew she'd not been a part of it. Molimo worked on his own escapes. They were led into the bowels of the ice palace. In spite of her plight, Kesira couldn't help but admire the intricate carvings in the walls, the way the floors had been delicately etched with patterns of birds and flowers and things pastoral and alien to this frigid environment.

"She wants you to see what her wrath can be like," said Nehan-dir. "While you do not deserve it, I offer you a chance for escape."

"What?" asked Kesira, immediately suspicious. "Why?"

Nehan-dir took a deep breath, as if trying to compose unsettled thoughts. "You are a worthy opponent in battle, better than many who carry steel swords and wear armor. For that, I offer you a quick death rather than entering there." His pale eyes betrayed a flicker of distaste for what Ayondela intended.

"You're offering to kill us cleanly so we won't have to endure Ayondela's tortures?" Kesira laughed. "A useless life is one that ends too early."

"Remember that when your mind burns and your soul cries out for release." Nehan-dir made a gesture and his soldiers obeyed. Molimo and Kesira were shoved into the cell.

The door slammed shut. A hissing sound came that at-

tracted Kesira's attention. Through the translucent walls
of the cell she saw some of the soldiers working with a bra-
zier and irons to melt shut the prison door.

"We're melted inside," she said to Molimo. He nodded.
"What did you do back in the throne room? To Ayondela? I
heard, or felt—it is difficult to describe the sensation—
words."

"These?" he wrote on his tablet, outlining the spell
given him by Toyaga.

"Not that, not exactly, but some of the words. I heard
them, as if you spoke. You didn't, did you?"

He shook his head sadly. Then Molimo wrote, "It is a
spell given me by a demon. It did not work over-well on
Ayondela. She had been told I was guilty, so the spell could
not be expected to function perfectly. Not against the
power of the jade."

"She recognized you, but she did nothing. She preferred
to take her revenge on poor Raellard."

Molimo vehemently denied this. Kesira had to agree.
Ayondela's wrath could not be sated with a single act of
sadism. Her insanity required her to punish the entire
world, choking it in snow and blinding it with storm. Kesira had missed her chance to plead guilty to the crime of
killing Rouvin. Now she and Molimo and Raellard and
probably everyone else were doomed.

"Why is this cell supposed to be so nasty?" she asked,
slowly walking around. Her hands found only slippery ice
walls and floor. The ceiling was of the same frigid material. "She traps us in the center of an ice cube, nothing
more."

Molimo took her by the shoulders and spun her around.
The look of concern in his eyes tore at her.

"I'll be all right," she said. "We are together. We can escape any cell. And remember, Zolkan is still free. He will
figure some way of getting us away from this awful place."
She put her arms around herself and shivered.

Then she screamed.

Melting through the wall came a beast of utter blackness. Its body rejected the material and embraced the nothingness of space. Midnight black pseudopods rippled forth
to surround her, to embrace her with lingering, painful
death.

Kesira shied away and bumped into Molimo. The expression on his face matched hers—and he stared in the opposite direction. Kesira couldn't look to see what menaced the man. Her own personal horror floated and fluttered and slithered to take her.

She screamed again.

Chapter Fifteen

THE ARMIES OF FROZEN waves marched ghostlike in the silvered moonlight beneath Zolkan like dutiful soldiers on parade. He wheeled about, spilled air under his left wing, and plummeted downward, only to swoop and soar upward again when he saw the Order of the Steel Crescent mercenaries closing in around Kesira and Molimo, swords prodding dangerously into their bodies. The *trilla* bird let out a squawk.

Find help, came Molimo's words. Then Zolkan heard nothing more.

"Help?" he complained to himself as his powerful wings took him toward the moon. "Help from where? Who is asshole stupid enough to help?" Even as the bird screamed this protest into the still night the answer came to him. His beak clacked open and shut, tasting the cool breezes, then he dipped his brightly crested head and started flying in earnest for the mainland.

The jagged ice fields that had once been the Sea of Katad disappeared under him, replaced by low hills, higher ones, real mountains. Zolkan spiraled about, looking, not finding. Tirelessly he continued his search until, just a bit before the sun reached its zenith, a pinpoint of brightness shone from the area near the Pharna River.

Zolkan clucked to himself and arrowed downward, a green-feathered messenger. He pushed hard against the air and braked, hanging almost stationary in the air above the decrepit traveler heating soup over a minuscule fire of dung chips. The derelict glared upward as Zolkan cut off his warming sunlight. An impatient wave indicated that

Zolkan should land. The *trilla* bird dropped like a stone and faced the man across the fire.

"He needs your aid," Zolkan said without preamble.

"How did you find me? I've taken pains to lose myself along the myriad paths of this lacy winterland." The man ran his slender, uncalloused fingers through snow and sent the white powder high into the air. Sunlight caught the individual crystals and sent forth tiny rainbows from the intricate shapes.

"Toyaga, he needs you. You cannot turn from him."

The man sighed and ran a hand over his eyes, as if a mighty headache assailed him now. "How you found me is a mystery, but then you always were adept at being the messenger, weren't you, Zolkan?"

"Some easier to find than others. Necessity drove me. He is caught by Ayondela."

"I gave him what I could. Has the spell worked?"

"It worked," confirmed the bird. "He needs more than simple spell. You received aid; it is your duty."

"This is one of the damnable things I hate about *trilla* birds. You have such long memories. You put even a demon to shame."

"Dangerous. Eznofadil as well as Ayondela on Isle of Eternal Winter."

"Your quick tongue works to convince me to never go to the Sea of Katad."

"You ought to know opponents."

"Ah, I know my enemies. They define me, they give my life substance and bounds. I do know them, Zolkan." Toyaga chuckled. "I suppose that if I had no enemies it would be a sign that fair fortune has overlooked me, which is certainly not the case."

"You have enemies," confirmed Zolkan. "You also have friends."

"And duty to them, yes, yes, Zolkan. You need not remind one such as I of this." Toyaga lounged back and spooned some of the hot stew into his mouth. A dribble went down his chin. The bird canted his head to one side, trying to understand this demon.

"Oh, sorry," Toyaga said. "When I play a role, I immerse myself in it totally." He wiped the spill off with a quick swipe of his hand. "I thought to wander among the unfortunate mortals for a while and find new inspiration for an epic poem of struggle and suffering."

"We must hurry."

"I suppose the poem can wait. I am barely rested from my last battle with Eznofadil and Ayondela. They are worthy foes." Toyaga heaved a sigh. "And you are so right. I have worthy friends, as well. Let's go see if we cannot prevail in their behalf, eh?"

Zolkan's colorful, delicately formed crest fanned out in the warm sunlight, then folded low. He hopped to Toyaga's shoulder and waited. The trip back to the Isle of Eternal Winter would be accomplished much faster than the flight away.

The black arms reached around her. Kesira shrieked and struck out with her fists. She found emptiness. The inky vacuum sucked her forward, against the nothingness of its chest. Kesira twisted and turned, then fell heavily to the floor as the creature made a wild grab to ensnare her. She tingled all over as the emptiness fell into itself and vanished as suddenly as it had appeared.

The ice wall remained untouched, whole. Kesira turned and stared at Molimo. The man had shifted into his wolf shape, snarling and snapping at thin air. She reached out to pat the wolf head, to calm him. He nearly took her hand off at the wrist. Kesira showed no fear as the teeth closed around her hand. One convulsive wolf twitch and she would be without a right hand.

"I am you friend. We must stand together, Molimo. Together. Against Ayondela. Against the jade demons." She betrayed no hint of pain as the teeth clamped down harder on her flesh when she mentioned the jade demons.

"It is terrible to be alone. I know that—I know a bit of what you feel. No parents, no family, the social hierarchy missing. The Emperor is far away and there is little that is honorable left in this part of the world."

The wolf's green eyes turned almost phosphorescent in their intensity.

"We can make the difference, Molimo. You and I, together." The wolf twitched nervously, getting free of the human clothing still hanging about its sleek, gray-furred body. Kesira noted that Molimo did not release her hand.

"All my life I have been alone, even among my Sisters in the Order. I sense that it is similar with you. We are different, Molimo. We do not fit the easy, accepted pattern of society. I was an orphan." Kesira started to point out the details of Molimo's affliction, then stopped. With the wolf instincts in control, she did not want to play too much on his pain and hardship.

Kesira didn't know what it was. The feel of the hot saliva on her hand turning different, a small jerking movement of the tail, some other small sign—but she gently withdrew her hand from the wolf's mouth just as the shape shift back to human occurred. She heaved a sigh as Molimo reappeared, a look of anguish on his face.

"You cannot help it," she said softly. "I know. I understand."

Molimo dressed in silence. Kesira couldn't help but watch as his naked body became clothed. He was such a handsome man, strong, intelligent, gentle when in human form. Her mind touched on all the fantasies about him she'd had before and added one or two new ones. To have him in her bed, intimately next to her, making love, when he shape-shifted. Kesira shivered at the forbidden thought. What would it be like with a wolf? And, even worse, one of the afflicted other-beasts caused by the actions of the jade demons?

She flushed guiltily when Molimo glared at her. She wondered if he read her mind or simply disliked all that had happened to them.

"Are you all right?" she asked Molimo. A curt nod was the only answer she received. "What was that monster? It came through the walls."

Molimo found his tablet and scribbled in an almost illegible hand, "Might be able to follow it through. Try?"

Kesira wasn't sure if she wanted to try or not. "Yes," she finally said. Anything had to be better than freezing in the ice cell.

"Will summon beast again. I will slip behind, distract it, then you come."

"This sounds dangerous," she said. For a moment she thought on it, then laughed. "Of course it is dangerous. It is dangerous merely being here."

Molimo rewarded her with a wry smile. His eyes had returned to their usual midnight black, and he carried himself with dignity once more. Whatever affront she had given him had been forgotten—or forgiven.

"How are you going to summon it?"

He waved her to the side of the tiny cell. She pressed her back into the frigid wall and waited. Somewhere—at the fringes of her hearing?—sounded a shrill whistle. The noise irritated Kesira as much as it reminded her of the singsong speech Zolkan used to communicate in his fashion with Molimo. The woman started to ask Molimo about this when the back wall turned gray, then black.

The creature surged through the wall once more.

And again, just at the edges of her senses, Kesira heard snatches of the spell Molimo had mentioned to her.

> *The world . . .*
> *. . . no eyes.*
> *Freedom . . .*
> *I fade . . .*

Only snippets came, but she had no time to think about this. The nothingness beast ignored Molimo, blundered past and came for her, tentacles reaching.

"Go, Molimo," she cried. Kesira had no chance to see if the man-wolf obeyed or not. He had to. This was his plan. She found herself dodging the long, vaporous reach of the groping black tentacles. One passed through the side wall and snaked around, coming back at her from an unexpected direction. When it touched her flesh, it was disgustingly substantial.

Kesira ducked down low, yanked her arm free and slammed hard against the wall where the door into the cell had been, before the mercenaries had melted it shut. As she faced the monster, Kesira felt a pang of guilt. At this instant of danger she experienced selfishness. She thought only of herself.

This was Ayondela's true torture: In adversity Kesira lost sight of her goals, of her teachings. Gelya would not have been pleased.

The world lay under a blanket of ice, shivering to death, robbed of warm summer breezes. Zolkan might have his freedom, but the dangers outside the ice palace were as great as those within. And Molimo. Where had he gone? To his death? Kesira did not know. Theirs might be the greater need and all she could think of was a cold black tentacle brushing along her skin.

"Time to leave," she said softly. Pseudopods flowed toward her from both sides of the creature. Inadvertently her feet helped her—she slipped on the icy floor, the cleated right shoe giving way. She fell heavily and slid past the black nothingness of the creature through the wall into darkness so extreme she had to push down a pang of fear that she'd gone blind.

Here.

Kesira looked about her at the sound of the word. She got to her feet and saw Molimo ahead, beckoning to her. The blackness danced about his body, repulsed by some force.

"You spoke!" she cried. No answer came. Kesira knew she might have imagined the single word. But she wasn't sure. Everything had turned upside down in her world. She rushed to Molimo yet her journey seemed endless, a trip ten times the distance from her nunnery to the Emperor's capital. When she finally reached him, thankful arms out-thrust to embrace him, Molimo had gone.

"No!" she shrieked. "Don't leave me like this. You can't, damn you, Molimo, damn you!"

Kesira stood alone in the dark. The impact of her predicament struck her anew. She had gotten back on the right path in the ice cell when facing the vapor-tentacled beast. The proper course to follow was not to think of herself, but to consider others. She was a part of the universe; an important part, due to a quirk of circumstance. She had to believe this. She knew the danger from the jade demons and had a way to alleviate some of the heartache they carried with them.

Only through her interaction with Molimo—and Zolkan and Raellard and all the others—might she triumph.

Even as she again found this point, Molimo returned to her side. He took her arm and guided her among hidden obstacles.

"How can you see?" she asked. Her voice sounded curiously dull and muted. "Did you truly speak to me? Before?"

His eyes flashed but carried no assurance. That had to

come from within. She simply accepted that Molimo's vision in this light-sucking black void was better.

Laughter taunted her. Molimo hurried her along even faster. She stumbled many times, but kept moving. Wherever they went, it had to be better than this. But strive as they did, they couldn't outrun the mocking laughter. It came from everywhere, and from nowhere. Kesira put her hands over her ears and even this did nothing to stop it. The nun felt as if it rattled inside her brain, forcing its way out.

"What is causing that?" she moaned. "Stop it, Molimo. Make it stop."

"Yes, Molimo, make it stop," the voice said. Kesira recognized it instantly: Ayondela.

"This is only some new torture," Kesira said. The absence of certainty had been snipping away pieces of her sanity. Knowing allowed Kesira to hold to what little she possessed. Failure came not from weak flesh, but from weak spirit. Over and over she told herself this. Her resolve strengthened.

And Ayondela sensed it.

"You will not escape my ice prisons. Never!"

"Please, Ayondela, listen to me. For just a moment. Take my life, if you will, in payment for your son's life. But lift the curse. Let the seasons grow naturally."

"All you mortals must suffer. Rouvin died for all of you, you must all die for him!"

"That's not so," protested Kesira. She tugged at Molimo's grip. He seemed to want to keep her from drawing more of Ayondela's attention. This might be the only chance Kesira got to explain. If any thread of rationality persisted in Ayondela, Kesira had to appeal to it.

"Oh?"

"We have an ordered society, one of hierarchies and duties," Kesira said, "and everyone knows their place in it, but I acted on my own, without authority from anyone." Tears welled up in her brown eyes. "Lenc killed my Sisters, my patron, all who would give me guidance. I acted on my own out of revenge."

"The one with you," said Ayondela. "He is so familiar. Who is he? He . . . he is responsible for Rouvin's death. Someone told me this. Who?"

Kesira heard Molimo grunting and mumbling deep in his throat. An instant of dizziness assailed her. She reeled, then straightened. She thought she heard the snippet of poem again. Something about freedom and nothingness and no more eyes.

"Ayondela, take me. Free the world."

The female demon's response startled her. It was as if Ayondela had forgotten all that had been said.

"Come, look upon my vengeance. A part of him dies every second. How long will he last? Not long. Oh, no, not long now."

Glare blinded Kesira; Molimo seemed to have expected it and had already shielded his eyes with one hand. A vista opened before them that made Kesira suck in her breath and hold it. She had been giddy before. Now she stumbled and fell to one knee, unable to stand without vertigo seizing control of her senses.

She and Molimo floated high above the floor of Ayondela's audience chamber. The demon's throne stood off to one side. Behind the throne, through a window of frost and ice crystal flickered the cold flame of Lenc's sigil. Immediately below—hundreds of feet below—stretched the icy floor with rank after rank of soldiers standing rigidly at attention. Kesira saw that Nehan-dir commanded them. The leader of the Order of the Steel Crescent had bared his chest and exposed the cruelly burned half-moon symbolic of his Order. Even though she was far distant, she saw the expression on the man's scarred face as if he were only at arm's length. He enjoyed all that happened and would enjoy her death even more, now that she had refused him his chance to kill her quickly.

The cathedral-high roof of the throne room brushed Kesira's hair; Molimo had to stoop. At some unseen command, they drifted lower. Ayondela pointed with her wand of blue ice. The light dancing forth in waves carried Kesira's attention with it, past the rows of mercenaries, past Nehan-dir, past the elegant and elaborate appointments in the room to a small alcove.

Molimo's fingers bit into her arm. He understood what torture Ayondela visited upon Raellard Yera long before Kesira did.

Raellard's arms had been pulled out to either side of his

body and chained securely. The links of that chain glistened and shone a milky white. Like so much else in the palace, they were of steel-hard ice. His legs were similarly attached, making all but the slightest of movements impossible.

He shrieked and moaned loudly.

Eznofadil's burning device used by the soldiers to cut through the frozen waves on the sea was now aimed for different parts of the farmer's body. Light from Lenc's flame entered a tiny window above Raellard, struck the curved reflecting surface and magicks bent the feeble rays into ones able to inflict intense agony.

"They're burning him with it. But no charred flesh appears when the ray touches him." Kesira felt faint, both from the idea that nothing beneath her feet supported her and that she drifted a hundred feet above her death, and from the obvious suffering Raellard endured.

"The burning takes place inside, when Lenc's flame is used as a source of energy. Sunlight," Ayondela said with obvious distaste, "produces only intense heat. This produces intense pain."

"He is innocent. I am responsible for Rouvin's death."

Molimo shook his head.

"No, Molimo," she said earnestly. "I cannot let another suffer for what we did." He put his hand over her mouth to stifle her words. Kesira's eyes widened in surprise. Molimo was no coward hiding in the dark, fearing the slightest of sounds, cringing from his own heartbeats. Time and time again he had risked his life for her and had done so without an instant's hesitation. Kesira found it hard to believe he could be so insensitive to Raellard's suffering.

Raellard might be a miserable person or worthy of deification—to Kesira it made no difference. He was a human and he suffered for something she and Molimo had done. Fair or not did not matter. This was a question of honor and duty.

"Stop it!" she pleaded.

"Focus the beam to produce more pain," commanded Ayondela, lounging back on her icy throne, enjoying the suffering. A woman of the Steel Crescent came forth and tinkered with the settings, tipping the dish-shaped part slightly. Raellard's shriek of misery cut through Kesira's heart like a knife.

"Continue. Until he is dead. Then we begin on them." Ayondela's green eyes burned like phosphorus as she pointed her scepter at Kesira and Molimo. They drifted lower until their feet touched the icy floor.

Chapter Sixteen

RAELLARD'S SCREAMS FILLED Kesira Minette's soul with searing acid. She resisted closing her eyes or putting her hands over her ears to block the farmer's hideous shrieks. That would have given Ayondela too much pleasure. The jade demon sat on her throne of blue-white ice, sneering, her tusks gleaming with shining green. Ayondela tossed her head and sent a cascade of hair floating out gently; she had been lovely once, Kesira knew.

Only stark, ripping hatred showed now.

"No wound appears—they are all within his mind," Ayondela boasted. "This is a fine instrument for wreaking the vengeance I need. You will be next, Geyla's slut. And then . . . then . . ." Her voice trailed off.

Kesira frowned. Ayondela had started to indict Molimo, also. But the female demon had lost the chain of her thought. Kesira looked away, gratefully, from Raellard's suffering and turned to Molimo. His eyes had the bleak, desolate look she had seen there so many times. But a curious triumph that fluttered here and there confused her. A tiny portion of the poem-spell came to her mind again. She saw Molimo's throat muscles working, as if he intoned the spell, but the words came not to her ears but directly to her mind.

"How can you do this to a man who has done no harm?" Kesira demanded of Ayondela.

"No harm? He helped you kill Rouvin. He is guilty and now is being punished!"

"He is a poor farmer, whose family is starving to death by slow inches because of your curse. He knows nothing of Rouvin or the Quaking Lands or Howenthal."

"He must be taught, then," came a new voice, a deeper, more resonant one. Molimo and Kesira watched as a thick green pillar of whirling dust formed between them and Ayondela. The miniature tornado spun faster and faster until an explosion blasted the windy walls apart to reveal a tall, well-muscled, handsome Eznofadil. The greenish complexion glowed in the light of Lenc's flame, giving Eznofadil an alien aspect that made Kesira shiver.

"Reason with her," pleaded Kesira. "You know I was responsible. I will die for it, if only she lifts her curse."

"Why should she lift her cold touch on the world in exchange for your confession? She already *has* you. You, my dear Kesira Minette, will be destroyed. You and your friends." Eznofadil blinked as he stared at Molimo.

Molimo tried not to appear nervous, but Kesira felt tenseness in the man's body. He moved slightly, so that she shielded him from Eznofadil's direct stare.

"What's wrong?" she asked, almost in a whisper. "Do you fear them?"

Molimo nodded vigorously.

"But you've confronted them before. Why do you fear them now?"

"He is . . ." Eznofadil paused, confused as Ayondela had been. "Let your friend revel in his anguish. Let him anticipate all that will be done to his precious body—and yours, my dear—with this fine implement of mine. Have you seen it at work? Ah, I see your other friend already samples its exquisite delights." Eznofadil laughed. No humor was contained within that sound.

Molimo tugged at her arm. She saw he had retrieved his tablet and wrote swiftly.

"The spell muddles their thinking, but Eznofadil is too powerful for it to last long. Their attention must not fall upon me. If it does, *we are lost!*" Molimo ran a bold stroke under those words to emphasize the importance of all he wrote.

Kesira frowned, unsure of the man.

"He cannot last much longer, can he, Ayondela?" Eznofadil pointed one slender, green-nailed finger in Raellard's direction. "Five minutes? Or less?"

Even as he spoke, the pale light playing over Raellard's body centered on his belly. The man's left hand sprang free

of his manacle; the heat of his fear and pain had melted
through the ice bracelet.

"My guts are on fire," he whimpered. Raellard clutched
at his stomach, made a curious coughing sound, then
slumped. The light from Eznofadil's infernal device continued to stroke over the man's unmoving body. Finally
Ayondela gestured. The woman behind the machine made
a few movements and the pale light winked off.

"He is quite dead, painfully achieving that sorry mortal's fate," said Eznofadil. "Ayondela, I do believe the
nun's . . . companion ought to enjoy the caresses next. He
is overly nervous. It will take his mind off other matters."

Ayondela barked out an order. Nehan-dir gestured and a
dozen of his followers seized Molimo. Kesira started to her
friend's aid, but was driven back at swordpoint. She
watched helplessly as the ice manacles were fastened on
Molimo's arms and legs.

"Please don't do this. He has suffered enough."

"Oh?" asked Ayondela. "How is this? Can he suffer
more than a mother shorn of her only son?"

"He can't cry out in pain for your enjoyment," Kesira
said bitterly. "Someone has already cut out his tongue."

"The silent scream is often the best," said Eznofadil.
"Commence with the ray."

Kesira felt pain as great as any Molimo might feel. She
sobbed and fought and found herself trapped within a magical bubble. Every time she tried to look away, the encap-
sulating bubble turned her around to face Molimo's plight.
His ebony eyes took on a haunted expression far worse
than anything she had seen before. Molimo was trapped
within himself, unable to communicate since his tongue
had been severed. His arms and legs strained against the
ice links, but those bonds held him firmly.

The light worked over his legs, thighs, groin. Molimo's
mouth opened in unvoiced pain.

"I begin to tire of this," Eznofadil said. "Ayondela, my
sweet, let me show the nun about. I promise to return with
her in time to see his demise."

The leer on Ayondela's face numbed Kesira even more.
The demons understood one another all too well. Eznofadil
was not offering her a guided tour of the ice palace; more
hinged on the request than she understood.

"Do so. Return within one hour. I doubt he will be able to last longer. Then it will be *her* turn." The scepter pointed directly at Kesira, sending needles of alternating heat and cold through her. "She will be made to last for at least a week. If I can draw it out to a month, all the better." Ayondela leaned forward on her throne and told Eznofadil, "Let her escape and it will be you suffering in the beam of the torture machine."

Eznofadil laughed lightly. "Never would I jeopardize such a valued ally's loyalty. She will be returned in one hour. After I have given her the full benefit of my expertise."

The bubble holding Kesira burst. She tumbled downward. Only force of will prevented her from screaming as she rushed toward the cold ice floor. Inches above the ground, another invisible force seized her and prevented her from being injured.

"So easy," Eznofadil said, "since I have walked the jade path. But then, so many things have become clear to me. Come. I want to share them." He made a careless gesture. Unseen hands lifted Kesira and hurried her along beside the jade demon.

"You only use her, don't you?"

"How's that? Ayondela?"

"Ayondela," said Kesira. "You taunt and torment her, make her bring the coldness to the land for your own reasons. What will you do when her need for revenge is past?"

"Feed it again. I think she has an infinite capacity for hating mortals. In spite of her protests, she and Rouvin's father were never in love. As much as can ever happen to a demon, she was seduced, raped, whatever term you wish to employ. This has caused a long-festering hatred of mortals. I rather suspect Ayondela was happy that you killed Rouvin." Eznofadil turned and stared curiously at Kesira.

"A nun did not kill such a warrior. Was it your friend—the one now enduring Ayondela's tortures—who killed Rouvin?"

Kesira said nothing, but her expression betrayed her.

"I feel as if I know—knew—that." Eznofadil frowned, thinking hard. "Can it be some spell at work, one I do not detect? While it is possible, I doubt any is of sufficient strength to befuddle me."

"No one except Lenc," she said, hoping to sow discord among the ranks of the jade demons.

"We have an agreement, Lenc and I. No, this is something more. Curious. I must look at your friend more carefully when we return. And he is dead."

The aura of green surrounding Eznofadil built in intensity, radiating like a gaseous envelope. Eznofadil's skin had not taken on the brittle appearance that Howenthal's had shown, but it differed greatly from normal skin, for either human or demon. The texture was somehow smoother, the strength tougher.

"You admire my . . . suntan?" Eznofadil smiled. "This is an alteration in my appearance I find distressing, but it is little enough to trade for the power I wield. Come. See what we do in the world. You owe it to yourself."

Kesira gasped as wind whipped around her body, catching the tattered gray robe and pulling it back as if she soared like Zolkan. Eznofadil strode out on the snowy ground, pointing to the far north where the Yearn Mountains rose majestically. The white blankets of winter covering them had never been more brilliant in sunlight.

"Those are but one facet of Ayondela's gemlike curse. I encourage such beauty. Don't you agree that the mountains are at their loveliest in winter? Can you deny such a glory to the world?"

"How did we get here?" Kesira wandered about, dazed by the sudden transition from the Isle of Eternal Winter to the Plains of Roggen. Kesira thought she recognized the location; Chounabel lay off to the southeast and Blinn nestled high in the mountains directly to the north. And to the north and west lay the Quaking Lands. The woman wondered if they still shivered and boiled with subterranean restlessness or if Howenthal's passing had stilled their temblors.

"You cannot expect a demon to waste time getting from one spot to the next. All of us are able to travel in this mode, to some degree or another. But only those of us who partake of the jade can bring along such valued guests." Eznofadil executed a mockingly formal bow in her direction.

"Ayondela thinks to change the seasons? This is beauty? The only beauty is in the hope that the following season brings something better. Summer melds into autumn and harvests. Winter allows rest for the work of the summer and fall. Spring breaks the monotony of storms and snow. Summer is filled with the exaltation of spirit from good, pleasing labor. Ayondela breaks the natural cycle and locks us into perpetual boredom."

"Boredom?" asked Eznofadil. "Do you find storms boring?"

Kesira tried to hold back her gasp of surprise as they again changed locations. Strong, cold winds tugged at her flesh, freezing and nipping and trying to tear it from her bones. Eyes watering, she looked down a sheer precipice to the world below. Kesira had no idea where Eznofadil had brought her.

"We are atop Mt. Pline. Perhaps you don't know it? The Emperor once had a summerhouse here." Eznofadil walked about, untouched by the fiercely raging storm. Occasional bolts of lightning lit his green skin and turned it into something truly evil. "The heat of Limaden drives him here every summer for rest. Normally, this place would be pleasant, a high meadow lush with grass and trees, a small brook. A spot of unsurpassed loveliness after winter releases its death's grip. I think Ayondela does the empire a service by forcing the Emperor to stay closer to his capital and tend to matters other than his own comfort."

Kesira pulled her tattered robe more tightly around her body, but it didn't help much—nor had any amount of shelter helped those servants of the Emperor's caught in the unnatural storms now raging. Kesira made out the snowy forms of a dozen men and women, frozen as stiff as marble statues, all lined up outside one of the sumptuous houses kept here for the Emperor's use. To Eznofadil their deaths meant nothing; the suffering of millions meant no more.

Kesira found herself unable to speak from the overwhelming realization of the demon's indifference to human misery. She stood and snow clogged her nose and mouth. Her eyes froze and heat seeped from her body, stiffening her.

She stumbled and fell as Eznofadil took her to another spot. While the cold winds did not blow as strongly here, she still felt the teeth of unnatural winter.

"Tropical isles fascinate me," said Eznofadil. "The Isle

of Eternal Winter used to be such, until Ayondela took possession. I do not understand her passion for ice and snow
but it is useful to me. The mortals cringe and cower. When
the curse is lifted, the one responsible will be a hero. They
will honor me as their patron. With the power of jade to
back me, I will rule all of the empire—and more!''

"Won't Ayondela and Lenc protest this small breach of
your trust?''

"Protest? Why, Lenc strives to kill me, even as I do him.
We are realists. There can be no quarter given, but it
might benefit us both to join forces now and again. Ayondela is a tool, no more. I use her to act as a lightning rod for
you mortals' fear and loathing. When she is no more, I will
ride in, the conquering hero.''

"You say you use Ayondela as your tool, but Lenc's
flame burns on the island.''

Eznofadil frowned. "It keeps him happy. I do nothing to
oppose him openly. Not yet. My power grows to the point
where I can destroy him without injury to myself.''

"The jade doesn't protect you?'' Kesira said, her voice
cutting sarcastically. She had nothing more to lose. Molimo might be dead by now—Raellard certainly was. Kesira saw no way of freeing the world from Ayondela's grip
or of destroying Eznofadil. Caustic comments gained her
nothing but a sense of finally striking back. It was feeble
and futile, but it instilled her with a small feeling of accomplishment.

"The jade is both a master and a servant. I cannot explain to you the transformation within me. With the
others removed, I will be its total master and its hold over
me will be as nothing.''

"Is that all you want? Power to rule? Why, after so many
millenia? The demons were revered and looked upon as
great teachers, not despots. The Emperor ruled and all
looked up to the demons. What has changed? Why do you
seek direct dominance?''

"It has taken a long time for me to understand my destiny. Petty mortals rule for a few briefs moments before dying. I can give a unity of purpose to the world. I will. And,''
he said, shrugging, "all this breaks the monotony of my existence. It becomes dull living for such a long, long time.''

"How can anyone think to bring himself happiness by

exercising power over another?" Kesira asked. "Gelya rightly taught that with power comes responsibility. Emperor Kwasian does not sleep soundly at nights worrying over the condition of his vassals. If you are to rule the world, can you worry over the lives of all the populace?"

"The will to power is strong," said Eznofadil. "It is more than an aphrodisiac. It is the ultimate aphrodisiac. I am happy to have discovered it."

The demon spun and looked out on the once-tropical island. A few people had gathered to see what disturbed the serenity of their afternoon nap. Eznofadil pointed. Four green pillars rose just outside the tight knot of natives. Shimmery curtains of light leaped out of the posts connecting one to the other. Screams came from within.

"It seems some of the mortals were caught by the diagonal sheets of energy," said Eznofadil, not really caring about their deaths. "Pity. But you wanted to see the cold removed from the land. Very well. For those lucky ones, it is."

Flames a thousand feet high leaped to sear the sky. The burning came so quickly none within the energy barriers had a chance to even cry out, as their friends had on being cut in two. Eznofadil watched with a clinical detachment that startled Kesira.

"You feel nothing for them," she said in a choked voice. "To you they are little more than insects."

"Less, actually," admitted Eznofadil. "Insects perform useful services. You mortals only clutter the landscape."

"And yet you want to rule us. Why?"

"Power is worthless unless it is used. While you are feeble, vain, venal, and shallow, you do have your uses. You mortals keep our existence from becoming unbearably boring."

Kesira paled when the demon turned toward her. His expression hadn't altered but the aura surrounding him deepened, as if the jade demanded even more mortal sacrifice.

"The ones like Ayondela are interesting, but mortals can be used and then discarded, with no more thought needed."

"The jade drives you now. Once, you were held in high

esteem by both the mortals who worshipped you and your peers. Don't you see how it changes you, Eznofadil?"

"For the better," the jade demon said. His eyes flashed wildly. He advanced, arms reaching for her. Kesira tried to run, to fight, to resist. Whatever Eznofadil did to her, it sucked away all power, if not her resolve. She stood as motionless as a statue, railing inside but outwardly immobile. Kesira almost fainted when the jade fingers lightly brushed across her cheek, her jawline, tracing back to the crease under her ear, lower. Wherever his digit touched, flesh burned—passionately.

Kesira sobbed as he parted her robe and discarded it. She stood naked to the waist as the demon moved closer, hands touching her now, sparking within her insane lust. She gasped and tried to thrust out her hips in wanton need.

"See what joys I can bring you?"

"The jade," she gasped.

"Gelya was a fool. He never visited his worshippers to learn what they might offer, other than feeble prayers and idiot looks of adoration for his parables."

The demon's outstretched finger drifted lower, teasing her, stirring passion within Kesira's loins unlike any she'd ever felt. Tears ran down her cheeks, and she failed to control them—or herself. All of the hours of meditation and control learned at such a cost abandoned her. Primal urges rose like inexorable tides within her moon-wracked body. Eznofadil jerked and the nun's robe fell off her hips to pile about her feet. She stood naked before him.

And she wanted the demon.

"This is nothing new to you, is it, my lovely one?" asked Eznofadil. "I see one of my colleagues has already sampled your delightful mortal wares." The tormenting finger traced over the mark on her left breast. Wemilat's kiss began to heat up, as if touched anew with a branding iron.

"My toadlike fellow demon must have done this to you." Kesira gasped. And felt nauseated when she realized she enjoyed it—wanted more. "Ah, he did, didn't he? And this?" The fingers stroked over her nude figure, stimulating, dipping deep and racing out once more until her body quivered with abject, forbidden need.

"No, you cannot do this to me. I forbid it!"

"The jade power demands it," Eznofadil said. "Now and again, I delve into a mortal's body and extract needed energy. Perhaps this is what Wemilat did. Perhaps he needed your energy to combat Howenthal? Yes, I think that must be what happened."

Kesira flushed with shame as Eznofadil moved even nearer. His smooth, hard body rubbed suggestively against hers. She commanded her legs to move; they remained rooted to the spot. Her arms did not lift. Eznofadil's spell dominated her totally.

"You must be a strange nun to enjoy ugly Wemilat's company and yet find mine detestable. We shall have to change that perception. You will tell me afterwards the difference. You cannot prefer him to me. You cannot."

Kesira knew the demon wove a spell of ponderous magicks around her, tangling her thoughts, confusing her emotions. How she wanted to be like Molimo in this instant, to change into a wolf and rip the demon's throat out! But she was held to his will, little more than the demon's slave.

"Yes, you do desire me now. I can tell." The hands brushed over her body, lewdly touching. "You will desire me with every fibre in that mortal body of yours even as I drain you and leave you a burned-out husk!"

His jade lips crushed into her flesh-and-blood ones. Kesira jerked against the potent spell holding her as hot arrows of desire lanced through her body. The demon's arms encircled her, held her, stroked over her nakedness.

The kiss broke off, leaving her gasping. Kesira dared not open her eyes. Eznofadil mistook this for true passion on her part.

"You warm to me. Perhaps I won't exhaust your vitality totally. Perhaps I will leave just a little to sample later, for a lightly erotic snack."

His lips again crushed down passionately on hers, then slipped lower, to her curving throat. To the deep valley between her breasts. The demon's insistent kisses set her ablaze within—and Kesira gasped, arching her back when Eznofadil's lips touched Wemilat's mark on her breast.

Through a veil of confusion, fear and unwanted lust, she remembered the brigand who had tried to rape her. He had put his lips to that spot and died.

Eznofadil was no mortal brigand.

Kesira gasped and hated herself as Eznofadil moved between her legs, having his way with her. The Kiss of Wemilat had not protected her this time.

Chapter Seventeen

KESIRA MINETTE stood motionless. Her mind reeled, but her body refused to respond to even her most desperate commands. Eznofadil had finished with her and stepped back. Fearfully, she opened her eyes, not knowing what she would see. The expression on the demon's face startled her.

She had expected to see contempt, or the remnants of lust, or triumph. All Kesira saw was confusion.

And that Eznofadil's lips had changed from their jade green color to a more normal flesh tone.

"What now?" she asked.

"I . . . I don't know." Eznofadil turned and started to wander off, then stopped. The jade demon's entire demeanor told Kesira that he had been deprived of his senses.

Even the spell holding her so firmly in place began to slip. The woman at first allowed the tingling sensation in her toes to remind her of her continued life, but then it spread, to ankles, past her cramped, knotted calves, up her legs. Strength flooded into her arms and body. Gasping with relief, she sank forward onto the cold ground, balancing herself on hands and knees. When the cold winds caused her to shiver, Kesira knew she had recovered from the paralysis inflicted upon her. Without asking Eznofadil's permission, she hastily put on her gray robe. Knotting the blue cord and tying the gold sash around her waist returned her to the known and made her more confident, in spite of all that the demon had done to her.

"What?" started Eznofadil, then recovered. He stared around him as if this island came as a complete surprise.

Kesira approached the demon warily. She had an idea as to what had happened to him, but she needed to know for certain. The brigand's leader had placed his lips over Wemilat's imprint on her breast and died horribly a few seconds later. But Eznofadil was neither human nor an ordinary demon. He had accepted the burden and gift of the jade stone, becoming incredibly powerful because of it. Wemilat's protection might not be powerful enough to kill Eznofadil, but it might have robbed him of his senses—at least for a while.

"Do you know who I am?" Kesira asked.

Eznofadil nodded.

"You know who your enemies are, don't you, Eznofadil, my demon lover?"

"Lover?" he asked, panic rising into his green eyes when he failed to remember what Kesira meant.

"Lover," she said firmly. "We are lovers, you and I. You are completely devoted to me." Kesira forced herself closer, her hand stroking over Eznofadil's lean, stone-hard body. She captured his hand and lifted it to her breast. He pulled back, but the movement did not show his true physical prowess. Kesira exposed her left breast with the lip imprint and pulled Eznofadil's hand directly over it.

"That feels good," the demon muttered.

"Yes," she said, hating herself, but hating Eznofadil even more. The fury of her emotions added strength to her limbs, to her conviction. Her strength flowed from his weakness. Kesira's control over Eznofadil grew. "We are lovers, and you will do anything for me."

"No," he said, but his negation carried no fire. Eznofadil was increasingly confused. He stared blankly at his hand and again tried to pull away. This time Kesira was strong enough to hold him. The jade green of his left hand had begun to lighten where the flesh touched Kesira's. The transformation back to more human-appearing flesh proceeded slowly, but it happened. His slightly parted lips took on highlights of pinks and reds, the green totally vanished. Such was the power of Wemilat's kiss.

"Yes," said Kesira. "I am in danger. You must help me. You want to. Only you, my demon love, can aid me now against my greatest enemy. Our *mutual* enemy."

"Who?"

Kesira held back the gloating she felt. "Ayondela. She desires me for her own. You would never willingly give me to her, would you? When it is only you I care for?"

"Never," the demon said. Animation returned to his voice. Kesira hoped that memory did not also come back with it.

"She wants me for her lover."

"No!"

"Then you must stop her, Eznofadil. Only you are strong enough. You can do it. For me. For me!"

"She cannot do this. I won't allow it."

"She thinks to bind me to her by hiding the world under a blanket of snow. This is wrong. I do not want it. You don't either, because it makes me unhappy."

"Why should I care?" asked Eznofadil, the confused expression returning. Kesira worried that the effect on the jade demon might be fleeting. She jerked his other hand to her breast and forced both into the pinkly glowing lip print there. "Why?" he asked again. "I do, though. I do care."

Eznofadil's hands had both returned to a more normal hue. The line of green began at his wrists now. The demon quaked and anger replaced the confusion.

"Ayondela cannot get away with this! She flaunts the power I have given her. How dare she! She must die!"

"Yes," said Kesira, emotions high now. "Destroy Ayondela. She must never be permitted to take me. I must be yours and yours alone." The woman played on what she hoped the demon believed deep down. She strove not to break the mood she wove about him, the mood engendered by the magicks of Wemilat's mark.

As quickly as they had arrived on the tropical island, they returned to the Isle of Eternal Winter. Kesira threw up one arm to protect her face from the glare. It was nearly noon and the sun shone off the snow with an eye-searing light. Somehow, the palely burning white flame reaching upward for the sky seemed to flicker as Eznofadil returned. Kesira prayed to Gelya—to any other patron willing to hear her—that this was not a warning device alerting Lenc that he might have defectors in his ranks.

"She is inside. You must stop her or she will take me."

"Stop her," said Eznofadil, as if in a deep trance. He turned and faced the side wall of the immense ice palace.

His hand lifted. For a moment, nothing happened. Kesira feared the demon had also forgotten the proper spells to cast, but it seemed only to be a function of his hands returning to their normal fleshiness. Power welled up and rushed forth in scintillant waves.

An entire wall of the palace vanished in hissing steam and flowing water. Eznofadil strutted forward toward the startled Ayondela, who sat on her throne off to one side of the new entryway into her palace.

Kesira trailed Eznofadil as he boldly stopped in front of the female demon.

"She is mine," he said.

"What do you mean?" roared Ayondela. "She is *not* yours. I will torture her to death!"

Eznofadil heard nothing past the refusal to turn Kesira over to him, body and soul. Already he summoned his power. The greenish aura about his body firmed and turned ominously darker. The sheet of energy radiating forth from his outstretched hands smashed against Ayondela's throne and melted it.

With a squawk more like a *trilla* bird than anything else, Ayondela jumped up, her blue scepter pointing. The next wave of Eznofadil's melting power was turned aside by the power of her own magicks.

"How dare you accost me like this in my own palace? How dare you?" Ayondela shrieked.

Kesira slipped around, fingers behind her and guiding her along the destroyed wall. Molimo hung in his ice chains across the room. To reach his side Kesira would have to boldly cross the expansive floor—and this looked impossible. Nehan-dir had summoned his soldiers the instant Eznofadil melted through the palace wall and ranked them to protect Ayondela. Seeing that it was the Order of the Steel Crescent's own patron, Nehan-dir hung back, watching and waiting.

But mostly the scarred man watched. Kesira could not hope for an instant of inattention from one such as Nehan-dir.

Molimo's head lifted and half-hooded eyes opened wider. Kesira's heart went out to him. How he had survived was a mystery. She saw the diabolical focusing device still at work on his body, inflicting pain he could not shriek against, injuries as much to the soul as to the body. Kesira covered her mouth with a shaking hand when she saw the flickerings in those midnight black eyes turning to specks of green.

"No, Molimo, please, no," she whispered. "Don't transform. They will kill you instantly if you do. Ayondela will know. She will!"

Her words came from too far away to have been heard by the man, yet Molimo understood. The green, dancing highlights faded; Molimo slumped against his chains. Kesira skirted the central portion of the audience chamber, keeping her back to the frosty wall, and hoped to reach Molimo unseen.

The commotion caused by the two arguing demons aided her cause.

"You cannot come in here and accuse me!" shouted Ayondela. She fended off another of Eznofadil's attacks with a wave of her ice-blue scepter, then rose up to her full height. The viridescent aura surrounding her made Ayondela appear as if she had cloaked herself in shimmering mosses.

"You overstep your bounds," said Eznofadil. "I will have her for my own. She wants no part of you." Eznofadil's hands shook as the greenish tint returned to them; his lips stayed as pinkish as they had been after he first planted them against Wemilat's mark. Kesira knew that some of the jade demon's power had been sapped by his attack on her.

Strangely, what Eznofadil had lost she felt that she had gained. Never stronger, never more daring, Kesira continued to make her way around the audience chamber to free Molimo while the demons continued their exchange of deadly magicks.

"You will hang beside him," came a low voice from behind her. Kesira spun to face Nehan-dir, his sword drawn and ready to lunge. "I offered you a clean death. You refused. Now you will suffer your friend's fate." Nehan-dir smiled crookedly. "I must admit to respecting him. Even if he'd had a tongue, I don't believe he would have cried out. He is brave—and foolish, like you."

Kesira did not wait for Nehan-dir to attack. She launched herself forward, only to slip on the icy floor.

Arms flailing, the woman crashed into Nehan-dir. They both tumbled to the ground, arms circling one another. Kesira stayed on top, got her legs under her and drove a hard knee into the man's midriff. Nehan-dir gasped, turned on his side and vomited.

Kesira reached for the mercenary's steel sword, then stopped. Gelya's edicts against using such weapons returned to her. "We walk by faith, not by sight. I must not give up my faith." She took the few extra seconds to clamber to her feet and kick Nehan-dir as hard as she could. He groaned weakly. He would not oppose her soon.

Kesira looked up and saw others loyal to the Steel Crescent closing on her. She turned and rushed to where the soldier still played the pale light from the magical device over Molimo's body and limbs.

Kesira struck the woman and sent her to her knees, but the soldier came up with a dagger. Without thinking, Kesira swung the dish-shaped device around. The light winked out, but the hard edge caught the soldier on the arm. The wounded mercenary spun to avoid a harder contact; Kesira gave her no chance to recover.

"Molimo," she gasped out, going to him. The ice links around his ankles and wrists had turned his flesh a sickly grayish white with frostbite. "I'll free you."

He lifted his chin and indicated something behind her. Kesira looked over her shoulder and saw a dozen of the mercenaries closing on her, swords drawn. Nehan-dir had to be supported by two burly men, but he made gestures indicating attack.

Save yourself.

Kesira stood, stunned. "You spoke!" she cried. Then the nun realized Molimo had done no such thing. The torturing beam focused in the dish had burned his lips badly. Even if Molimo had had a tongue in his head, speech would have been impossible. "How?"

The soldiers came closer.

Kesira took a few precious seconds to compose herself, to achieve a level of concentration that might permit her to see new solutions to the problem of their escape. She opened her eyes and found nothing changed.

The ring of soldiers around her still threatened. Eznofadil and Ayondela traded strange magicks in the center of the audience chamber. Around them the ice walls and floor melted and refroze as first Eznofadil and then Ayondela attacked. The two demons were oblivious to anything else in the icy room.

"The dish," she said. "I can turn it on them."

The soldiers of the Order of the Steel Crescent now stood between her and the magical device.

"Get her," came Nehan-dir's choked words.

Kesira stood firmly, mind settled. Her only weapons might be hands and feet, but she would not die easily.

A loud squawk pulled her level, appraising gaze from the advancing soldiers to high up in the chamber where she and Molimo had floated only hours before. A bright green bird spiralled around, screeching and swearing.

"Zolkan!" she cried.

A thunderclap blasted the chamber, and the resultant heat bowled over the soldiers almost upon her. Kesira managed to protect Molimo the best she could, then saw it had been a mistake. Where she had not thrown herself in front of him, the heat had melted his manacles. Molimo's right arm and leg had been freed.

"You have gone too far this time, Ayondela," came a loud voice. Toyaga strode arrogantly and confidently into the chamber. "You, also, Eznofadil. You cannot imprison such as he." As Toyaga lifted his hand, both of the jade demons ceased their squabble and turned the full fury of their magicks against the intruder. Toyaga staggered under the impact of such torrential outpouring.

"No!" the handsome demon cried. "You will not triumph so easily."

He fought, but Kesira saw immediately that there was no possible way Toyaga might defeat the combined power of Ayondela and Eznofadil. Those two drove Toyaga ever backward, wore him down until his face turned a pasty, sickly white, battered his defenses inch by slow inch and closed on him.

The mercenaries got sluggishly to their feet. While they were still groggy, Kesira hit them low. She skidded along the floor on her belly and slammed into their still shaking legs. They went down heavily—and she found herself by the torture machine.

Kesira hazarded a quick look at Molimo, who shook his head and waved at her, as if trying to warn her.

"Get yourself free," she called to him. Molimo clumsily bent and brought a sword closer with one toe until he was able to wrap numbed fingers around the hilt and lift it. Kesira decided he was not in immediate danger; Toyaga was.

She spun the bulky dish around, trying to find some control on the back that fired the device, that sent out the punishing pale light. She frantically pulled levers and turned dials. Nothing happened. From above, Zolkan cursed loudly and fluidly, then hurtled down and perched on the top of the dish.

"Reflections only. They used Lenc's flame as source. You cannot turn it against them, not from here."

Ayondela saw Kesira. Horror widened Kesira's eyes as the female demon smiled wickedly, the fangs gleaming bright green now. The scepter rose and pointed directly at Kesira.

Reflection.

"Reflection!" she cried, spinning the dish around and pointing it directly at Ayondela. The demon's potent stream of cold impacted on the dish, fell into itself and rushed back—but not directly to Ayondela. Kesira had inadvertently turned the dish.

"Toyaga!" squawked Zolkan, trying to reach the woman's arm with his claws. But Kesira saw her mistake too late. She caught the demon battling to free her and Molimo squarely with the beam. Toyaga stiffened, then fell forward. He hit the ice floor and shattered as if he has been built from glass.

A hush descended on the chamber. Then confused mutterings came from the soldiers. But Ayondela showed no hesitation. She turned on Kesira, her scepter again spewing forth its frosty death message.

Kesira gasped, her entire body caught in the beam. She stiffened, joints freezing, limbs unable to move. More solidly than she had been held by Eznofadil's magicks, this frigid ray immobilized her.

Seeing only straight ahead, Kesira was treated to the heady sight of Ayondela spinning angrily and directing her attack against Eznofadil. The jade demon had paused only an instant in his attack—and he perished under the female demon's attack. As Kesira had done, Eznofadil stiffened and froze into position.

Kesira wanted to shout with joy as Ayondela went to Eznofadil, then swung her scepter with all her might. Pieces of jade that had been the demon blasted all over the room.

Eznofadil was dead.

And Kesira Minette was forever cradled in winter's embrace.

Chapter Eighteen

Sorrow. Loneliness. Isolation. Sorrow.

Intense sorrow filled Kesira Minette as the cold crept through her body and froze through to the core of her being. She had failed, and she was all alone now. That would be her eternal punishment: unendurable solitude.

Eznofadil might have died, but Ayondela's curse still lay heavy on the world. The woman stared sightlessly into the ice chamber and drifted off to a deep, deep slumber. One day her spirit might return, and when it did she would carry the burdens laid upon her this day.

And they would be heavy. Heavy.

Light intruded on her sleepless dreams, assaulting her eyes, making her want to blink. The spell of ice and immobility held her too firmly to allow any movement whatsoever. Pain started at the backs of her eyes when she failed to shut out the light, and the pain spread.

Legs, arms, body. Kesira tried to scream; her voice had been frozen, too.

Resist, came the oddly distant command. It was both familiar and unknown to her. Kesira puzzled over this paradox. Only slowly did she remember. She had heard such a voice before, when she had entered the audience chamber with Eznofadil. It had seemed to her that Molimo had spoken. But that was impossible. He had no tongue. Yet it had been Molimo, of that she was sure. Another paradox. A world of them. Kesira wanted only to slip back into her dark repose.

"She thaws," came another familiar voice, this time to

her ears and not only her mind. Zolkan. It had to be the *trilla* bird. Pain again came, this time to her shoulder.

"Go 'way," she muttered. Her tongue had turned to rubber and filled her mouth totally. Simply swallowing presented problems too vast to be overcome. Again the pain, a familiar one. Zolkan's talons biting into her flesh. "Stop it," Kesira said more plainly.

"She returns to us," the bird said.

Light faded, flowed, turned into a crazy kaleidoscope of vivid colors. When the scene focused it was the one Kesira remembered last. The throne room.

Other memories rushed back to her. Eznofadil. Ayondela. Toyaga. Their battle.

"Molimo!" she cried. Misery rocketed through her but Kesira moved. The pain a companion, the woman moved, twisted, turned, got circulation flowing throughout her veins once more.

"She returns from land of frozen living," said Zolkan with some pleasure.

Molimo held her upright. Her legs no longer supported her easily. With tender care he lowered her to a sitting position on the icy floor.

"What happened? I saw Toyaga die. I . . . I focused Ayondela's spell directly on him."

"Stupid," said Zolkan. "Tried to warn you. Stupid shit."

"Zolkan!"

The *trilla* bird shut up, but did not look the least bit contrite.

"All right," Kesira said, sighing. "It was stupid of me. And Toyaga died, didn't he?" She read the answer on Molimo's face. True sorrow found a home behind those ebony-dark eyes. "I'm sorry. I only tried to help him." Molimo put a comforting hand on her shoulder, but Kesira was not comforted.

"Ayondela gone," said Zolkan. "Eznofadil died and she left palace screaming mad. Ordered all soldiers to accompany her."

Kesira saw the scene of the battle among the three demons. Toyaga had died, shattering like glass. Ayondela had turned instantly against Eznofadil and frozen the con-

fused demon. He, too, had broken like a dropped clay pot.
Tiny fragments of jade pulsed and shone across the floor—
all that was left of Eznofadil.

"Where did Ayondela go?"

"Just left. Shrieks of betrayal."

"She might have gone to seek out Lenc," said Kesira.
"Eznofadil had turned on her. She might fear Lenc will do
the same."

"He will."

"You're right, Zolkan. He never intended for her to be a
true ally. Eznofadil told me they only used her powers,
that they held no place for her. Lenc is the true winner in
this battle. Ayondela has eliminated a powerful foe in Eznofadil, perhaps the only one able to challenge Lenc for su-
preme control of the world."

"Winter gets colder outside."

"Her curse."

Molimo had retrieved his tablet. He wrote and held it up
for Kesira to see. "You can lift the curse. Only you."

"But, Molimo, I tried," she said. "Ayondela wouldn't listen to me. She . . . she tried to torture you to death and
would have done the same to me. Even at this, she
wouldn't have been sated. Rouvin's death unbalanced her.
She is running amok now."

"Not that," Molimo wrote. "*You* can lift the curse. You
have the power. I feel it within you."

"What do you mean?"

Molimo hesitated, then wrote much slower than before,
as if carefully choosing the words. "After you were with
Wemilat, did you not feel different?"

Kesira's hand involuntarily went to cover the spot on
her left breast where the ugly demon's kiss had been
burned into her flesh. The woman could only nod.

"He drained power from you, but he also gave you some.
The process is not one way."

"And?" she said, her voice cracking now. Kesira thought
she knew what Molimo would write next.

"You were responsible for Eznofadil's confusion. He
gained power from you, but it was not the kind he expected. You gained from him. More than you suspect."

Kesira wanted to cry in humiliation. Was it so apparent to Molimo what the jade demon had done to her? It had to be. She felt dirty, used, wretched beyond words.

"You have power of jade within you," spoke up Zolkan. The bird muted his voice, pitched it softer than Kesira had ever heard. She looked at him. A topknot of feathers fanned out, then folded flat against his head. Zolkan had always prided himself on his appearance; he badly needed cleaning now and seemed not to notice. He had been through much. He didn't complain.

And Molimo? He had suffered for long hours under the agony of the torture device wielded by the soldiers of the Steel Crescent. Raellard Yera had died. None of them had had an easy time. Why should she feel sorry for herself?

But Kesira did.

"I can't do anything. I don't feel up to it."

"Look." Zolkan reached over and bit down on her ear, twisting until she cried out. He jerked her head around so that she stared out the window above where Molimo and Raellard had been chained. The pale dancing flame still reached for the heavens, still burned with its unnatural coldness. The pale white fire taunted her, mocked Kesira for being weak, only a mortal, not worthy of a patron as knowing and kind as Gelya.

Gelya had taught that great works are accomplished not by strength of arm, but by perseverance. The body may be frail, but the will must be strong. Kesira trembled in her weaknesses, but her resolve firmed.

"I feel no different," she said.

"You are," wrote Molimo. "There is more within you than you realize. Reach for it. It won't fail you."

"What do I have to do? I can lift Ayondela's curse?"

"You can. The flame is keystone holding the spell together. Cause the flame to falter, and the power of nature reasserts itself."

Kesira stared at the leaping flame and wondered how she could ever disrupt its flow, even for an instant. Step into it?

No!

Kesira swung about, looking at Molimo. She thought he'd spoken, but he only wrote the word on his tablet.

"You can do it without destroying yourself."

"Show me."

She, Zolkan, and Molimo left the ruined ice palace and stood on the tiled walk circling the flame pit. No fuel fed the fire. No heat radiated outward. No living being might survive within the flame's boundary. Yet Molimo had confidence that she might be able to break its cycle.

"Lenc supplied this as more than symbol," said Zolkan. "It powers Ayondela's curse. If for even small instant flame dies, the world returns to normal."

"How do you know this, Zolkan?"

"Do it," was the only answer she got from the bird.

"But I don't know how. What is it I am supposed to do?" She closed her eyes and dropped into a meditative state. No matter what she would be called on to do, it all began from this point. Calm. Settling down. Tranquility. Thoughts moving in precise paths. Ideas popping up spontaneously.

Molimo took her hand. Zolkan moved closer to her cheek. She was no longer alone, not with them. She depended on them as they did on her. She was a part of something greater, something more complete than any individual could hope to achieve.

"They conquer who believe they can," she muttered.

The source of the white fire came to her in a dreamlike state. And more. She saw the magicks feeding it, how Lenc had established it to burn forever. Kesira was unable to create fire on her own, but she knew the mechanisms, the magicks, the driving forces.

But how to unlock them, how to undo all the jade demon had set into motion?

She needed a spell to shut off some of the cold fire.

From a distance, she heard the poem Molimo had shown her.

> *The world about me,*
> *There are no eyes.*
> *Freedom of the air and sky,*
> *I fade into nothingness.*

She embraced the spell, followed the magical threads,

found new ones. It became hers. Part of the flame wavered into the nothingness promised by the spell. The intensity of the fire wavered, but it did not go out completely.

Zolkan. Molimo. They were with her. In a curious way, so were all her Sisters, now long dead, their spirits claimed by Lenc. They burned within the flame; Kesira joined them with her spell of negation.

She stood watching even as she stood at a long distance, detached and watching herself. The dichotomy lasted for only a few seconds before Kesira felt whole again.

Kesira rubbed her eyes. The flame had vanished.

"It is done," said Zolkan.

"No," Kesira shrieked. "It's returning. Look!"

Fingers of coldness worked at the bottom of the pit, coalesced, then rushed upward once again to burn with frigid white intensity.

"The curse is no more," insisted Zolkan.

"He is right," wrote Molimo. "You interrupted the flow of power long enough. Let the flame burn now. It doesn't give energy to any spell."

Even as Molimo wrote, Kesira felt a warm wind blowing from the mainland. She looked out across the Isle of Eternal Winter to the frozen waves on the Sea of Katad and beyond to land. It was only her imagination, she knew, but the wind *did* carry the scent of summer with it.

"Storm," cautioned Zolkan. "We must leave now. Across sea before it melts. Too dangerous if icebergs still float."

Kesira walked to the edge of the precipice and stared down at the waves, still trapped in rigid formations below. But she looked forward just a few hours and saw the heating caused by summer robbing those frozen waves of their stiffness, letting them fall regularly into themselves, to smash on the beach with aquatic fury.

"We must get across them soon," she agreed.

But Kesira didn't see the trip back through the icy waves; she saw her own failure. Ayondela still raged against the death of Rouvin. Lenc still schemed to rule all the world, to pass from demon to god using the evil jade.

She had come so far, and so many had died. Her Sisters in the Order, Raellard—what of Parvey Yera and her son?—Toyaga and the others. All gone.

Kesira Minette called out to Molimo and Zolkan, but her words were swallowed by the wind.

BIO OF A SPACE TYRANT
Piers Anthony

"Brilliant...a thoroughly original thinker and storyteller with a unique ability to posit really *alien* alien life, humanize it, and make it come out alive on the page." *The Los Angeles Times*

Widely celebrated science fiction novelist Piers Anthony has written a colossal new five volume space thriller—**BIO OF A SPACE TYRANT:** *The Epic Adventures and Galactic Conquests of Hope Hubris.*

VOLUME I: REFUGEE   84194-0/$2.95
Hubris and his family embark upon an ill-fated voyage through space, searching for sanctuary, after pirates blast them from their home on Callisto.

VOLUME II: MERCENARY   87221-8/$2.95
Hubris joins the Navy of Jupiter and commands a squadron loyal to the death and sworn to war against the pirate warlords of the Jupiter Ecliptic.

VOLUME III: POLITICIAN   89685-0/$2.95 US /$3.95 CAN
Fueled by his own fury, Hubris rose to triumph. Obliterating his enemies and blazing a path of glory across the face of Jupiter. Military legend...people's champion...promising political candidate...he now awoke to find himself the prisoner of a nightmare that knew no past.

Also by Piers Anthony:
The brilliant Cluster Series—
sexy, savage interplanetary adventures.

CLUSTER, CLUSTER I	01755-5/$2.95 US /$3.75 CAN
CHAINING THE LADY, CLUSTER II	01779-2/$2.95 US /$3.75 CAN
KIRLIAN QUEST, CLUSTER III	01778-4/$2.95 US /$3.75 CAN
THOUSANDSTAR, CLUSTER IV	75556-4/$2.95 US /$3.75 CAN
VISCOUS CIRCLE, CLUSTER V	79897-2/$2.95 US /$3.75 CAN

AVON Paperbacks

Buy these books at your local bookstore or use this coupon for ordering:

CAN—Avon Books of Canada, 210-2061 McCowan Rd., Scarborough, Ont. M1S 3Y6
US—Avon Books, Dept BP, Box 767, Rte 2, Dresden, TN 38225

Please send me the book(s) I have checked above. I am enclosing $ _____
(please add $1.00 to cover postage and handling for each book ordered to a maximum of three dollars). Send check or money order—no cash or C.O.D.'s please. Prices and numbers are subject to change without notice. Please allow six to eight weeks for delivery.

Name _____

Address _____

City _____ State/Zip _____

ANTHONY 1/85

FANTASY AND ILLUSION

A READER'S GUIDE TO FANTASY   80333-X/$2.95
Baird Searles, Beth Meacham and Michael Franklin
A comprehensive source of writers and works—from the magical
to mystical to supernatural—for every lover of fantasy, with full
listings of authors, titles, series, categories and award-winners,
plus a fascinating overview of fantasy's past, present and future.

THE FANTASTIC IMAGINATION:
An Anthology of High Fantasy   32326-5/$2.25
Edited by Robert H. Boyer & Kenneth J. Zahorski
THE FANTASTIC IMAGINATION II   41533-X/$2.50
From another world beyond our own where epic quests and ritual evil
challenge the gods and seduce the spirit...where witchwomen and
unicorns, sorcerers and swordsmen vaunt and court and do battle...
come these brilliant collections of the best in fantasy literature,
chosen from the most popular works of the past 150 years.

THE PRISONER OF BLACKWOOD CASTLE   88005-9/$2.50
Ron Goulart
When an American millionaire is mysteriously kidnapped, ace detec-
tive Harry Challenge is called on to rescue him...but finds himself up
against a team of deadly robots and a mad doctor, amidst swords and
sorcery, werewolves and automatons.

QUARRELLING, THEY MET THE DRAGON 89201-4/$2.95
Sharon Baker
A compelling fantasy novel of mystery, passion, and horror on a distant
planet where a slave's quest for freedom takes him on an unforgettable
adventure into the realm of the Off-Worlders...and to a destiny
stranger than dreams.

THE FIRE SWORD   88718-X/$3.75
Adrienne Martine-Barnes
An epic fantasy novel of pageantry and ritual, of a beautiful young
woman transported into the mysterious world of 13th century England,
and of her mission to reinstate the King of Light to the throne using
the magical powers of faith, courage and love.

AVON Paperbacks

Buy these books at your local bookstore or use this coupon for ordering:
....
Avon Books, Dept BP, Box 767, Rte 2, Dresden, TN 38225
Please send me the book(s) I have checked above. I am enclosing $ _____
(please add $1.00 to cover postage and handling for each book ordered to a maximum of
three dollars). Send check or money order—no cash or C.O.D.'s please. Prices and numbers are subject to change without notice. Please allow six to eight weeks for delivery.

Name _____

Address _____

City _____ State/Zip _____

Fantasy 10-84